JUST DUCKY

A Lexie Starr Mystery

Book Five

Jeanne Glidewell

Cover and Book design by eBook Prep
www.ebookprep.com

First Edition, January 2014
ISBN: 978-1-61417-518-6

ePublishing Works!
www.epublishingworks.com

DEDICATION

I'd like to dedicate this book to my sister, Sarah Goodman, who has supported me throughout my writing career. It was she who convinced me I should write a cozy mystery series and encouraged me to do so. Along the way, she's been my proofreader and sounding board. Sarah has been the best sister anyone could ever wish for, and I feel very fortunate to have her in my life. Thanks sis!

ACKNOWLEDGMENTS

I'd like to thank my talented editor, Judy Beatty, of Madison, Alabama, for being such a pleasure to work with, and Nina and Brian Paules, with eBook Prep and ePublishing Works, for their expertise and commitment to excellence.

CAST OF CHARACTERS

Alexandria Marie Starr, a.k.a. Lexie – Her perseverance, creative scheming, and impulsive behavior, make her a murderer's worst nightmare, but her lack of fear sometimes makes her even more dangerous to herself. If she doesn't get herself killed, while taking it upon herself to investigate a crime, it isn't for lack of trying.

Stone Van Patten – When this bed and breakfast proprietor married Lexie Starr, he knew what he was getting into, but he loved her too much to turn away and run for the hills, as he was often tempted to do. Stone's patience, and peace of mind, is tested time and time again, until he does the only thing he can think of to protect his wife—he joins her in her quest to catch a killer.

Detective Wyatt Johnston – This hulk of a police officer has become a close friend of Lexie and Stone's, which makes him a valuable asset to a determined sleuth who frequently finds herself in need of being rescued. A human eating machine, Wyatt finds a never-ending supply of coffee and sweets at the Alexandria Inn. Could Lexie be feeding him to keep him in her corner?

Bertha "Ducky" Duckworthy – An eccentric enigma, this spunky librarian is ready to retire, but finds a hang up in her retirement plans she hadn't anticipated.

Wendy Starr – Lexie's daughter, who makes a living as the assistant to the county coroner, Nate, and makes a valiant effort at trying to keep her mom from sticking her neck on the line nearly every time a body drops, against its will, in Rockdale.

Andy Van Patten – Stone's nephew, who followed in his uncle's footsteps by relocating to the Midwest from South Carolina, is a part-time pilot, part-time rancher, and full-time boyfriend of Lexie's daughter.

Paul Miller – Part-time library employee, and bodybuilding cage-fighter. Lexie's seen mimes who talk more than this man, which makes conversing with him a challenge.

Carolyn Aldrich – When things get too hot at the library, this amicable young lady, and part-time library employee, decides it's time to make a career change.

Tom Melvard – A contract custodian, who is good at cleaning up messes.

Angus & Olivia Spurley – Nebraska Senator, and his wife, are paying customers at the Alexandria Inn, who like all the other guests, are spoiled and pampered, well beyond the call of duty, helping make the bed and breakfast a thriving lodging establishment.

Detective Clint Spurley – A rookie cop, whose dispassionate, and surly, personality rubs Lexie the wrong way, until she realizes there might be a good reason for his offensive behavior.

Colby and Mrs. Tucker – Director of the county library system, who rarely bites off more than he can chew, and his wisp of a wife, who has the challenging job of keeping her husband full. Lexie can be counted on to make an unforgettable first impression on her new boss.

Quentin Duckworthy – Ducky's husband, loves his wife, but not so much that he can't pursue other interests. Is he a ruthless killer, or just a gentle old man who makes wooden toys for sick children in the hospital?

Barbara Wells – Is this postal clerk, a buxom blonde, one of the other interests Quentin Duckworthy is pursuing, or someone with her own interests at heart?

Elroy Traylor – Rockdale City Manager, whose hobbies include land development, bass fishing, and getting under Ducky's skin.

Tina Traylor – Elroy's wealthy wife, whose book collection is worth more than the Rockdale Public Library's, but she's not done collecting yet.

CHAPTER 1

Boredom had set in on me like a thin layer of congealed fat on a bowl of brown gravy. With autumn leaves falling gently from the tree limbs, business at our bed and breakfast had slowed down tremendously. I almost wished I had a couple loads of laundry to do. I thought about rewashing a load of bedclothes I'd just washed yesterday. You know what they say: you can't be too rich, too thin, or get sheets too clean. I even considered driving to Pete's Pantry because we were running low on turmeric, a spice I used about once a decade, whether I needed to or not. Our last guests had left nearly a week ago and the intervening days had dragged on like a silent movie, or a foreign film with subtitles. I wasn't one who handled idle time well.

Stone Van Patten and I had fallen into a comfortable routine at the Alexandria Inn. Everything from the front door out was his responsibility and everything from the front door in was mine. The only exception was when something broke, leaked, or made odd noises it shouldn't make inside the house. Then the responsibility shifted from me to Stone. He seemed to actually look forward to these occasions with great anticipation. Nothing excited him like a small kitchen appliance gone haywire. It usually resulted in a trip to Wal-Mart to buy a new one, after Stone had disassembled the faulty one and been unable to recall how to put it back together again. But in the meantime, it kept him happily occupied and he always enjoyed the challenge.

It was early on a Monday morning. Stone and I sat at the kitchen table sipping on fresh coffee and reading the *Rockdale Gazette*, the local newspaper that Howie Clamm had just recently flung into the thorny bushes out in front of the massive Victorian mansion we'd renovated in the historic section of Rockdale, Missouri. Stone had purchased the mansion after deciding to sell his online jewelry business in Myrtle Beach, South Carolina, and move to the Midwest to be closer to me. We'd met while I was on the East Coast, investigating the death of my ex-son-in-law's first wife. It had been twenty years since my first husband, Chester, had died of an embolism, and I had finally been ready to allow myself to form a new relationship with a man that wasn't strictly platonic.

"What do you have planned for the day?" I asked Stone, more to make idle conversation than any real interest in his plans. He traded me the business section for the sports page, and set his empty cup down on the table.

"Wyatt's stopping by for coffee, and I thought I'd see if he wanted to go to the RV and Boat Show in Kansas City today. He wants to buy a new bass boat with a more powerful motor." Stone's light blue eyes sparkled in delight at the idea of a faster boat.

"Why would he need more power? So you can get to your fishing hole in three minutes instead of five?"

"It's a man thing. You wouldn't understand."

"No, probably not. It just seems like an awful waste of money to me."

"You mean waste of money like purchasing that new pair of black leather shoes last week, even though you already have ninety-eight pairs of shoes, many of them leather, and most of them black?" Stone said, with a wink to indicate he was merely messing with me. "And, my dear, what is up with this new shoe fetish of yours? Before we got married you had one pair of old black heels that I was beginning to think you were saving to bequeath to your daughter in your will. Now you need an entire walk-in closet just to house your massive shoe collection."

"Okay, okay, point taken! Having a shoe fetish is a woman thing that you wouldn't understand. And I can't believe how many years it took the importance of a extensive shoe selection to hit me. Thank God for Veronica's desire to bring me up to speed, or at least where shoes are concerned," I replied. "Her attempts to modernize my make-up regimen failed miserably."

"Thank God for small favors! And, I have to say, when the female foot fashion fetish finally hit you, it hit you like a Mack truck doing ninety in the passing lane. I suppose like that old antiquated pair of heels you once depended on for any occasion that arose, all these new shoes will be with us forever," Stone said, with a purposely long drawn-out sigh.

"Yes, of course they will. Throwing away a pair of shoes, even my old dependable, antiquated pair, as you called them, is like losing a good friend," I replied, in defense of my new obsession with shoes. "I have learned that a lady simply needs a specific style of shoe for any occasion that's apt to occur. For instance, one can simply not be caught dead in a pair of white heels after Labor Day. I actually shudder when I think of the events I attended in those hideously-inappropriate black heels."

"Good Lord, do you ladies have to memorize a whole list of rules and regulations on what shoes you are, or aren't, allowed to wear on any given day?"

"Pretty much! And, even more crucial, is what type of event or function you're attending. The list of do's and don'ts regarding that aspect of shoe protocol is even lengthier. Like I said, it's something only women understand."

"You're absolutely right. I'll never understand the shoe fetish thing, or a zillion other different things about women, and, now, I'm not sure I'd want to," Stone replied, as he ran his fingers through his silver hair. "I don't even want to start on women and their obsession with their hair; curling it if it's straight, straightening it if it's curly, adding extensions if it's short, and adding highlights if, God forbid, it's all the same color. You don't even want me to get started on the need to make it some color other than the one they were born with."

"You're right, I don't want to get you started on the importance of having our hair be the perfect shade for our complexion."

"By the way, I also need to get a haircut one of these days before I have to get this mop permed," Stone said.

I instinctively ran my hand through my own short, brown hair, realizing that it really was about time for me to get a perm. I still had a lot of highlights in my hair from my last appointment with Beth at the Klip Joint in downtown Rockdale, but the trim she'd given me on the same day had pretty much cut off what was left of the perm I'd gotten in late July. I decided that visiting the beauty salon would be a more productive way to spend time than loading up on spices I had no idea what to do with.

"Could you make me an appointment at the barber shop with Bruce for tomorrow? I'll probably be with Wyatt for most of today," Stone said. After my nod, he continued. "So, what's on your agenda?"

At the mere mention of Detective Wyatt Johnston's name, I'd already headed for the pantry to pull out some Danish pastries I'd bought at the bakery over the weekend. Wyatt was a human garbage disposal, about six-and-a-half feet of pure muscle fueled by nearly constant calorie consumption. The martial arts training he participated in to keep fit for his job probably helped him wear off those extra calories. He wanted to be able to defend himself if the situation arose, he'd told us one morning while we were having coffee and discussing his incredible physique.

Wyatt had been a member of the local police department for over fifteen years, and had become a close friend of ours after his involvement in the investigation of two murders that had occurred at the inn, and also the murder of the pastor of our church just days before he was to officiate our wedding in the spring.

Wyatt and Stone had both tried valiantly to keep me from getting involved in the investigation of those murders, with little to no success. I had a personal reason in each instance to want the perpetrator brought to justice, and I took great pride in the fact that, in all three cases, my involvement had been instrumental in apprehending and arresting the killers. The authorities were not impressed with my infinite wisdom and dogged determination, but I was. It was on rare instances such as these that I truly amazed myself. Of course, most of my success was more a matter of dumb luck and uncanny timing than investigative skill, but that was beside the point. My perseverance had paid off in each case.

As I poured a refill into both of our cups, I considered Stone's question about my plans for the day. I tried to think of all the tasks I needed to accomplish and could come up with exactly nothing.

"Well, I, um, need to, um, probably should, um," I mumbled. "Crap! I can't think of one damn thing I need to do today. However, I was thinking I might go to the grocery store and stock up on turmeric, and maybe even some fennel. You never know when I might need either of those for a recipe I'm experimenting with. We have absolutely none of either one of those spices in the pantry."

Stone had the gall to laugh at my response. "Good God, Lexie! Don't tell me we're in the midst of a rarely used spice-shortage crisis? What in the world are we going to do? How are we going to survive this precarious predicament?"

"Okay, okay, wise guy. I didn't exactly say it was a crisis, just something I thought we should have on hand." I didn't appreciate the way he was getting his jollies at my expense. If he was as bored and restless as me, he'd be at Home Depot stocking up on every size and shape of screw, nut, and bolt they offered.

"Really?" He asked sarcastically. "Lexie, I think you need to get a job!"

"A job? Did you just tell me to get a job?" I asked. I stared at the man I thought I knew, wondering when he'd taken leave of his senses.

"Sure," Stone said. "Why not? And why are you looking at me like I just asked you to go rob the Jazzy Jigger Liquor Mart?"

"Well, for one thing, I thought I already had a job here at the Alexandria Inn," I said. "And, secondly, if we need the money, why don't you go get a *real* job?"

"We don't need the money or I would get a 'real'

job," Stone said, chuckling at my over-reaction to his teasing. "And, yes, of course you have a job here. I didn't mean it as an order, just a friendly suggestion because I love you. You wouldn't need a full-time job, or even necessarily a paying job. But you've been uptight and antsy, and complaining about being bored during the fall as business is slowing down. Winter will be even slower, so why not find something you'd enjoy doing to help fill some of your spare time? I'll be busy remodeling the suites upstairs that I didn't have time to mess with when we renovated this old place. I'd also like to replace all the old plumbing in the restrooms upstairs, and lay new tile in the showers. I might even replace all the existing toilets with the low-water flush ones. I'll have enough to do to keep me busy until business picks up in the spring. But you might need a reason to get out of the inn and do something to keep your mind and hands busy. The inactivity around here for days on end might drive you nuts. And from what I'm seeing here today, it might be a very short drive."

"You know, that's not a bad idea," I said, after a little consideration. "Wendy just told me yesterday that she'd heard the head librarian at the Rockport Public Library was getting ready to retire and they were looking for someone with librarian experience to handle the job during the interim, while they interview applicants for a permanent replacement."

My twenty-nine-year-old daughter, Wendy, who worked as the assistant county coroner, had mentioned the opening in passing, knowing I'd volunteered for several years as an assistant librarian in my hometown of Shawnee, Kansas. Now that I thought about it, she was probably hinting at the same thing Stone had just suggested. They must have realized even before I did that I was going stir-crazy.

Maybe it was watching me re-arrange the spices in the pantry into alphabetical order that tipped them off. But how else would I have discovered our lack of crucial spices like turmeric and fennel? If it wasn't my spice obsession, then maybe it was their finding me sorting all the books in the bookcases by genre that made Stone and Wendy think I'd missed working at the little local library in Shawnee.

"Maybe you should consider applying for the job. It would get you off the couch. You know those scintillating old re-runs of *The Love Boat* you've been watching in the afternoon? I can DVR them for you if you're afraid you might miss one."

"I've seen every episode three times, but thanks for offering. I get what you're saying, Stone. I really do. But, even though we're not booked solid, we do have occasional guests here at the inn, you know. What about them?"

"I can handle things here until spring," Stone assured me. "Once we get them settled into their suites, basically our only real responsibilities are to feed them and clean up after them. All the other things you do for them are above and beyond our obligations."

"Well, I guess you could handle things if I was gone during the day. I'd be home early enough in the evening to prepare supper for any guests we might have, and us too, of course. I'd also have time to spruce up the suites after the guests depart and prepare them for newly arriving guests."

"And I'd be happy to help out in any way I could," Stone said.

The Alexandria Inn, which my husband of just a few months, Stone Van Patten, had named after me, had been restored from an old Victorian mansion in ill repair into a thriving lodging establishment, a charming bed and breakfast in the small town of Rockdale, Missouri. We had both enjoyed the challenge and the hard work we'd poured into the project.

My name is Alexandria Marie Starr, by the way, but I'm known simply as Lexie. At fifty years old, I was enjoying being a newlywed, having recently married Stone, the second love of my life. I'd also enjoyed the challenge of running the inn, efficiently and effectively, which had been filled to capacity nearly all spring and summer.

But now it was late October, and business was waning as people stayed home and anticipated the approaching holidays. I felt like I was rattling around aimlessly in the huge inn, which encompassed half a city block. I liked the idea of getting an opportunity to use the skills I'd acquired as a volunteer librarian assistant in my old hometown. I'd had to give up that endeavor when I moved to Rockdale right before our wedding, because it would have been a long commute of over an hour each way.

"You know, Stone, I think I might just see about putting in for that job. I'd be out of your hair and have something to do to fill my spare time. Obviously, I couldn't apply for the permanent position, because of the nature of our seasonal business, but filling in during the interim would be fun and challenging. And the timing couldn't be any better. They will surely have hired a permanent head librarian by the time we get busy in early spring. Are you sure you wouldn't mind me being gone during the day?"

"Of course not," Stone said. "I know you're happiest when you're busy, and this opening at the library is the perfect solution. After all that happened this last spring, you could probably use something more tranquil and less nerve-wracking to do with your time."

"That's for sure. Having Pastor Steiner killed just days before our wedding, and having to find a replacement in such a short time, while investigating his death, took a lot out of me," I agreed.

"And it, no doubt, took ten years off my life just from worrying about you," Stone said. He had still not completely gotten over my insistence at becoming involved in the search for the pastor's killer. I wanted to change the subject before we got embroiled in a debate about my reckless impulsiveness, a character trait I'd finally learned to live with, but one Stone was still trying to accept and get accustomed to. I'd surely given him plenty of opportunities to work on that lofty goal.

"I think I'll head over to the library this morning," I said, just as Detective Johnston came in through the back door of the inn.

I would soon find out there would be little tranquility to be found working at the local library. If only I'd known what I was about to get myself into, I may have just stayed home and rewashed those clean bedclothes, or spent the day watching the wallpaper fade in the parlor, while ingesting entirely too much caffeine as I was prone to do.

CHAPTER 2

While chatting with Detective Wyatt Johnston over one final cup of coffee, I mentioned my plan to apply for the interim head librarian position at the Rockdale Public Library.

"I wondered when you were going to find something to do to cure the restlessness you've developed. I've gained ten pounds in the last two weeks," he said, as he popped an entire oatmeal cookie into his mouth. Obviously, he had noticed my symptoms of boredom too. Even with no customers at the inn, I'd been baking enough pastries, tarts, cream puffs, and fruit pies to feed an army of Wyatts.

"Speaking of which, I have a fresh pineapple upside-down cake cooling in the pantry for you to take home for you and Veronica. And, by the way, Stone has threatened to have you issue me a restraining order, not allowing me to get within fifty feet of the oven," I said.

"Yeah, I can see why," he replied, glancing at Stone. "He may have gained even more than I have."

"Twelve pounds and counting," Stone said, patting

his slightly protruding belly. Two or three inches below six foot, Stone tended to be slightly too short for his weight. As he had a habit of saying, he wasn't overweight, just under-tall. But at just five foot two, and a few pounds over my ideal weight, I had a tendency to be under-tall as well.

"Patrolling all over Rockdale on a daily basis, I hear a lot of things, Lexie," Wyatt said. "I've heard the Meals on Wheels organization is looking for drivers to deliver meals around town, and the nursing home on Spruce Street is always in dire need of extra help. Just something to keep in mind if the librarian job, for some odd reason, doesn't pan out."

I nodded in response, knowing there was no way on earth I could volunteer at the nursing home. It took a special kind of person to work at one, and I was pretty sure I wasn't quite that special. I couldn't walk from one end of a nursing home to the other without crying, puking, or both. I had a weak stomach as it was, and something about a nursing home made my stomach roil, and really tugged at my heartstrings. I wanted to visit with every single resident I passed, and sneak them, in their wheelchairs, out the back door, if possible, as if I were breaking them out of prison. I knew nursing homes served a valuable purpose, but I've never seen a resident of one that seemed truly thrilled to be there. It was if they had just resigned themselves to reside there while they waited patiently for the inevitable. I knew I'd find it sad and depressing, and I'd opt for boredom before those two emotions. However, the Meals on Wheels idea was definitely feasible. If I could manage to fit a few meals into my little sports car, I could certainly deliver them to disabled and elderly folks around town. It would be very self-satisfying to help the senior citizens who were unable to prepare meals for themselves, and feed the less fortunate.

"Thanks, Wyatt! That's good to know, because there's a good chance they already have someone in mind for the library job."

"They do," he said. "You!"

"What do you mean?"

"I ran into Bertha Duckworthy, the head librarian, the other day, and she told me she was going to retire, on or just after the last day of October, if she could find someone to fill in by then. I told her you had volunteered as a librarian assistant for a number of years, and she asked me to mention the opportunity to you the next time I saw you. I was going to do that today, but Wendy obviously beat me to it!"

"Thanks Wyatt. It sounds promising, doesn't it?" I asked.

"It's right up your alley, and you're a shoe-in for the job, Lexie," Wyatt answered. "She'd hoped you apply for the permanent position, but I told her the likelihood of that was remote due to your work here at the inn."

"I'm going down to the library this morning to speak with her. What did you say her name was again, Wyatt?"

"Her name is Bertha Duckworthy, but most people just refer to her by her nickname, Ducky."

"She goes by *Ducky*? She sounds like she must be a real character."

"She's one of a kind, all right. She's the type you either love or hate, but to me she's just Ducky," Wyatt answered. "I think you'll get along with her just fine as long as you remember to take whatever she says with a grain of salt, and try not to take any of it personally."

I wasn't sure what to make of Wyatt's advice, but I was anxious to go speak with Ms. Duckworthy, so I told the men to enjoy their day at the RV and Boat Show, and excused myself to go change into something other than the well-worn sweatpants and *Miller Lite* tee shirt I was wearing. I wanted to make a good first impression and this outfit hardly screamed, "Hire Me!" It more likely made the statement, "If you give me the job, I promise I won't chug beer until I'm off the clock."

Half an hour later I was in my blue convertible heading to the library, dressed in a knee-length pastel yellow dress, trimmed with black piping, and my brand new terribly uncomfortable, black leather heels. I knew there would be a critical reason I'd need to wear them when I bought them last week.

I'm not sure why, but I'd even chosen to put on a pair of pantyhose, which I detested and normally only stooped to wearing to funerals and weddings of people with whom I was very close. I also slipped on some dangly earrings and a matching emerald necklace Stone had given me for my birthday. It had been years since I'd applied for a job, and I didn't know the current dress code for such an occasion. Plus, it was important to me to make a good first impression on Ms. Duckworthy, and I didn't want to look like I'd just come from the gym, or a weeklong camping trip.

As I introduced myself to the head librarian a few minutes later, I knew I had over-dressed for the occasion. Ms. Duckworthy was wearing an old pair of baggy, faded jeans that ended several inches above the top of her beat-up hiking boots. She also donned a stained, light blue sweatshirt that had a Kansas City Royals 1985 World Series Champions emblem on the front and was frayed around the collar. To complete the ensemble, she wore an Isle of Capri Casino ball cap.

The head librarian had short salt and pepper hair, more salty than peppery, and wore thick horn-rimmed glasses. She was several inches shorter than me, probably an inch or two shy of five foot, and couldn't have weighed more than ninety pounds. Yet, for some odd reason, I instantly felt very intimidated by her, as if I were introducing myself to a drill-sergeant on the first day of boot camp.

"I'm Lexie Starr, Ms. Duckworthy. I believe Detective Wyatt Johnston spoke to you about my experience as an assistant librarian in Shawnee. I volunteered there for several days a week for a period of almost four years. He told me you were retiring and looking for someone to fill in as acting head librarian while applicants were being interviewed for the permanent position. The detective thought it might be right up my alley, and actually I was looking for something to do in my spare time while business at our bed and breakfast was in a seasonal slump," I said. As I babbled on, she stared at me like I had "*village idiot*" tattooed across my forehead. "So, um, anyway, I guess I've come to speak to you about the position and apply for the job."

"Really?" she asked. "I thought maybe you were on your way to a cocktail party, dressed in that fancy get-up, and all."

I laughed nervously at what I thought was meant as a joke. She didn't laugh, smile, or show any emotion at all. I turned slightly to my left, on the verge of walking right out of the library, and back to my car, knowing my face was flushing in embarrassment. I took a step toward the door when Ms. Duckworthy's next words stopped me in my tracks.

"Okay, lady, you've got the job," she stated. "When can you start?"

"But, don't you want me to fill out an application, or, perhaps, be interviewed first?"

"Naaa, the cop's word is good enough for me. It's just temporary after all, so you don't have to be the sharpest knife in the drawer."

"Well, then, Ms. Duckworthy, I guess I can start whenever you'd like me to." I wasn't sure if I should be insulted by her "sharpest knife" comment, so I chose not to be, since I really did want the job, and Wyatt had suggested I didn't take anything Ducky said personally. "Tomorrow's Tuesday. Will that work for you?"

"Yeah, that will work fine. I'll see you tomorrow morning around nine. Don't be late. I'll want to show you the ropes for a few days before I leave you on your own. This library ain't much different than any other library, but your responsibilities here might be somewhat more diverse than what you're used to," she said. "So don't go thinking you know everything there is to know about running a library."

I nodded. "Oh, yes ma'am, of course. I only worked as an assistant, so there are a lot of things I'll need to learn, but I promise I'm a fast learner."

"You'd better be," she retorted. "I'm not planning on baby-sitting you for very long. I'd like to be out of here by Friday, which is Halloween, if at all possible. Bring a notebook with you to take notes so I don't have to repeat myself."

"Yes, ma'am."

"And put that dress back in the closet and pull out something you can work in, like I got on," Ms. Duckworthy said, with a touch of sarcasm in her voice. I made a note to myself to come to work tomorrow looking like I'd just come from the gym, or a weeklong camping trip, as I'd tried so valiantly not to do today.

"Yes, Mrs. Duckyworthy, no problem there. This is not how I typically dress."

"Thank God! And one final thing, don't every call me ma'am or Mrs. Duckworthy again, and don't even think about calling me Bertha. Bertha makes me sound like an old lady. It's just Ducky from now on."

CHAPTER 3

"I'm sorry to disturb you," I said the next morning, taking notes as I sat next to Ducky, who was pecking around on the computer keyboard. She'd told me she had a requisition form she needed to fill out and fax to the main office before she continued "jacking around" with me.

"What did you call that cataloging software again?" I asked.

Ducky looked over the rim of her reading glasses for a few moments before answering. There was a menacing arch to her eyebrows. This was the second time I'd asked her to repeat herself, and I'd gotten "the look" both times. I'd hesitated to ask her to repeat herself again, but it was important I knew the correct name of the software program required to get the job done properly. I'd rather get the look a hundred times than screw everything up once Ducky left me on my own.

"What's another word for *quantity*?" Ducky asked, a few minutes later.

"How about *number*?"

"Naa, try again."

"Amount?"

"Yeah, that'll work."

For a moment, I thought she might be working on an online crossword puzzle, but quickly realized she wasn't the type to spend her time at work so frivolously. "Why do you ask?"

"Oh, this antique keyboard is a piece of crap," she answered. "The 'B' key sticks and you have to hit it repeatedly sometimes to make it work, and the "Q" key is completely defective and doesn't work at all. I've put in a work order for a new keyboard every week for the last two months and haven't received one yet. My boss is a piece of work, I'll tell you. He's one of the main reasons I'm retiring."

Keyboards are cheap enough, I thought, so I made a quick notation in my notebook to purchase a new one with my own money as soon as possible, so I didn't have to use my copy of *Roget's Thesaurus* every time I made entries on the computer. I wondered for a moment if I'd be working directly for Ducky's superior. It stood to reason I would, and now I was not all that anxious to meet this man who would have authority over me. I shook off my trepidation and continued to concentrate on everything Ducky was explaining about the cataloguing software program I'd be using.

After another hour of computer tutoring, Ducky led me over to the large-print section of the library. I noticed, despite her petite size, she walked with the heaviness and clumsiness of an inebriated elephant. Her outfit today was even tackier than the one she'd worn the day before. I had dressed-down significantly, but there was no way I could show up to work at the library in clothes so cruddy that even Goodwill would turn their noses up at them if I attempted to donate them. I was relieved when Ducky had made no comment after giving me the once-over when I walked into her office. She'd merely shrugged and pointed to a hook where I could hang my jacket.

Ducky started out by introducing me to Paul Miller and Carolyn Aldrich, two part-time employees, already busy with their responsibilities. Paul, who I guessed to be in his early thirties, was helping a customer find a specific book she was searching for in the rear of the library. I could tell instantly he was a man of few words. After telling him I was pleased to meet him and looked forward to working with him, he merely nodded, shook my outstretched hand, and turned his attention back to the customer he'd been assisting. Paul's muscular frame and large stature reminded me of Detective Johnston. He absolutely dwarfed Ducky, and looked like he should be employed at the local lumber mill instead of working at the library.

Carolyn, a gregarious local college student, was sorting returned books into categories to assure putting them back in their given places would be more efficient. I knew instantly I would enjoy working with her, and hopefully Paul, as well. Carolyn welcomed me to the library, and we spoke for a few minutes about nothing in particular. As we meandered away from Carolyn, Ducky muttered under her breath. I could only make out a few words, and "chatterbox" was one of them, so I knew whatever she'd said was not complimentary. I didn't know if she was referring to Carolyn or me, but I really didn't care either way.

Following the introductions, Ducky gave me an abbreviated tour of the building. It was an older lodge-styled, cedar-sided structure that looked as if it belonged in the Colorado Rockies next to a rippling trout stream. We started in the basement, which was dark and musty, with no windows and only a few light bulbs scattered about. There were quite a few boxes, no doubt filled with old library books, and a metal shelving unit with cleaning supplies on each shelf, and a wet mop, dust mop, and broom leaned up against the concrete wall.

Ducky told me an elderly man named Tom came in on Tuesday and Friday nights to do custodial work in the library and that Tom had been cleaning the library since he'd retired and moved here from Kentucky four years ago. He did contract work, cleaning a number of businesses around town in the evenings.

In the far corner of the basement was a shiny weight-lifting apparatus that looked to be fairly new. There was a bare bulb hanging on a chain above it, providing the only source of light in the area.

"Are you pumping iron in your spare time?" I asked Ducky, in jest.

"Of course not!" She answered, not amused by my teasing. "I let Paul put that down here a few months ago. He works out here sometimes after work. He's been such a reliable employee for all these years, I figured letting him use it down here was no big deal. He and his girlfriend live with her folks in a small apartment, and they don't have room for it at their place."

"Does Paul have a key to the library?" I asked, just in case the situation ever arose when I needed to get in the library and couldn't locate my key.

"No, it wouldn't bother me if he had one, but it would be against library policy," Ducky said, as we walked back up the stairs and then turned off the light switch.

We meandered through the back break room, and on to the main section, where all the books were shelved. This room had what appeared to be at least fifteen-foot ceilings, with large log beams traversing the room. Ducky led me to a little nook with several overstuffed chairs, and a comfy-looking sofa, situated around a floor-to-ceiling river rock fireplace that was being utilized on this cool October morning.

A young woman was curled up on the sofa, absorbed in the novel she was reading. Observing the cozy scene, I felt certain I'd enjoy working in this old-fashioned, but alluring, library. We stopped momentarily while Ducky rather curtly instructed the young reader to get her shoes off the couch. The twenty-something gal apologized profusely and put her feet on the floor. When the patron turned to glance at me, I merely shrugged apologetically. I couldn't see how she was doing any damage to the already well-worn leather couch.

When I expressed my impressions of the library to Ducky, she replied, "Too bad everyone doesn't have such a positive opinion of it, or at least of its location. The city manager, Elroy Traylor, wants to raze the building and have the city build a modern one down on Mulberry Street, which would be a very inconvenient location for a public library."

"That's for sure," I agreed. "I can't imagine why anyone would want to eliminate this building. One of Rockdale's charms is its abundance of historic homes, antique shops, and quaint little mom and pop shops. The library is the perfect complement to the very things that draw tourists here, and tourism is one of Rockdale's primary sources of income."

"I don't think Traylor cares about what's best for Rockdale and its citizens. As you know, there's a shortage of long-term rental properties in this town. He wants to build an apartment complex on this property, and the vacant lot next door, which he already owns. He's convinced the owners of the

Subway on our other side to sell out to him if it comes to pass, but fortunately so far, Elroy's been unable to convince the city council to appropriate the funds a new library would require. Traylor's nothing but a pompous prick. We've been at odds for years. It's a mutual dislike between us that goes far beyond the fate of the library."

I didn't know what their mutual dislike was based on, if not just the location of the library, but I felt a bit sympathetic for anyone who had the misfortune to be on Ducky's shit list. I was doing everything I could do to stay off that particular list.

I spent the next two hours walking on eggshells, afraid to do something that would result in being chastised by Ducky. She seemed to go out of her way to be unpleasant toward me, as if she resented the fact I was going to replace her in a few days. I had to remind myself on several occasions that I'd only have to work with her a couple more days before her retirement took effect, which was now scheduled for Friday.

As Ducky explained all the intricacies of the Rockdale Public Library to me, people were milling about, studying at the tables provided, and occasionally returning or checking books out at the front desk. After watching Ducky handle the first customer, she let me assist with the rest; something I was very accustomed to doing. She only scolded me twice; once for making needless small talk with a customer, and then again for taking a short bathroom break. I guess I was expected to pee on my own time. I wondered if Paul and Carolyn were forced to wear catheters to work. I guess that's why some, no doubt incontinent, individual invented Depends. At least while I was in charge of the library, visits to the restroom would be at one's own discretion.

Unfortunately, one could not always accurately schedule bowel movements.

Later I was checking out a couple of newly released mysteries to a young college-aged man when I saw Ducky involved in a heated conversation with a tall, raven-haired woman, who appeared to be very fit and quite striking in appearance. I couldn't tell what the dispute was about, but even though they were in the far corner of the library, I could hear raised voices and saw Ducky pointing her index finger in the other woman's face. After a few minutes of arguing, the other woman turned and rushed out the front door in obvious discontent.

When Ducky returned to the front desk, she didn't mention the confrontation. Despite my curiosity, I didn't want to ask her about it in the event it was a personal matter, entirely unrelated to the library. If she wanted me to know what the quarrel was about, she'd tell me. I was disappointed when she didn't. The woman may have just asked for the hours the library was open, and it rubbed the temperamental librarian the wrong way. "There's a sign on the front door. Read it, and don't waste my time!" I can imagine her shouting at the woman. I'd come to learn that any given transgression, no matter how insignificant, could result in a tongue-lashing from Ducky.

By lunchtime, I'd relaxed somewhat. I'd chosen to heed Wyatt's advice and take anything Ducky said to me with a grain of salt, turning a deaf ear to her when she snapped at me over something inconsequential. I asked her to repeat herself several more times, and actually, felt a little disappointed the one time she forgot to give me "the look."

While Ducky sat in her office and ate a sack lunch, I went next door to get a turkey sandwich at Subway. I reflected on what I'd learned throughout the morning and realized I was getting anxious to begin my tenure as the acting head librarian. There would be a few things I'd have to learn, but for the most part it would be repetitious of the tasks I'd performed during the duration of my volunteer work as an assistant. I wasn't thinking I knew everything there was to know about running a library, as Ducky had insisted I not do. But, I did feel I knew enough to muddle through while I learned the intricacies of the job.

After lunch, we picked up where we'd left off. By mid-afternoon, I was beginning to find Ducky almost endearing as she loosened up and talked about some of the things she looked forward to doing during her retirement. Some were quite predictable. She wanted to do a little traveling, and take up a couple of hobbies, such as needlework and gardening. And, not surprisingly, she wanted to spend more time with her grandchildren, Melissa and Barney.

But a few of the things on her bucket list I found almost unimaginable, if not ludicrous. Motivational speaking? Yeah, right. What could she possibly inspire an audience to do? Drink poisoned kool-aid en masse? That was one dream she fostered that I knew would never come to fruition. But, I guess it never hurt to dream.

And ballroom dance lessons? Really? Ducky was married, or so I presumed by the wedding ring on her left hand, so a dancing partner was probably not an issue. But, sprightly as she was, I couldn't quite picture her waltzing around the dance floor, with her having been blessed with the gracefulness of a newborn giraffe.

Last, but not least, skydiving? Seriously? I didn't even want to try to picture her abandoning a plane three thousand feet up in the air. It sounded like a disaster waiting to happen. Was that not a prelude to a hip replacement at her age, which I guessed to be in the mid-sixties, if she even managed to survive the plummet to earth? I guess I just couldn't understand why anyone would want to exit a perfectly functioning airplane, that didn't have its wheels on the ground at the time.

But the item on her bucket list that amazed me the most was her desire to have a Harley Davidson logo tattooed across the top of her left breast, which I imagined pointed straight to the ground when not secured in place by an industrial strength Playtex Cross-Your-Heart bra. For a tiny lady, she was well endowed in that department, which should be a real thrill for the local tattoo artist, a twenty-five year-old skinhead named Max, who had recently inked a small rose on Wendy's left ankle. I tried to picture Ducky lying on a table with her chest bared, while Max performed his artistry above her ample breast. I couldn't even go there in my mind without feeling highly amused and slightly repulsed.

Apparently, her husband, Quentin, had a Harley Big Boy. He and Ducky planned to take a coast-to-coast excursion on the bike, and then commemorate the trip with matching tattoos. Quentin planned to get his inked on his chest too.

While I was trying to picture Ducky getting a tattoo, she bent over, tugged her slacks down a few inches, and flashed me the top of her left butt cheek, revealing a tatted depiction of a half-full hourglass, and the phrase *Carpe Diem* below it. Ducky was turning out to be a surprisingly eccentric character, and I didn't doubt her desire to seize every single day of her retirement.

Just before the end of the workday, she surprised me yet again by telling a joke while we stood in the "how to" section of the library.

"Do you know where we keep the books about suicide?" she asked.

"No," I replied, a little taken aback by her question.

"Well, they should be right here, but once we check them out, we never see them again." She nearly lost her balance, as she slapped her knee, and laughed at her own joke. I chuckled along with her. Even though her joke was a bit distasteful, it was also kind of amusing, especially since I'd never have imagined she'd even tell one to begin with.

I thought back to Wyatt's comment that Ducky was the kind of person you either loved or you hated. Well, I couldn't honestly say that I was beginning to love her, but I did find myself developing a little fondness for her. I certainly didn't despise Ducky, as I had feared I might by the end of the week.

As I prepared to leave for home, Ducky raked me over the coals for straightening up her desk without permission.

"Now how in the hell do you expect me to find anything tomorrow? I had everything exactly where I wanted it. When you take over, you can do anything you want with this desk, but in the meantime, please refrain from rearranging my stuff." She had practically snarled at me. I, of course, apologized, and then let her disdain run off me like water off a "Ducky's" back. I chalked it up to her almost bi-polar personality. I would probably never understand her, but I was learning how to deal with her turn-on-a-dime mood changes.

Ducky was still muttering to herself about my audacity in moving things around on her cluttered desk, when I wished her a pleasant evening and left her to lock up the library. In the parking lot there were only two other cars, and they were situated on either side of mine. I tried to guess whether Ducky drove the pale yellow VW Bug, or the shiny black one-ton pickup. With Ducky, I figured either one was possible, and neither was what I'd expect a tiny, senior citizen librarian to drive.

I headed home with a much brighter outlook than I'd arrived at the library with earlier that morning. I was anxious to get back to the inn so I could tell Stone all about my day. Having a husband to go home to at the end of a long day was so nice after twenty years of living alone. I knew he'd be pleased with my renewed spirit, and relieved I'd found something as sedate as working at the local library to cure my boredom.

CHAPTER 4

Suppertime found Wendy, and Andy, Stone's nephew, at our dining room table. The two had been living together for several weeks now, and seemed to be growing closer with each passing day. I couldn't wish for a better son-in-law than Andy, who was so much like Stone, and I prayed the relationship would result in a marriage some day.

Andy had sold his private charter business back in Myrtle Beach, South Carolina, where both he and his Uncle Stone had formerly resided. He'd purchased a cattle ranch near Atchison, Kansas, and moved to the Midwest to be closer to his uncle, and also to my daughter, I'm sure. He still owned his five-passenger Cessna, and occasionally picked up charter flights as a side-job. Andy had drastically changed his lifestyle so seamlessly it was hard to imagine he hadn't been a cattle rancher his entire adult life.

As I was placing bowls of au gratin potatoes and peas, and a fish-shaped ceramic platter of grilled flounder on the table, Andy was telling Stone and Wendy a story about a couple he'd flown to a private airstrip outside of Climax Springs, Missouri, so they could attend their daughter's wedding. Their daughter and son-in-law lived near the fifty mile-marker on the Lake of the Ozarks, and owned a number of alpacas.

Andy was now negotiating with the newlyweds to purchase a pair of two-month olds, which were descendants of a herd in Ecuador. They were a smaller version of llamas, with expressive eyes, and valuable fleece that could be any of a number of colors, Andy explained. He was enamored with their curious personalities, and their friendly, gentle nature, and was hoping to raise them on his ranch.

I didn't comment, but was hoping Andy wasn't gradually taking on more than he could handle, even though he was a young, energetic man with a good head on his shoulders. When Andy bought the ranch, which encompassed a full section of land, he not only took on a large herd of cattle, he'd also inherited hogs, chickens, and a goat. He'd even adopted the previous owner's golden retriever, Sallie, who, along with his mastiff, Rebel, now followed Andy around like the pied piper.

After giving it some thought, I decided two more animals to take care of would probably not alter his day-to-day responsibilities all that much. And by the remarks Wendy was making, I could tell she was encouraging him to purchase the animals. She loved babies of any variety, and I knew she was picturing how adorable a newborn alpaca would be.

After supper, we all sat in the living room, chatting over cups of coffee, and pieces of apple crumb-cake. We discussed the couple who'd be checking in for a few days in the morning. Angus, a Nebraska state senator, and Olivia, a retired teacher, were attending a political fundraiser, and would also be celebrating their fiftieth wedding anniversary over the weekend.

I'd spent an hour sprucing up the nicest suite in the inn for the Spurleys. I also put a bottle of champagne and a vase of red roses on their nightstand to commemorate their milestone anniversary. A congratulatory card hung from a ribbon around the neck of the bottle of Dom Perignon. Stone and I took special pride in our reputation for going the extra mile to indulge our guests. Word of mouth advertising is what had brought most of the customers to our lodging establishment.

I ruminated over what else we could do to make the Spurley's stay special, while Wendy discussed the gruesome details of a head-on collision on Highway 36. As usually was the case, Wendy told us the drunk driver, who'd crossed through the median strip and caused the crash, had walked away from the accident without a scratch, and the law-abiding young woman with two toddlers at home, who was driving the other car, had been killed upon impact. Thinking about the Spurley's impending arrival distracted me enough to block out Wendy's colorful descriptions that were making it hard for me to keep down the perfectly prepared fish Stone had grilled, and I didn't want to hurl and spray everyone in the room with the peas I'd eaten, like bullets whizzing out of a machine gun. Something like that could throw such a wrench in a dinner party.

After Wendy spoke at length about the autopsy that resulted from this horrifying wreck, I wanted to lighten the mood and steer the conversation away from severed appendages and ruptured spleens, so I told everyone about my day at the library, and all about the head librarian I'd be replacing temporarily. I may have embellished a bit, as I had a tendency to do, to make the story as entertaining as possible, but it didn't take much exaggerating to portray Ducky as the enigmatic creature that she was.

Everyone laughed at my description of my day. After the lively discussion, my daughter said, "I'll bet you'll be relieved to see the last of her!"

I explained that dealing with Ducky was much easier once I'd paid heed to Wyatt's advice to take her with a grain of salt, but I had no way of knowing how prophetic Wendy's statement would turn out to be.

I woke up early, anxious to get to work and start another day of on-the-job training. I drank far less coffee than my caffeine addiction hankered for, but I didn't want to take the chance I might actually have to dispel any of it during my working hours. As small as Ducky was, I suspected she had a bladder the size of a camel's, for I'd yet to observe her visiting the restroom at the library. Perhaps she'd invested in a case of Depends at the drug store across the street, I mused.

She'd promised to give me free rein today while she observed me from a distance. I wanted to impress her with the fact that I'd paid attention to all she'd told me, and had a few tricks of my own up my sleeve from several years of working at a library. I suspected that, with Ducky, one or two of those tricks might come back to bite me in the ass.

I'd found a nearly new book at home in the inn's library, about herb gardening, something Ducky had expressed a desire to learn more about, and I was going to give it to her as an early retirement present. Giving a librarian a book as a retirement gift seemed kind of redundant, like giving a box of blueberry muffins to a baker, or a fedora to a milliner, but it was all I could come up with at the last minute. I picked it up off the kitchen table, drained my one meager cup of coffee, and kissed Stone goodbye before heading out the back door of the inn.

When I arrived at the library, the only other vehicle in the parking lot was the Volkswagen Beetle, parked in the same spot as it was the day before. I had actually guessed the car to belong to Ducky the day before, because of her diminutive size, but I'd learned over the course of the last two days that there was nothing predictable about her. I wouldn't have been at all surprised to see her tooling around town in the massive truck that had been parked beside me the previous evening. How her feet could reach the pedals, or her eyes could see over the dashboard of the massive truck, was beyond me, but I had to smile at the image the thought provoked.

I was surprised to find the front door of the library locked. Maybe the yellow VW wasn't Ducky's, I thought, because she must not have arrived yet. I cupped my hands around my eyes to peer in through the window, situated to the right of the door. The mirror-like finish on the outside of the glass made it difficult to see inside without shielding out as much sunlight as possible. I didn't see Ducky, but I did see a ten-to-twelve-foot ladder propped up against the wall in the section that housed the young adult books. I found this odd, knowing it hadn't been there when I'd left the previous evening. I'd spotted the extension ladder in the back storeroom earlier in the afternoon when Ducky toured me through the building. She told me she often used it to reach a book on the top shelves of the bookcases, but I couldn't imagine why Ducky would have placed it there before she locked up the library. Paul had returned all the books to their rightful places on the shelves before he'd left to go home a half-hour earlier.

I instantly felt something was wrong. Had Ducky decided at the last moment to retrieve a book from the top shelf to take home with her? Had she then fallen off the ladder? I couldn't see the base of it, or even the top, due to the pitch of the roof, but it looked a bit askew, and the sight of the off-centered ladder sent a chill up my back.

I dug furiously through my fanny pack until I came up with a spare copy of the front door key Ducky had given me right before I'd left the night before. I nervously fumbled with it as I tried to unlock the door. After several unsuccessful attempts, I finally got the key to turn in the lock and pushed the door open.

I rushed in through the door and headed directly toward the ladder. What I saw next took my breath away. I gasped in horror as I caught sight of Ducky's lifeless body dangling from a braided rope, attached to a log beam, just a few feet from the library wall where the ladder was propped.

Her head listed to the left at an unnatural angle, her skin a pale blue, and her eyes were opened slightly. She had on the same plaid flannel shirt, and tattered khaki slacks she'd worn the previous day. It became instantly clear to me she'd never left the building the night before.

My hands were trembling, and I could hardly catch my breath. I knew there was nothing I could do for Ducky at this point, so I pulled my cell phone out of my back pocket and dialed 9-1-1 as quickly as I could. I was not surprised when Detective Johnston was the first officer to arrive just moments later. He knew I'd accepted the job at the library and would have naturally responded when the call was dispatched to the officers on patrol. He had a tendency to always be the first responder to the scene of any death I'd been unwittingly involved with.

"Lexie, are you okay?" This was the first question Wyatt asked me when he walked in the door. I assured him I was all right physically, but shaken and horror-stricken by the turn of events. He led me to a chair and had me sit and put my head between my legs for a few minutes, fearing I might pass out in reaction to the mortifying scene I'd just witnessed.

I tried to calm my nerves by sitting quietly as the library began to fill up with uniformed officers. I heard sirens approaching as I watched a pumper truck pull up in front of the building. When I saw Nate, the county's medical examiner, and my daughter, who worked as Nate's assistant, enter the room the finality of the situation hit me like a wrecking ball. Ducky was dead. Sawing her open might be the topic of conversation at our next family gathering, as Wendy would relate every gory detail of the autopsy she and Nate performed on this intriguing woman I'd just become acquainted with. What in the hell had happened after I'd left the building the previous evening? I wondered.

Photos were being taken from every conceivable angle, as detectives scoured the room for any sign of what might have transpired there the night before. As far as I could tell, nothing out of the ordinary was detected other than the ladder leaning up against the wall and the corpse hanging from the ceiling. I tried valiantly to determine if anything else had been disturbed since I'd last been in the library.

Sitting with my head down, and my hands covering my face, I heard someone approach me. I looked up at a police officer I'd never seen before. I recognized the name on his badge as a new-hire Wyatt had told us about just days before. I answered questions as precisely as I could, and hoped that my being possibly the last person to see Ducky alive other than her killer, did not make me a prime suspect should her death be ruled a homicide. I also was the one to discover her dead body, which might not bode well for me if I were to become a murder suspect. I knew in my heart it was precisely that—a murder—someone had to have killed Ducky. The word "suicide" was being bandied about by every person in the room, and I wanted to scream out in anger that this was not possible.

I was explaining to Detective Travis in great detail what had taken place the evening before, which included nothing out of the ordinary as far as I knew, when I felt someone's hands on my shoulders. I turned my head to see Stone with an anxious expression on his face. I'd been too shook up to call him, but assumed either Wyatt or Wendy had done so, knowing I would need him to help quell my agitation.

"Did Bertha Duckworthy seem upset, overly emotional, or out of character in any way while you were with her yesterday?" Detective Clint Travis asked me.

"No. She was often agitated, and her emotions ranged from one extreme to the other, but for Ducky I don't think that would be considered out of character. In fact, I think it probably would have been uncharacteristic of her to have behaved any other way."

"Did she seem concerned, worried, distracted, or maybe even depressed?"

"No, not at all. In fact, quite the contrary."

"Did you notice anyone hanging around the library when you were preparing to leave for the day, or see anything unusual in any way?" He asked.

"No, not that I can recall. Ducky and I were the last ones here. I meant Mrs. Duckworthy and me."

"Whatever! Everyone in town called her Ducky, I've heard," he said.

"And when I left, Ducky was left here alone," I

continued. "But someone must have come in after I left."

"Yeah, right, lady. Did she receive any calls that you know of during the day?" The detective ignored my last statement and kept scribbling notes in a small notebook he'd taken out of his shirt pocket.

"No, but she did have a confrontation with a woman earlier in the day. However, she didn't tell me who the woman was, or what their conversation was about."

"And you didn't think to ask her?"

"No, Detective Travis, I didn't think it was any of my business. And, I don't have strong enough physic powers to have known Ducky would be found dead the following day, making their argument have any significance to the police department." I knew I was coming off as rude and sarcastic, but I didn't appreciate the detective implying I should have made it my business to find out what the two women had said to each other.

"Okay, fine. But could you tell me what you remember about the confrontation, just witnessing the incident from across the room?"

I told him what I could recall about the argument between the two women, even though there wasn't much to tell. They quarreled verbally, and then abruptly parted ways. Ducky didn't appear to be shaken after the incident, as if it were an everyday occurrence.

"Probably *was* an everyday thing if this Duckworthy lady was as cranky as everyone is saying. But, because I know the Chief will want a description of her, could you describe the other woman to a sketch artist?" He asked, still scribbling in the notebook.

"Yes, but not in great detail, as I was busy with a customer at the time," I said. "She was a pretty, well-built woman, with long straight jet-black hair and bangs, is about all I can recall."

"Okay, it's probably a moot point anyway, as it appears to me and the other investigators, as well as the coroner, that things are just as they appear, and Ms. Duckworthy took her own life."

"What?" I asked, incredulously. "No way! I can't believe she'd kill herself the very week of her retirement."

"All the evidence points that way, but it's still early in the investigation," the officer said, as he turned to walk away. I grabbed him by the arm and turned him back around to face me. As I began to speak, I pointed to an area on my left butt cheek.

"Yesterday Ducky showed me a tattoo which read 'Carpe Diem' right about here on her backside. Why would anyone so happy to show off a tattoo that stood for 'seize the day,' commit Hara Kari just a couple hours later? That makes no sense at all!"

"Yeah, whatever," Detective Travis replied. "The old lady could have had Wonder Woman tattooed on her ass, but that wouldn't mean she could fly, or fling a magic lasso around you that'd make you reveal all your secrets, would it?"

I was so dismayed by his sarcastic and incredibly insensitive remark, that I couldn't even form a response. All I could think about was Ducky's tattoo, and how her hourglass had just run out of sand. I turned into Stone's embrace, with tears in my eyes. He rubbed my back, and held me for a long time, until another officer approached us and asked me to make up a sign to hang on the library door, which read, *Closed until further notice.*

This was an ominous beginning to my "tranquil" time working at the library. It suddenly occurred to me even my job was up in the air now. If the library were allowed to open again in the near future, would

Stone be agreeable to me working there after what had just taken place? Did I ever even want to enter this building again?

Thinking back to the joke Ducky had told the day before about 'books regarding committing suicide' sent a chill up my spine. Little did I know she would be suspected of doing that exact thing just hours later. However, I refused to accept the idea that Ducky might have taken her own life. This did not even seem to be within the realm of possibility to me, and I intended to press that point to Detective Johnston when I got the chance.

I suddenly had the overwhelming desire to go home and consume an entire pot of strong coffee while I ruminated over the bone-chilling events of the morning.

CHAPTER 5

"Are you doing okay? I'm totally stunned, so you must be absolutely blown away by what awaited you at the library this morning." While Stone spoke, he lovingly caressed my back as I sat hunched over the kitchen table in quiet disbelief.

I was comforted by the touch and words from my husband of just over five months. When I couldn't form a verbal response, I shook my head and wiped a tear off my cheek that had just escaped from my overflowing eyes. I was not normally highly emotional, but I'd just met the deceased, and was beginning to bond with her. I felt it was a very unfortunate way for one's life to end, just a couple of days before a long-awaited retirement. I still believed her fate had been at the hands of another individual, and not a decision Ducky had made for herself.

I was having trouble wrapping my head around the very idea Ducky might have decided to end it all by hanging herself from the rafters after I'd left the building the previous evening. Was I being naïve by denying it was even possible? Did I just not want to believe she could do such a thing, despite the fact that every piece of evidence indicated she had? It was not unheard of for me to bury my head in the sand when I didn't want to face the truth.

Ducky could be crotchety and disagreeable much of the time, but my thoughts kept slipping back to how impassioned she was when telling me of her plans for the future. Would someone who had just expressed a desire to spend her coming days gardening and jumping out of perfectly good airplanes, suddenly decide that life was not worth living? I didn't think it was likely. Just as I was about to share these thoughts with Stone, Detective Johnston entered through the back door and strode into the kitchen.

"Hey, Wyatt," Stone said, as the detective pulled his favorite chair out from under the table and took a seat. He had long ago adopted the chair, which allowed him to sit with his back to the wall, a cop habit thoroughly ingrained in him.

"Hi guys," Wyatt replied in greeting.

Like Stone, Wyatt's first order of business was to ask how I was faring. I assured him I was all right, but very shocked and dismayed at the untimely death of Bertha Duckworthy. "I can't help but think that under the circumstances, if her death turns out to be something other than a suicide, I will be the prime suspect. Am I right?"

In response to my question, Wyatt reached out and patted my trembling hand that was resting atop the table. "Relax. I don't think that will be an issue, Lexie. Her death has been unofficially classified as a suicide. We're still waiting for the results of the autopsy, of course. I believe Wendy said it would be performed this afternoon. Right after you left, a suicide note was found. Apparently, after you left the library last night, Ducky typed out a short note, certainly not a manifesto or anything of that nature. Then she printed it off and placed it on her chair before pushing the chair up under her desk. It looks as if she then carried out her final mission."

"What exactly did the note say?" I asked. I was still very skeptical about the true nature of her death, and felt a little uncomfortable knowing my daughter would be involved in slicing Ducky open like a watermelon in a few short hours.

"Just that she could not face the changes in her life that retirement would entail. For many years, her world had revolved around spending her days at the library and the idea of nothing but idle time spent in the company of her husband was more than she could bear," Wyatt explained. "I didn't actually read it myself, but was told that she basically said she'd lost the will to live, and was apologizing to her loved ones for ending her life."

"Ducky had no intention of *idling* around the house with her husband. She planned to spend time enjoying her grandkids, Melissa and Barney. And she and Quentin were going to learn ballroom dancing together," I said. "Well, let me take that back. *She* was going to take ballroom dancing lessons and I assumed Quentin would be her partner."

"She must have had a change of heart," Wyatt said. "When push came to shove, those desires may not have been intriguing enough to ward off her sudden despair. Severe, overwhelming despair can come on in an instant, causing the affected person to react without giving their decision much thought. Having been in the department for many years, I've been involved with quite a few suicides, and this incident seems very reminiscent of many of the cases I've seen in the past."

"But she had a lot of plans and dreams for her

retirement that she told me about, with great enthusiasm I might add. I certainly didn't sense any 'overwhelming despair' from her. She could hardly wait for her retirement to commence."

With a little chuckle, Stone said, "She told Lexie she wanted to go sky-diving and get a Harley Davidson tattoo."

Turning to me, Wyatt asked, "And you believed that?"

"Well, yes. She already had a tattoo on her bum, and you know how eccentric she was. I felt like, with Ducky's personality, anything on her bucket list was apt to be odd and unusual."

"I guess you've got a point there," Wyatt said. "She once told me she kept a pet iguana named Pookie in her bathtub, and was looking for a mate for her. I have to admit, I know very few senior citizens who breed iguanas in their tub. Like, exactly no one other than Ducky."

"I can picture that," I said. "But didn't her husband have a say about her desire to house an entire family of iguanas in their bathroom?"

"You would think so. One has to wonder what kind of character Quentin is, being married to Ducky, and all. He and Ducky had only been married a couple years though. I do know Ducky and her first husband went through a very nasty divorce about five or six years ago. There were several domestic dispute calls involving the two of them during that time. If I remember right, her ex-husband's name is Bo Reliford. I'm not positive about the first name, it could be Bob, but I know Bertha's last name was Reliford for many years."

"Have you ever met her ex?" I asked.

"Yeah, I went out on a couple of those calls, and he was a real hot head and very abusive and belligerent when he'd been drinking, which was the majority of the time. He was arrested one time after a serious bender for assaulting a police officer, who just happened to be my partner at the time. Bo went after Clayton with a broken beer bottle, but in his drunken stupor, he stumbled to the ground and cut his own leg with it. He was a real schmuck, but I think he moved to Lee's Summit not long after that incident."

"Hmm, that's interesting," I said. "I can't imagine why Ducky stayed with him as long as she did. She didn't seem the type to put up with that kind of behavior, and tiny as she was, I can't see her being so afraid of anyone that she would be reluctant to leave an abusive husband in fear of retribution. Have you met her current husband?"

"No, but that's about to change. Quentin's coming in to the station for questioning in about twenty minutes. Even in the event of a suicide, it's not uncommon for family members to be interviewed. In a case like this, it's almost mandatory. That reminds me, I need to get going or I'll be late, and I don't need the Chief on my case. I really just stopped by to check on your welfare, Lexie."

"Thanks, Wyatt, I appreciate your concern. Would you like a cup of coffee and a doughnut to go?" I asked. I'd never seen this goliath of a man turn down food, and this time was no different.

"I think I'll pass on the coffee, but I might take a long john with me. It might be a while before I can grab some lunch."

The house phone rang a few minutes after Wyatt left to return to the police station. As I suspected, it was my daughter calling. She was also just checking in to inquire about how I was doing. I told her I was coping as best I could, considering what had happened earlier in the day.

"The body's in the cooler at the moment, but the autopsy is scheduled to begin in an hour or so," Wendy told me. Sadness overtook me as I marveled at how one could be a lively, complex, and vibrant human being known as Bertha "Ducky" Duckworthy, one day, and referred to as simply "the body" the next.

"Do me a favor and look for signs of defensive wounds on *the body* during the autopsy. I have very strong doubts about Ducky killing herself, and I know she would not have gone down without a fight."

"Why are you so certain she wouldn't have committed suicide, as the detectives concluded in their initial investigation this morning?" Wendy asked me.

I went on to tell her what I'd just told Wyatt and Stone. I listed off all the things Ducky had told me she wanted to do after she retired, repeating some of what I'd told everyone, including her, at the supper table the previous night. I described the excitement Ducky displayed while uncharacteristically chattering on about her plans. I described the tattoo she'd so proudly shown me. By the time I was through, I could tell Wendy was harboring some doubt about the validity of the librarian's death being ruled as a suicide.

"That is awfully strange," Wendy said. "I suppose she could have been trying to throw you off with all her bucket list talk, but what would she have stood to gain by that? I will run it by Nate so he will also be on the lookout for any signs of a struggle on the body during the autopsy."

"Thanks. I'd appreciate it. And please don't call her 'the body.' I find it unnerving, and somewhat offensive."

"Sorry, Mom. It's a force of habit from working in the coroner's lab every day. I didn't mean to sound disrespectful."

"I know, honey. I'm just stressed out right now."

"As well you should be."

"Call me this evening with the results of the autopsy, okay? I'm very anxious to see what you discover," I said.

"Of course. Now go sit on your back porch with your ever-present cup of coffee, and try to relax and unwind a bit. I'll give you a ring this evening."

After the call ended, I decided Wendy's suggestion was a good one. I put on a sweatshirt and retreated to the back porch with a cup of steaming fresh-brewed java. Stone soon joined me with his own cup, and we sat quietly, saying very little as we were both engrossed in our own thoughts. I found myself unwinding somewhat, but knew I would never relax while the cause of Ducky's demise was still up in the air. I considered scrounging up a load of laundry, just to keep myself occupied, until Wendy called with the autopsy results, but soon realized I was too bone-weary to remove myself from the lounge chair. Before long Stone was snoring in the other chair and, eventually, I too drifted off into a fitful slumber.

Somewhere between dreaming that all my teeth were falling out one by one, while unsuccessfully trying to get a huge wad of bubble gum out of my mouth, and Stone giving me the Heimlich maneuver while I was participating in a hot dog eating contest against Pee Wee Hermann and Mean Joe Green, I dreamt I was being chased down a dark alley by a scary, wild-eyed man with a broken beer bottle in his hand. Even after the man morphed into a childhood friend of mine, and then finally into my late former mother-in-law, I kept running in sheer panic. I then stopped briefly at a café to purchase a cup of coffee before continuing my terrifying sprint down a dark, deserted highway. Apparently, even during my darkest hour, I had a caffeine addiction that couldn't be denied.

When Stone shook my shoulder an hour later, I was still damp with sweat and my heart was beating as if I'd just sprinted up the stairs to the top of the Empire State building. According to Stone, I'd been murmuring in my sleep, and tossing and turning in the lounge chair. Despite the nonsensical quality of my dreams, I was disturbed by the fear factor embedded in them. It was time to get up and go search through the inn for items I could justify washing, just to keep me busy while I tried to clear my mind.

I was deep in thought, while rinsing off the dishes after serving supper to the Spurleys from Nebraska, who had checked in about three o'clock. I was aware the tuna casserole I'd made tasted more like saturated sofa stuffing, with just a hint of lemon pepper, than anything a person would actually want to eat, but fortunately, our guests didn't complain. I wondered for a moment if turmeric would have enhanced the flavor, had we had any on hand. The Senator and his wife seemed like a kind, laid-back couple, and knew from our dinner conversation that I'd had a traumatic morning. They were very sympathetic about my emotional distress.

And Stone was too much of a gentleman to ever criticize my cooking, no matter how God-awful the new recipes I attempted turned out. He never failed to kiss me after every meal and thank me for preparing it. The closest he'd ever come to objecting to a dish I'd served, was when he referred to my seven-layer lasagna as a "valiant effort." Even I couldn't choke down that culinary catastrophe, and from years of eating my own cooking, I could force down some really offensive vittles.

When the phone rang, it startled me. I dropped a wine glass into the porcelain sink, shattering it. I didn't even hesitate to consider the mess. Instead, I dried my hands quickly with a dishtowel and rushed to answer the phone. As I'd hoped, it was Wendy calling in regard to the results of the autopsy.

"Hi Mom," she greeted me. "I told Nate about our conversation earlier, and he agreed that from your conversation with Ducky yesterday, she didn't sound like someone on the verge of ending their life. And we did find multiple hematomas on her arms."

"Hematomas?"

"Bruises, basically. But as you surely know, when a person ages their skin gets considerably thinner. Sometimes an insignificant bump against a doorframe can cause major discoloration in the skin of a person Ducky's age or even yours. Because of the nature of these hematomas, they might be considered suspicious, but can't be definitively considered defensive wounds. And other than that, there was really nothing of any significance to be found, other than the telltale ligature marks around her neck that had the characteristic inverted 'V' shape, which indicates suicide rather than homicide."

"How's that?" I asked.

"When a body is already deceased, as in the event of having been murdered before the hanging, the ligature mark is nearly always a straight-line bruise. However, in the event of a suicide, where the person is still alive when the hanging occurs, the bruise is typically in the shape of an inverted 'V,' as was the case with Ducky. The bruising in the entire neck region was fairly extensive, but not inconsistent with the type of bruising associated with thin skin, like we saw on her arms."

"Well, I don't know what to think now," I admitted. "Because she had on long sleeves yesterday, I didn't see if there were already any hematomas on her arms before I left, but I'm still not one-hundred-percent convinced Ducky's responsible for her own death, despite what the evidence suggests."

"You might have to just accept it and let it be. We are waiting for the results of a tox screen, however, looking for signs of things like chloroform, or perhaps Rohypnol, Ketamine or GHB."

"What are those?"

"Date rape drugs."

"Oh, good Lord. Wendy, please tell me Ducky wasn't raped too," I said.

"No, she was not sexually assaulted. These drugs could render her unconscious, or unable to defend herself. But there are a lot of drugs out there that could knock a person out. We don't suspect this was the case, however, because we found no visible injection sites. The tox screen results are due back tomorrow morning though, and I'll call you when we get them."

"Good. Thanks honey!"

"Don't get your hopes up, Mom. It's not likely anything will show up that will point to anything but a suicide. Had we found definitive signs of her being dead prior to the hanging, we'd surely have a case for murder. But, Mom, do you realize how hard it would be for an individual to physically carry another person, no doubt kicking and screaming for all they were worth, up a ladder and then carry out the actual hanging? Ms. Duckworthy was for certain still alive prior to her neck being broken as a result of the hanging."

"Yes, I've considered the logistics involved, and do find it difficult to imagine. I don't recall what the noose was constructed of, do you? I was in shock at the time."

"It was crudely made out of a rope. There were quite a few particles of vectran found on her clothing and in her hair, as well as a few equine hairs. The rope was probably around a horse's neck before it was around Ducky's neck. Did she mention owning horses to you? Do you know if she lived on a farm?"

"No, but we never discussed where she lived. I assumed it was right here in town and never inquired."

"Ducky would most likely have brought it to work with her, since it isn't something you'd typically find in a library," Wendy continued. "That points to a pre-medicated, well-thought-out plan, and not a spur of the moment decision to kill oneself."

"I didn't see any rope in the library, but Ducky got very irritated when I messed with the stuff on her desk. I guess it's possible she didn't want me discovering the rope in one of the drawers, probably already tied into a noose. Had I stumbled across it, I would have naturally questioned her, and if not satisfied with her response, I might have called Wyatt to come check it out. And Ducky probably would have guessed that'd be my reaction."

"True," Wendy agreed.

"Still, I'm having trouble accepting her death as a suicide. If it was, she did one hell of a brilliant job of acting when she discussed her future with me. I'm not going to let this drop until I delve into it a little deeper."

"I was afraid you'd say that," Wendy said, with a long drawn-out sigh of dismay. "Mom, please don't get involved in this incident. The detectives will thoroughly go through every little detail and come up with a conclusive answer. They'll be able to come to a qualified and accurate determination about what occurred last night in the library, I promise you."

"We'll see," was my short reply. I could hear my daughter groaning in exasperation as I hung up the phone.

After a restless night, I got up early the next morning and joined Stone in the kitchen for coffee. He was always up and about at the crack of dawn, and usually had the paper read before I even woke up. He stayed just long enough to ask how I was doing, and then went upstairs to do some measuring for his remodeling project.

I flipped through the paper, not really concentrating on anything I read, and finished off three cups of coffee. I read the front-page article about Ducky's "suicide" several times and found nothing of significance in it. I then spent the next couple of hours dusting every horizontal surface in the entire inn. The floors needing vacuuming, too, but I wanted to make sure I could hear the phone when it rang. So instead, I scrubbed every toilet in the place with a bleach-based toilet bowl cleaner solution, ruining my sweatshirt and favorite pair of jeans in the process. They now had little white blotches where the solution had splashed on them and bleached out the fabric. Once the toilets were sparkling, I started in the kitchen washing the windows, and proceeded through the inn, room by room, until there wasn't one streak on any glass surface, including the bathroom mirrors.

Exhausted, I poured myself another much-needed cup of coffee, and sat down at the table while coating chicken breasts and thighs to fry later on for supper. I was rinsing blood off my index finger, from a self-inflicted paring knife wound, when the phone finally rang at about ten-thirty.

"Hello," I said breathlessly into the handset, after

seeing Wendy's number on the caller I.D. monitor.

"I was right, Mom. Nothing on the tox screen report to indicate Ducky had anything unusual in her system. Nate has signed the death certificate and put down 'suicide' as the C.O.D."

"I'm shocked, and somewhat disappointed to hear that, I must say."

"I knew you would be, but that's the way it is. I'm sorry. I know how badly you didn't want to believe Ducky could kill herself," Wendy said.

"I still can't honestly say I'm totally convinced, but I do appreciate you calling me with the results. Say, did you by chance read the suicide note?"

"No, I just heard the gist of it."

"Do you know where it is now?"

"I'd assume the police department has it."

"Okay, just curious," I said.

"Uh—huh. I'm sure that's all there is to it. You do know what curiosity did to the damned cat, don't you, Mom?"

"Oh, don't be silly. I'll let you get back to work now, and talk to you later." I hung up before Wendy could climb up on her soapbox and start lecturing me about the hazards of my doing a little investigating on my own, as she was prone to do. I quickly picked the phone back up, and waited for a dial tone, before punching in Wyatt's cell phone number. After exchanging a few pleasantries with the detective, I got around to why I'd placed the call in the first place.

"While I have you on the line, Wyatt, do you have access to Ducky's suicide note?"

"I think Detective Travis has the note on his desk. He was just finishing up the paperwork on yesterday's 9-1-1 call. Why do you ask?"

"I was just hoping to get an opportunity to read it. I don't think I can let it go without reading it, and trying to come to grips with Ducky's reasoning, in her own words, for ending her life."

"And that's all there is to it?" He asked, with a hint of mistrust in his voice.

"Of course," I replied. Wyatt was known to get on that exact same soapbox as Wendy, and Stone, for that matter, so I tried to cut him off at the quick. "I'm not sure I like Detective Travis very much. He was quite rude and insensitive while questioning me yesterday. What's your impression of him? I know you haven't had the opportunity to work with him yet."

Wyatt nodded, before replying. "Well, Clint seems very driven and anxious to succeed, but also very introspective. He doesn't interact much with the other officers, but he doesn't know any of us well yet, either. So really, I have very little to base an opinion on so far. He probably was just uptight because it was the first fatality case he'd been involved in."

"Oh, okay. That makes sense," I said. Actually, it made very little sense to me. The new officer hadn't seemed uptight or upset about Ducky's death, but more as if he were totally unaffected by it. He seemed concerned about something, but it certainly didn't have anything to do with the librarian's death, I was pretty sure. I was about to drop the subject and ring off, when Wyatt's next words stopped me.

"I'll see if I can make you a Xerox copy of the note and drop it by later after my shift. I guess letting you read the note can't bring any harm to you, and maybe you'll feel more assured after you've seen it with your own eyes."

"Thanks, Wyatt. It might be best if you didn't tell Detective Travis who you're making a copy of it for. I got the impression he didn't care for me any more than I did for him."

"I don't know how Clint could dislike you, or hold

any bias against you at all, but if it makes you feel better, I'll just make the copy when he's out on patrol."

"Thanks, Wyatt. I appreciate it."

It was early in the evening when Wyatt walked in the back door and sat down at the kitchen table. I turned the burner off from under the frying pan so the chicken wouldn't burn while I visited with the detective.

"Would you like a cup of coffee? I just brewed a fresh pot," I said.

"Sure, why not? What's one more hit of caffeine? Since I've started visiting you here at the inn almost every day, I've gotten very little sleep. Why in the world would I want to start now?"

While I was getting a clean coffee cup out of the dishwasher, Stone joined us in the kitchen, so I snatched another cup off the top rack and closed the door. I placed the cream and sugar decanters in front of Wyatt, and then set down the full coffee cups. Before I sat down myself, I placed a plate of snickerdoodles in the middle of the table, knowing Wyatt liked sweet treats with his coffee, and Stone could never resist a cookie either.

Stone shot Wyatt a look of disapproval after the detective had placed a piece of typing paper in front of me and said, "Here's the Xerox copy of Ducky's suicide note that you requested."

"Does Detective Travis know you got this for me?"

"No, he was out on a call, I'd guess. I haven't seen him all afternoon," Wyatt said.

"Do you really have to encourage Lexie?" Stone asked Wyatt. "I can already see where her interest in this situation is heading."

"Well, it's no longer an open case, Stone. It's more of a cut, dried, and closed case of suicide. I didn't really see what harm could come of Lexie reading the suicide note, and I can understand her interest in it."

"Okay, I just had a bad feeling about it. My intuition regarding Lexie's intentions has always been pretty spot-on, so I am probably just over-reacting," Stone said.

For Stone's benefit, I read the note aloud.

> *"To Whom it May Concern. I have willingly made the choice to end my life because I can't seem to accept the idea of a life without a job to go to every day. Spending endless hours doing nothing with Quentin is not my idea of contentment, although this is not the fault of my husband in any way. It's just something in me that can't stand the idea of too much idle time. I'd like to express my love for Quentin, my daughter, and, of course, my beautiful grandchildren, Marissa and Bernie, and I apologize for the fact I'll no longer be a part of their lives. I'm afraid I'd be so adversely affected by the idea of being retired that I wouldn't be very good company to any of them, anyway. I never have dealt well with change, and know I couldn't cope with what would have been the biggest change ever in my life. Please forgive me for taking the cowardly way out.*
>
> *Sincerely, Bertha Duckworthy."*

There were tears running down my cheeks by the time I'd finished reading the note I held in my trembling hand. Nothing about it rang true to me, and I couldn't shake the feeling this wasn't a note Ducky would have contrived, but it tugged at my heartstrings, nonetheless. There was something else about it that troubled me, but I couldn't put a finger on it at the time. All I could do was shrug my shoulders, and thank Wyatt for getting me a copy of it to read.

I knew I needed to get back to preparing supper, to have it ready to serve on time, so I went back to the stove. I turned chicken breasts and thighs in the sizzling skillet in silence, sipping at my coffee occasionally, as Stone and Wyatt discussed Stone's renovation plans for the inn. My mind was a thousand miles away from schedule forty galvanized pipe, and the advantages of low-water flush toilets. I was startled when I felt Wyatt's hand on my shoulder.

"Thanks for the coffee and cookies, Lexie. Delicious as usual. I hope seeing the note for yourself will help you accept Ducky's death. I don't want it to eat at you, because that kind of stress can adversely affect your health, and there's nothing you can do about it, anyway."

"I know. But I do appreciate you bringing the copy of the note over for me. There's something about her note that's bothering me, but it's probably just my mind playing tricks on me, due to the tragic nature of the whole thing. Thanks again, and we'll see you later," I said.

Supper was a subdued affair. I didn't feel very talkative, and Stone and the Spurleys seemed to sense my melancholy, keeping the conversation to a minimum.

I went to bed shortly after cleaning up the kitchen. I lay awake most of the night with the words of Ducky's note reverberating in my mind. I finally drifted off to sleep in the early hours of the morning, dreaming about working at the Rockdale Public Library, once it was allowed to re-open. I saw myself checking out books to patrons, helping people find the novel they were searching for, going to the bathroom anytime I felt like it, and typing out requisition forms...

CHAPTER 6

"That's it!" I said out loud as I sat up in bed around four in the morning.

Stone turned over in alarm, awakened by my exclamation. "What's wrong? Are you okay?"

"Yes, I'm sorry I woke you," I said, apologetically. "But I was just dreaming about filling out requisition forms at the library and it hit me what it was about Ducky's suicide note that was bothering me."

"What's that?" Stone asked, with a hint of exasperation in his voice.

"It was the names!"

"The what?"

"The names in the suicide note," I said.

"What are you talking about, honey?"

"Well, for example, Ducky mentioned her husband by name!"

"And you think that confirms she couldn't possibly have killed herself?" Exasperation was clearly more evident in his voice now.

"Yes! You see, her husband's name is Quentin!"

"Okay, and that is important because..." Now the

exasperation dripped off every word he spoke. Stone was clearing losing patience with me and wondering why I'd woken him from a deep sleep.

"The keyboard on Ducky's computer is faulty. The 'B' key, as in Bertha, sticks and often has to be pressed numerous times to work, and the 'Q' key, as in Quentin, doesn't work at all, and hasn't worked in over two months. Ducky couldn't have keyed in that note on the computer at her desk!"

"Aren't there other computers there for library patrons to use?"

"She had turned off the computers, and shut out the lights in the computer lab before I left. I can't see her doing that if she intended to go back in there and type out a suicide note a few minutes later. I can't really see her using any of those computers, anyway. Despite the problems with the keyboard, I think she probably always used the computer on her desk, no matter what she was working on," I explained.

"Okay, I suppose I see your point," Stone said, sitting straighter up in bed. "But the note could have been typed anywhere. If she had been planning to kill herself, she could have used her home computer to produce the note."

"I know, I thought of that. But it's much more than that. I'm almost positive she told me her grandkids were named Melissa and Barney, not Marissa and Bernie, as stated in the suicide note. I remember thinking her grandson had the same first name as my cousin in New Mexico," I explained. "And no grandmother is going to forget her grandchildren's names."

Stone shook his head as he contemplated the situation. "That is rather curious, I'll admit. But grandmothers under duress, as anyone writing a suicide note would surely be, could accidentally mistype a name, even a grandchild's name. If she was typing rapidly, a few typos are not out of the question."

"It just seems like too many questionable inconsistencies to me to not warrant a closer look. And frankly, I can't imagine her signing her note 'Bertha Duckworthy' because she adamantly insisted that I never refer to her as 'Bertha,' but only as 'Ducky.' She told me she hated the name 'Bertha.' I can't see her using it in her final note, unless it was some kind of document that required giving your full legal name. And that's not a typo. That was just plain out of character for the woman."

"Hmmm. Well, let's go down and have some coffee. I know I'm not going to go back to sleep, and you don't look like you've slept at all. You can call Wyatt after eight when he reports to work, and tell him what you just told me," Stone suggested. "I'm seriously beginning to think you may be on to something. Ducky killing herself seems too unlikely, and, like you, I also believe that the official cause of death deserves another look."

I was relieved that Stone agreed with me there was too much skepticism regarding the manner of Ducky's death to arbitrarily classify it as a suicide, without taking the time to dig a little deeper. I, for one, was going to dig deeper, even if no one else would. As the last person, besides the potential killer, to see Ducky alive, I felt like I owed that much to her. Because if Ducky didn't end her own life, she deserved justice against whoever did, as did her family!

"And, one more thing, sweetheart," Stone said, as he got out of bed.

"Yes?"

"Why do I dream about catching huge bass, walking on beautiful beaches, and of course, big-busted women, while you're dreaming about filling out requisition forms? I'm beginning to think you need a little more joy and excitement in your life!"

If he hadn't ducked just then, he'd have been hit squarely in the face with one of the colorful throw pillows on our bed that he detested so much!

"What?" I asked Wyatt later that afternoon when he stopped by for a few minutes to speak to Stone and I. "You've got to be kidding!"

"I'm sorry, Lexie. I happen to agree with you that Ducky's death needs to be explored further. But unfortunately, that's not my call to make. Chief Smith doesn't think there's enough evidence to warrant a full-on investigation at this time. He thinks the suicide note could have easily been created on Ducky's home computer and, in her distressed condition, typos would not only be possible, but also expected. He did agree, though, to re-open the case if anything else significant comes to light that points to anything other than a suicide."

"Oh, jeez. No offense, Wyatt, but that seems a little lame and unprofessional for the Chief of Police."

"Well, there have been a string of break-ins on Main Street, and he has all hands on deck looking into who the culprit, or culprits, might be. Just last night the department store got robbed after the back door was kicked in."

"So the fact that a comb might have been pinched from the five and dime takes precedence over what is potentially a murder case?" I asked a bit sarcastically, due to my current disgust with the police department.

"It's more than the theft of a comb, Lexie," Wyatt said. "Narcotics, like Percocet and Oxycodone, were stolen from the pharmacy the night Ducky died, and it's only a matter of time before someone gets injured, or worse, by the perpetrators. Still, I agree with you that a couple of detectives should be freed up to pursue the possibilities surrounding Ducky's death."

"Well, then the way I see it, there's nothing preventing me from pursuing those possibilities on my own," I said, more to myself than anything.

"No way!" Detective Johnston and Stone said in unison. Both reacted with so much vehemence that Stone spit coffee across the kitchen table, and Wyatt removed the half-eaten long john from his mouth and sat it down on the table. I'd never seen this eating machine remove something already in his mouth and I sat back in my chair in surprise.

"We are not going through this again," Stone said. "Nothing good has ever come from your nasty habit of stepping into the middle of police cases."

"Totally untrue," I replied, in my own defense. "How about the arrests of murderers for starters? And from what I'm hearing from Wyatt, this is not a police case at all. Apparently it's not important enough to be considered a 'police case,' Stone."

"You know what I mean, Lexie! Your life has been threatened on a number of instances, and you've been to the emergency room on numerous occasions because of the cases you've gotten yourself involved with. Please let well enough alone!" Stone pleaded with me.

Pointing what was left of his half-eaten long john at me, Wyatt said, "I agree with Stone. It would be best if you stayed out of it completely."

"Best for whom? Certainly not for Ducky! She deserves justice!" I nearly shouted at our guest. "What about her family? They deserve justice too, and they deserve to know the truth. How else will they find closure?"

"Justice for what? The chances she was murdered

are still remote, Lexie. And you have my word that if anything comes up that says differently, the police department will check it out. I know her family deserves the truth, but my hands are tied."

I nodded without much enthusiasm. Wyatt's word was the best I was going to get at this stage of the game. But, I still felt like I owed it to Ducky to ask around and see if I could find something even more substantial than the inconsistencies of the suicide note. Something concrete enough that the police department could not deny indicated Ducky's death was not self-inflicted.

I stood up and walked to the refrigerator to begin peeling potatoes for supper. I had a rump roast in the oven, and wanted to serve it with all the trimmings, including freshly snapped green beans, big, fat fluffy rolls, and even a homemade blueberry pie for dessert. After all, staying at the Alexandria Inn did not come cheap, and the Spurleys deserved the same attention we showered on all our paying guests. I didn't want to ignore them in my quest to uncover the truth. I was deep in thought when Wyatt patted me on the shoulder.

"I really am sorry I couldn't do more. As always, thanks for the coffee and doughnuts. I'll see you two later." He tipped his hat as he walked backward toward the door leading out to the rear porch. I nodded, but was already thinking about the various people I wanted to find a way to speak with. As usual, I was going to have to go about it as covertly as possible, so as not to upset Stone. I wanted to at least get through the newlywed stage of our marriage before Stone realized he'd made a monumental mistake by marrying me.

I spent the rest of Thursday evening sulking and

pouting between bouts of furiously attacking housecleaning chores. By the time I went to bed, I'd decided nothing beneficial would be accomplished by throwing a pity party for myself, and also for Ducky, who for obvious reasons, was unable to attend.

I then began scheming and thinking of ways to investigate Ducky's death, without tipping off Stone and Wyatt. Despite the pleas for me to leave everything to the police, I was not going to let the matter drop until I, too, was convinced she hadn't been murdered. It was clear to me the detectives considered her death to be immaterial, and not worth their time or effort. With any luck at all, I'd stumble upon some piece of irrefutable evidence that would be impossible for them to ignore.

I found the little notebook I referred to as my "Sherlock Holmes pad," which I'd used several times in the past to jot down a list of people who I thought it might be worthwhile to speak with. That was the easy part of my plan. The more difficult part was figuring out how to accomplish that goal and that audacious task would take a little more thought. But coming up with clever ways to make those conversations happen, was a talent in which I not only excelled, but also thoroughly enjoyed. Let the inquisitions commence, I thought.

CHAPTER 7

"Ms. Starr?"

"Yes, this is she," I replied, to an unfamiliar voice after answering the landline telephone early Friday morning.

"This is Colby Tucker, with the county library system. I'm sure you already know about Mrs. Duckworthy's death."

"Yes I do, Mr. Tucker. I'm afraid I was the one to discover her body when I reported for work Wednesday morning. It was incredibly shocking. What a terrible thing to happen, don't you think?"

"Yeah, sure," he replied, with little or no emotion. "Bertha reported to me, and now you'll be doing the same as the interim head librarian until we can find a suitable person to fill the position full-time."

"Okay," I said. "I look forward to meeting you, and I promise I'll do the best job I'm capable of doing."

"Yeah, sure." My new boss repeated. "Mainly, I'm calling to let you know the library will be closed all next week and reopen the following Monday. You need to pass this on to the other employees there, because I'm about to go on a break, and I really don't have the time. Did Bertha give you a key to the front door, or am I going to have to interrupt my busy schedule to get one to you?"

"I have a key. Ducky made certain I got one. She was very professional, you know. And I will contact Paul and Carolyn as soon as I get off the phone with you. Do you happen to know when and where Ducky's funeral services will be held?" I asked. I had promised Ducky I'd never call her Bertha, and even now that she was dead, I would feel a sense of guilt in doing so. It seemed to me Mr. Tucker was using the despised name almost mockingly. But then, I was finding it hard to give him the benefit of the doubt considering the dispassionate manner he was displaying.

"No, I don't know anything about the services, but I'm sure it will be in the paper tomorrow if it wasn't already in there today." It was obvious Colby Tucker neither knew, nor cared about, the details of the services. He sounded like he didn't even give a rat's ass that the woman was dead, responding as if I'd asked him if he knew when asparagus would be going on sale at Pete's Pantry.

With a brisk and impersonal farewell, he rang off, leaving me to wonder if I'd be able to tolerate this man's demeanor, even on a temporary basis. So far, I had to agree with Ducky's assessment of her boss. He was a first class jerk! I couldn't imagine what kind of motive this man might have to kill Ducky, but I was almost wishing I'd discover he was the guilty party. I'd take great pleasure in seeing him arrested and prosecuted.

If nothing else, I now knew I had about ten days to devote to doing a little investigating on my own before my days would be filled with library work.

* * *

I couldn't find a Paul Miller or a Carolyn Aldrich in the phone book, but I kind of recalled Ducky telling me Paul lived with his girlfriend and her parents, and it stood to reason as a student at the local community college that Carolyn likely still lived with her parents. I decided to run down to the library to scour through Ducky's desk for their contact information.

When I pulled into the library parking lot, there was an affluent-looking black man surveying the property. He was standing next to a transit attached to a tripod. A plumb bob hung down from the center of the transit. The gentleman was making notations in a notebook, and shouting instructions to a younger man who was standing at the far end of the property holding a measuring rod.

I walked over to the man, introduced myself as the interim librarian, and politely asked him what he was doing.

"I'm planning on buying up this property in the near future, and I'm trying to determine how many apartment buildings I'll be able to fit on this lot, as well as the others I'll be purchasing for the project," he said.

"You must be Elroy Traylor."

"That's right," he replied. "I'm the Rockdale City Manager."

"That's nice, but I was not aware this property was for sale."

"It isn't. Not yet, anyway. But it will be in the near future. The untimely demise of Mrs. Duckworthy will undoubtedly speed up the process," he said, with a look of satisfaction. I could easily see how Ducky's issues with this man went "far beyond the fate of the library," as she had expressed to me.

"Not if I have anything to do with it!" I said. I didn't

like his pompous attitude and lack of concern about Ducky's death. I immediately wondered if he'd had anything to do with the *untimely demise* of the woman who'd been standing in the way of his new apartment complex development. Elroy Traylor seemed like the type of person who'd let nothing stand in the way of him getting what he wanted. My respect for Ducky went up a notch for standing up to such an intimidating individual, who was a little too full of himself for my taste.

"Trust me, you won't have anything to do with it!" He practically spat out at me. The very notion had me wiping imaginary spittle off my face with the sleeve of my sweatshirt.

With that rather rude retort, Traylor smugly turned away, dismissing me. I turned and strode purposely toward the library, using my key to gain entrance into the now ominous-feeling building.

It felt cold in the library, even though the thermostat had a digital reading of sixty-five degrees. I could still picture Ducky's body dangling from the rafters, and I couldn't wait to find Paul and Carolyn's phone numbers and leave. I would call them from home so I didn't have to remain in the building any longer than necessary. I had the sense I was being watched, although I knew it was just a figment of my overactive imagination.

I felt a bit like Nosy Nellie searching through Ducky's desk. She had planned to clear out all her personal papers and items today, her official day of retirement. It would be up to me now to box up her stuff and take it all to her husband, Quentin Duckworthy. If I could get past the eerie sensation I wasn't alone in the building, I'd come back over the weekend, and get that task taken care of, so I could concentrate solely on business matters when the library reopened.

I combed through the top drawer of Ducky's desk, and discovered she'd had a fondness for sweets. There were dozens of Tootsie Rolls in various sizes scattered about among paper clips, ballpoint pens, memo pads, and other assorted office supplies. I was often afflicted with chocolate cravings myself, so I unwrapped a small Tootsie Roll and popped it in my mouth before continuing my search. I could almost hear Ducky chastising me from beyond for messing with the stuff in her desk without her permission.

When I didn't find the employee contact information in the top drawer, I opened the second one, and didn't have to look long before I found, below a layer of candy wrappers, a folder containing time sheets, copies of W-9's, along with addresses and phone numbers of the employees. I'd forgotten about the man who performed janitorial duties on Tuesday and Friday nights. His name was Tom Melvard, and from his address, I could see he lived about two blocks down the street from the Alexandria Inn. I thought it'd be best if I called him right away from the phone in the library, since he was probably wondering if he'd be expected to report for duty later that evening.

Mr. Melvard answered the phone on the second ring. I repeated what Colby Tucker had told me, and explained to Tom he wouldn't be expected to return to work until Tuesday of the following week.

"I just can't believe she's gone," he said, with a catch in his voice. "I'm so sorry you had to be the one to find her that way. I don't know what I'd have done if I'd been in your shoes at the time."

"Did it surprise you to hear she took her own life?" I asked. "Because it sure did me. In fact, I'm going to try to prove somebody killed her."

"Oh really? Well, it really didn't surprise me at all.

She'd mentioned to me a few times how unhappy she was with her life. She shouldn't have married Quentin on a whim the way she did. But, I'd hoped she'd work things out and find happiness, despite the fact that I don't think her and Quentin's marriage was a match made in heaven."

"I didn't see any sign of unhappiness in her," I replied. "But I'd only had that one day to get to know her, and I'm sure she was a very complex individual."

"Yes, she was definitely complex, and had been all the years I'd known her. I can pretty much assure you she was not beyond committing suicide. In fact, I'd pretty much bet on it," Tom said with a sniffle. He was distraught, and I didn't want to upset him any further, so didn't press Tom for any more personal observations about his old friend.

"I'm so sorry for your loss, Mr. Melvard. I hope I'm still here next Tuesday evening, when you report to work, so I can meet you in person."

"Okay, thanks for calling," he said. "And I'll be sure to show up early Tuesday, because I'd like to meet you too. I'll see you then."

"Wait," I said, before he could hang up the phone.

"Yes?"

"Did you report to work this last Tuesday, the night Ducky died?" I asked.

"Um, no, I didn't. Something came up and I couldn't get to work. I'm sorry, ma'am, I meant to call in and let someone know."

Tom Melvard didn't appear anxious to expound on why he couldn't make it to work, but I'd deal with that matter later. "I see here that you normally clean the library from about six to ten in the evenings."

"Yes, that's correct," Tom said. "I usually got there just as Ducky was leaving. You know, I really do wish I'd been able to come in Tuesday evening. I might have been able to protect her had I been there. I kind of had a crush on her, and tried to get her to go out with me for years, until she met Quentin, of course. But, even then, our close friendship never wavered. Well, thanks for calling, Ms. Starr. Like I said, I'm looking forward to meeting you."

I hung up, wondering what Tom Melvard had meant by "protecting" Ducky. Did he mean protect her from her own demons, as in talk her out of killing herself? Or did he mean he might have been able to protect her from an assailant? Did Tom know more about Ducky's death than he was saying? Did he have reason to believe someone he knew about might have a motive to kill her? Or could "protect her" just have been the phrase that came out of his mouth with no ominous meaning whatsoever? Was he kidding about the "crush on Ducky" thing? He seemed sincere, but I mean, a crush on Ducky? *Really*? Could Ducky's death possibly have been a crime of passion? I found this possibility very hard to fathom, but all those questions just begged for a more intense conversation with the custodian.

Since nothing, or no one had slithered out of the cracks and crevices of the library and attempted to drag me up the ladder, which was still conveniently propped against the wall adjacent to the log beam Ducky's body had hung from, I decided to call Paul and Carolyn before I left the building, so I could mentally cross it off my to-do list.

Carolyn's mother answered the phone and informed me her daughter was at the community college enrolling in some business classes. Carolyn had decided the recent events at her workplace were a sign for her to move on, her mother told me. Her only child had always dreamed of owning her own beauty salon, and Mrs. Aldrich and her husband had promised to put her through cosmetology school, as long as she continued to live at home and enrolled in some business classes that would surely benefit Carolyn in accomplishing her goal. In short, her daughter would not be returning to work at the library, and it would probably be my responsibility to find someone to replace her.

After Mrs. Aldrich and I had discussed the tragic death of the head librarian, I hung up and immediately dialed Paul's number. His girlfriend answered the phone and handed the phone over to Paul when I requested to speak to him. I told him when the library would reopen, and asked him how he was handling the loss of a co-worker he'd spent a great deal of time with over the last fifteen years. I was prepared to console him and comfort him as best I could.

"I'm fine," he simply said. Then with an astonishing small amount of words, Paul managed to tell me he would be looking for a second job, and hoped we could re-arrange his hours working at the library to incorporate those of his future second job. The pay he was earning as a part-time employee was not sufficient enough for him to make ends meet, he told me. He wanted to propose to his girlfriend, but was unable to support them with his current income.

"Wow, this could turn out to be a case of perfect timing, Paul. I might have just the solution to your problem, and you might also be the solution to one of mine." I went on to tell him about Carolyn's decision to change course in her career path, and my dilemma of finding someone to replace her.

When the only response I got from Paul was a low-pitched guttural sound, that didn't sound like any word in the English language that I was familiar with, I continued. "If it would work out all right for you, I will check with the powers that be, and see if I can offer you a full time job, instead of hiring another part-timer to take Carolyn's hours."

"Okay," Paul replied. I took it he was agreeable with my suggestion, but I'd expected a bit more enthusiasm and gratitude in his response. However, being a man who was extremely stingy with his words, as if he was preserving his vocal chords for a debut on Broadway, I had to be content with the belief it might turn out to be a beneficial situation for both of us.

When I exited the library, the transit was still located in the corner of the lot. Elroy Traylor, and the other younger man, who looked enough like Traylor to be his son, were pouring over a set of blueprints, laid out on the hood of a Cadillac Escalade at the far end of the parking lot. I refused to acknowledge his presence, and got in my car to drive back to the inn. I had a list of things I planned to do that day that didn't include pummeling the city manager because he'd made the grave mistake of pissing me off.

An hour later, after stopping by the inn, and consuming enough coffee to keep a dozen people awake for a week, I pulled up in front of a two-story, old, but well-kept brick home, located at the end of a dead end road. I'd found the address in the phone book under "Q. Duckworthy." I knew the chances of there being another Q. Duckworthy in the small town of Rockdale were slim to none. In fact, another Q. Duckworthy in the entire state of Missouri was highly unlikely.

When no one answered the door, I walked around to the rear of the home where an odd whirring sound seemed to be coming from. I found the source of the odd noise when I rounded the corner. Standing over a wooden picnic table, operating a hand-held belt sander, was a bald, average-sized man, in a pair of old coveralls. He was so engrossed with smoothing the edge of an elaborate birdhouse that he didn't notice me approach him. I didn't want to startle the man, so I waited for him to turn off the sander and set it on the table.

"Mr. Duckworthy?" I asked softly. When he didn't respond, I repeated myself, louder this time. He spun around quickly, with his arm cocked back as if he were going to deck me. I stepped back in alarm. He was in his early seventies, I was sure, but as buffed up as a man half his age. I knew he could easily knock me into next week. I held both hands up as if to signal I had come onto his reservation in peace. "I'm so sorry I startled you. I certainly didn't mean to."

"That's okay; it's not your fault. I served with the Special Forces in Vietnam, and although my PTSD has improved with time, I still have a tendency to react defensively when surprised. Can I help you?"

"First of all, I'd like to extend my condolences on the loss of your wife. You are Quentin, aren't you?"

"Yes, thank you. And you are?"

"I'm Lexie Starr, and I was hired to take over at the library until a permanent replacement is hired."

"Oh sure, Ducky told me about you," Quentin said, without elaborating on his statement. I was afraid to ask him what she'd told him about me, not too certain it was something I'd want to hear. 'Chatterbox' and 'not the sharpest knife in the drawer' were personal descriptions that came to mind.

"You must be devastated, and totally in disbelief, at what happened," I said, hoping for an insight into Ducky's frame of mind about her retirement, which had been scheduled to take place that very day.

"Well, yes and no. Of course I'm absolutely devastated, but as I told the police, I'm not altogether surprised by her decision to take her own life," he said. "Deeply saddened, naturally, but not completely taken off guard."

"I don't mean to be nosy, but what do you mean by that? It seemed to me like she was greatly anticipating her retirement, spending time with her grandchildren, gardening, ballroom dancing lessons, and all that." I was a little hesitant to mention the skydiving and Harley Davidson tattoo, for some reason.

"Ballroom dancing? I don't know about that, but she did mention she didn't get to spend enough time with Melissa and Barney. I'm sure she was putting on a brave face. She was very unhappy about being forced to retire before she was ready," he said.

"Forced to retire? By whom? She never told me it wasn't her own decision, just that her boss was part of the reason she was retiring."

"Pride, no doubt. She was nearly inconsolable for a week after Tucker told her to take early retirement, or be fired. She wouldn't give that blowhard the satisfaction of firing her, but putting in for retirement was very difficult for her to do. She was the type who had to keep busy or go completely insane," Quentin explained. Keeping busy or going insane, was something I could easily relate to, as I suffered from the same condition.

"Wow, how awful to hear Tucker gave her an ultimatum like that." Colby Tucker had just graduated from "jerk" to "royal asshole" in my totally biased opinion.

"Say, Mr. Duckworthy, were you familiar with the custodian at the library, Tom Melvard?"

"Oh, I heard Ducky mention him a time or two, but can't say I ever met the man. Why?"

"Just curious. He indicated to me on the phone he'd been interested in pursuing a relationship with her before she met you, but I'm sure he soon realized you were the best man for Ducky. She, of course, showed no interest in Tom, and nothing resulted from Tom's attraction to her." I had to be careful I didn't get Tom Melvard threatened, harmed, or worse, by implying the wrong thing to a potential killer, who might be enraged by the idea another man was lusting after his late wife.

I was surprised when Quentin showed no anger whatsoever, but merely laughed, and scoffed at the very notion of Ducky being involved in any way with another man. He said, "Melvard was sniffing up the wrong tree, I'm afraid. Lucky for him, Ducky had all the man she could handle at home."

"Yes," I said, chuckling softly to echo Quentin's demeanor. "I've no doubt she was very satisfied with her marriage."

"As was I," he replied. I was touched by the sight of his eyes welling up, and patted his arm as he wiped a tear off his cheek. I wondered if the tears were genuine, or just a show put on for my benefit.

"I am so sorry for your loss, Quentin. If there's anything I can do, please let me know."

"Thank you. I feel so guilty for not picking up on any signs she was suicidal. If I had, I could have gotten her some help and treatment for her mental and emotional well-being."

"I'm really curious about why you didn't report your wife missing when she didn't come home from work on Tuesday night," I said, hoping to look more curious than accusatory, even if the latter term was more accurate.

"I wish I'd been here to know she didn't come home, but I wasn't. I was elk hunting in Wyoming with my brother. In Wyoming, they have a drawing every year for elk tags, and we were both lucky enough to get bull tags for the first time in six years. Clyde got his bull on Monday, and I had a chance at a six-by-six on Tuesday, but missed my target. We headed home late Tuesday night, arriving home Wednesday morning. I got the message about Ducky being found dead in the library, just as we crossed over the Missouri border. I feel so guilty about not being here, but I guess it wouldn't have changed the outcome any."

"That's true, and you couldn't be expected to know what would happen while you were away. I sure hope you can prove your whereabouts, just in the slim chance the detectives ask you for an alibi in the course of their investigation," I said, hoping to draw a reaction out of him.

"Why in the world would I need an alibi because my wife committed suicide?" He asked, with an expression of pure dismay on his face.

"Oh, I'm sure the chances of that happening are slim. But, Quentin, I have to tell you, I'm not convinced she took her own life, and I am searching for evidence to prove otherwise. I feel your wife deserves a full investigation into the circumstances surrounding her untimely death."

"I don't expect to have to prove my whereabouts to the police, but I'm sure my brother can substantiate my alibi if it were to come to that," he said. I was not surprised to hear him say his brother would vouch for Quentin's whereabouts. Who's to say his brother wasn't in on Ducky's murder? For that matter, if someone I dearly loved, such as my only sister, told the homicide detectives she was having lunch with Elvis Presley at the time of a murder, I might be tempted to vouch for her too.

"Yes, I'm sure it won't be an issue for you. Are there any other reasons you'd think your wife could have actually hung herself?" I asked.

"Ms. Starr, are you sure you should get involved in

this matter? It could put your own well-being in danger, you know," Quentin asked, with what appeared to be genuine concern.

"I'm aware of the risks. I'll tread lightly and use common sense. And, of course, I'll take the utmost precautions to guard against putting myself in harm's way. Don't worry about me, I'll be fine," I assured him. If Quentin knew anything about me, at all, he'd be laughing hysterically, knowing that when I was in the middle of a murder case such as this, all common sense flew out the window. And as far as treading lightly, I was more apt to approach the situation like a herd of Thomson's gazelles fleeing from a pride of hungry lions. But for now, that was my story and I was sticking to it.

Quentin seemed to weigh my words for a few moments before speaking. "You know, Ducky had been suffering from depression recently, even before she was forced to retire, and unfortunately, one of the side effects of the medication she was on is suicidal thoughts."

It sounded like an oxymoron to me to take a medicine to help improve your mood that could also cause you to go hang yourself from the rafters at the library. It would make a handy excuse for Ducky's death, but I didn't believe for a second that's what caused her death.

"Also," Quentin continued, "Ducky had been very rattled and upset the last few weeks since her ex, Bo Reliford, moved back to this area from Lee's Summit. We heard he's living in a rental just outside town. Because their relationship was so rocky, and Bo was often abusive, Ducky was terrified of him. She told me a couple of times she thought she'd recognized him in an older-model Jeep, custom painted in a desert camouflage design, following her as she drove home from work. Most likely, it was just her mind playing tricks on her because of her fear of him, but it still had a deeply disturbing affect on her. She had me driving her to work for over a week after she convinced herself he was stalking her. Perhaps you should speak to Bo, if you get the chance."

Had Ducky been right about Bo stalking her? Did he think Ducky wouldn't see him following her if his vehicle was camouflaged? Stupid man, Rockdale was not located in the desert. I think I'd be more apt to notice a camouflaged Jeep driving behind me than a white or black one, or even a bright orange one. Quentin was probably right that it was just stress causing her to imagine Bo might be stalking her. But what if it wasn't? I didn't want to just disregard the possibility as a figment of her imagination.

I wondered how I could find him, and what excuse I could invent to speak to him. Making up flimsy excuses was something I usually was very good at. The fact that anyone believed the crap I came up with sometimes amazed me.

"Hmm, I think I saw a vehicle like that parked in front of a house out on that two-lane county road just west of town. I wonder if that was Bo's car," I said, lying with as much nonchalance as I could muster.

"Could've been, I guess, but we heard he moved into a place on that gravel road that heads north, the one just past the Casey's Convenience Store on Locust. I drove out there hoping to confront him after the second time Ducky thought he'd followed her through town, but I didn't spot any Jeeps, and wasn't sure which house he was renting."

I sat down on the bench of the picnic table, because I was feeling a bit light-headed with all Ducky's husband had just related to me.

"Are you okay?" Quentin asked. "Would you like a

glass of water?"

"I'll be okay in a moment, but thank you anyway." I pointed toward the impressive birdhouse Quentin was working on. It was not your typical birdhouse, but nearly a work of art, with amazing architectural design and craftsmanship. "That's really quite something! You must be a carpenter, by trade."

"No, actually I worked as a honey dipper the last twenty years before I retired last spring. Woodworking is just a hobby of mine. It helps me relax when I'm stressed out."

"Honey dipper?"

"I cleaned out porta-potties for a living," he said, almost apologetically. "It was a shitty job, and didn't pay worth a crap, but someone had to do it!"

I smiled, knowing he was most likely making a joke with his play on words. But I didn't want to make that assumption and laugh out loud, taking the chance of insulting or demeaning him.

"I'm sure you were the best man for the job," I replied, diplomatically, realizing too late it was probably the most insulting and demeaning thing I could possibly have said. But, fortunately, Quentin took my remark as friendly teasing and slapped his leg in amusement.

Before I gave myself an opportunity to make another stupid remark, I stood up, stuck out my hand to shake his, and said, "It was nice to meet you, Quentin. Again, I am so very sorry for your loss. Even though I'd just met her, it was obvious to me that Ducky was a remarkable person."

"Well, that's one way to put it," was his ambiguous reply. I didn't quite know what to make of his remark, so I asked him for the details of the funeral services to change the subject. I also sat back down, with renewed interest in what Quentin had to say.

"She's being cremated, and there won't be any formal services," he said. "However, there will be a small memorial for her when we scatter her ashes in the flower garden in front of the library."

"She'd really like that," I said. I couldn't really imagine anyone "liking" having their body reduced to ashes and spread anywhere, but it seemed like the thing to say. I wondered if Ducky had mentioned to Quentin in the past that she'd prefer cremation, but figured it really didn't matter one way or another. After death, the body was just a useless shell, and she'd be in heaven and just as dead either way.

"Her daughter called me about an hour ago with the time and date of the memorial. Let me run in and get that information for you if I can remember where I put it."

I thanked him, and wondered how you could misplace the details of your spouse's memorial, as if that scrap of paper you wrote it down on was as immaterial as a gas receipt, or a grocery store shopping list.

As soon as the back door closed behind Quentin, the cell phone he'd left on the picnic table started playing the theme from "Shaft." The phone was lying face down on the table, so I picked it up and started to run after him with the phone, until I noticed an image of an extremely good-looking blonde on the caller I.D. under the name "Barbara Wells." I was a bit curious who the beautiful woman was that was calling Quentin, even though I realized it could be nearly anybody considering the recent death of his wife. Surely, a great deal of condolence calls were being made to him.

When the ring tone stopped, I picked up the phone and quickly brought up a list of the last dozen or so incoming phone numbers. All but two of the numbers matched that of the blonde who'd just tried to reach Quentin. As soon as I began to place the phone back down on the table, it rang again. The same number and photo popped up on the screen again. Perhaps she'd thought she'd dialed the wrong number. I laid it, with the theme song from *Shaft* still playing, face down on the table as Quentin had left it, and ran to the door to holler in to Quentin that his phone was ringing.

"Oh, thanks," he replied, as he stepped back out on the patio. He looked at the screen, turned off the ringer, and quickly put the cell phone in his pocket. With a grimace, he said, "Just my brother. I'll call him back later."

My first thought was that his brother was one exceedingly effeminate-looking fellow, and certainly not the elk-hunting type. My next thought was that I'd never met a gentleman named Barbara before that looked like he could be Pamela Anderson's twin sister. I made no comment, but wondered why Quentin was lying about the caller. He hadn't appeared happy Barbara Wells was calling, but perhaps he was just disturbed about the timing. Quentin then began to recite the information scribbled on the post-it note in his hand.

I took a pen and checking deposit slip out of my fanny pack, and notated the details of the memorial, which was not to be held for two weeks, and jotted down the female caller's name when Quentin looked away, along with the words *Casey's, North,* and *Locust.*

I then excused myself and walked back to my little blue convertible with more questions than answers. I was convinced there a great deal more to Quentin's story than he'd told me, and I had every intention of getting to the bottom of it. In the meantime, I had a camouflaged Jeep to track down.

It wasn't even noon yet, so I figured I had a couple more hours before Stone started worrying about me. I'd let him think I was going to a two-day clearance sale at Kohl's, at the Legends shopping area in Kansas City, Kansas. It would take over an hour drive each way to go shopping at the Legends, and stopping for lunch could easily fill another thirty minutes.

I was supposedly looking for a new pair of jeans because marriage had put a couple extra unwelcome pounds on me and some of my clothes were getting a little snug. Shopping for jeans could definitely consume a lot of time, because everyone knows a woman has to try on several dozen pairs of jeans before she finds a pair that she doesn't think makes her butt look fat. And with those recent extra pounds, that always seem to find their way to my posterior, finding a pair of jeans that didn't make me look as if I had way too frigging much junk in the trunk could prove to be impossible. So coming home without a new purchase could be reasonably explained.

I didn't like not being totally honest with Stone, so I disguised my little white lies with statements like, "Unless I find something better to do, I was thinking about going shopping for new jeans at the Legends. Kohl's has a two-day sale I just might decide to check out."

I actually was thinking about going shopping at Kohl's the day I got the flyer about their sale, and then again while I was searching for an excuse to get out of the house for a few hours. But, as I thought might happen, I did indeed find something better to do. Where's the lie in that? The only thing I forgot to mention was that instead of going shopping, I might decide to go tracking down a ruthless killer.

Now I found myself driving toward the new coffee shop on Locust Street to get myself a cup of coffee. I felt a bit daring, so I thought I'd broaden my horizons, and probably also that fat ass I was just mentioning, and get a large cup of Mocha Malt Frappuccino with whip cream on top. It was no doubt, guaranteed to contain a full day's worth of calories, or your money back.

Once I'd soothed my nerves, and gathered up my courage, at the coffee shop, I'd drive next door to Casey's and fill up with gas, and then head north on the gravel road that ran alongside the convenience store. With any luck at all, I'd spot the Jeep in a driveway and come up with a viable reason to stop and talk to its owner.

I drove for at least a couple miles with no success. I finally pulled into a long-winding gravel driveway to turn around and head back to town. As I started to back around, a rapidly moving vehicle passed from behind me, heading north. It was a Land Rover, painted in desert camouflage, and looked close enough to a Jeep that I felt certain it was Bo Reliford driving it. There were not many vehicles with that paint design traveling the roads around Rockdale, Missouri, and Ducky could have easily mistaken a Land Rover for a Jeep.

I quickly turned my wheel, backed in the opposite direction, and then tried to catch up with the Land Rover. It was moving fast and erratically, so I stayed just far enough back not to lose sight of the cloud of dust enveloping the car. When the car turned into the driveway of an old mobile home in ill repair, with a large lean-to shed beside it, I slowed down.

In the middle of the front yard, which was comprised of ninety-percent dirt and dried up weeds, and ten-percent smashed beer cans, was a big black contraption with a row of cylinder disks. A piece of cardboard, with "Four Cell" scribbled in paint on it, was propped up against the unusual object. I wasn't sure what it was called, or even totally sure what the thing was used for, but I was suddenly thinking that I might be interested in purchasing it.

I pulled into the driveway behind the Land Rover, unrolled my window, pointed at the piece of farm equipment and misspelled sign, and asked, "Hey there, sir, is that thing still for sale?"

An older man with a long, scraggly gray beard, and greasy ball cap, stepped out of his car carrying an opened Miller Lite in one hand, and a nearly empty case of beer in the other. It was obviously not his first drink of the day. He stumbled a little, looked at me with rheumy eyes, and replied, "Yep. Wanna buy it?"

"Um, kind of depends on how much you're asking for it."

"Fifty bucks! So, whatcha say? Ya wanna buy it?"

"Well, I'm sure that's a fair price, but I need to look at it a little closer first."

"Help yourself. Got a tractor?" he asked, listing a little too far to the left before he caught himself and straightened up.

"Of course," I replied. Just because I was driving a little sports car didn't mean I couldn't have a John Deere in my barn at home. But, even as I spoke, I could feel my nose growing longer. I started nonchalantly cracking my knuckles in an effort to appear more like a laid-back farmer's wife, and less like a anxiety-ridden liar on a furtive mission.

"Don't think that harrow will fit in your trunk, lady," he said, slurring his words a bit. Was he catching on to my ploy? I wondered. Or, in his drunken stupor, could I tell him I had a secret compartment in my car where I stored farm implements, and have him not bat an eye.

I wasn't sure just how tanked he was, so I just politely laughed. "Oh, my husband will pick the harrow up in his truck tomorrow, if I decide to buy it. My name's Lexie, and I'm sorry, but I didn't catch yours."

"It's Bo. Wanna beer, Betsy? We can go in the house and visit over a few beers, and I'll tell ya all about the harrow."

Betsy? Well, that was close enough for me. And even though I knew he was now flirting with me, I felt safe enough going into his trailer alone with him. Even with a beer or two in me, I felt sure I could handle myself if he tried to do anything other than talk. He was old, and so drunk he could barely walk. I could surely outrun him, if not roll him and steal his wallet in the process.

I agreed to stay just long enough for one beer, hoping to drill him with questions about Ducky. As looped as he was, he'd probably have a fairly loose tongue, spilling vital information he didn't have enough wits about him to know he was spilling. I followed him up the rickety stairs, to a dilapidated wooden deck, and on into the trailer. It reeked of not only booze, but also of garbage, mold, and dirty old man. When I felt the cream in the Frappuccino I'd drank begin to curdle in my stomach, I almost turned around and walked back outside, but I decided I could tough it out for a few minutes if it meant getting some useful information out of the old polluted geezer.

"Hey, Betsy, I also got an old toilet I wanna sell out in the shed if ya be interested." I really had to concentrate to make out his words. He handed me a beer and opened up a new bottle for himself before speaking again. "It got a little cruddy over the years, so I went and got me one of them new-fangled crappers, you know, with all the bells and whistles. But, don't worry, the old one's still usable and only leaks a little bit when ya flush it. And since ya is such a nice lady, I'll let it go for twenty bucks."

I just smiled, trying not to upchuck and spew the pricey Mocha Malt Frappuccino across the trailer. Bo motioned for me to sit right next to him on his filthy, tattered couch. I decided to sit on the other side of the room on a metal chair, where it was harder for bacteria to grow, while trying not to imagine a toilet so "cruddy" that this man would refuse to use it.

Just the mention of the word *toilet* had my bladder demanding to be emptied. All twenty-two ounces of that damn fancied-up coffee must have raced through my system to my bladder, bypassing my kidneys altogether in its haste. I crossed my legs and tried to ignore the feeling of urgency.

"I'll give purchasing the toilet some thought, Bo. Say, what's your last name? You look so familiar to me. I know I've met you somewhere before." The longer I conversed with this man, the longer my nose felt like it was growing. Before long, I'd have to tilt my seat back in order to drive my car home. I really didn't like lying to anyone, even soused strangers, but sometimes it was necessary, and usually not at all malicious, or apt to cause anyone any harm.

"Name's Reliford," he answered, although it came out sounding more like "really bored" because of his current condition.

"Hmm, I knew a lady whose last name was Reliford before she got married a few years ago. Her name was Bertha. Poor lady was found dead in the library a couple days ago. Was she any relation to you?" I asked, innocently.

"Yeah, she was my old lady for a long, long time. Went by the name Bert, and now I hear she goes by

Ducky. Always hated the name her mama give her. Too bad about the dying thing. I heard she gone and hung herself."

"Yeah, that's what the investigators said. She didn't seem like the suicide type to me, though. Did she to you?" I asked.

"Dunno. Never could figure that broad out, myself."

"Were you two still on good terms? When was the last time you saw her?"

"Ain't talked to Bert since the divorce was final," Bo said. He had drained his last beer in two or three gulps and opened up another bottle. He seemed in somewhat of a stupor, as he continued, "But I think I might have seen her in (hiccup) town a couple weeks ago. I pulled up behind a (loud juicy belch) VW bug at a light, and the driver looked like that old (very graphic adjective) bitch, so then I (incoherent muttering) so I could teach her a lesson."

"You must be very angry about the divorce. I'm sure you didn't deserve to be dumped that way," I said, hoping to get him stirred up and elaborating, no matter how crudely, on how he, in a drunken rage entered the library after I left, got involved in a heated argument with Ducky, or Bert, as he called her, and decided to drag her up the ladder and hang her from one of the log beams. Afterward, to save his own hide, he typed up a suicide note on one of the computers designated for library patrons to use, printed it out, and left it on the chair at her desk. That's what I hoped to hear and be able to decipher, amid all the hiccupping, belching, cursing, and even, occasionally, noxious farting. With all the sounds emitting from him, this old fellow was a one-man band.

If I could get him started confessing his sins, I would activate the voice recorder app on my smart phone, and then drive his recorded confession straight to the police station. I was very proud of the plan I'd developed, and was mentally patting myself on the back for a job well done. So naturally, I was then terribly disappointed when instead of reciting a detailed description of how he'd murdered his ex-wife, he merely passed out cold on the couch, dropping his nearly full beer on the linoleum floor.

Watching the beer flow out of the bottle onto the dark, grimy floor, creating a large puddle, the urge to urinate became more than I could control. As much as the thought disturbed me, using this man's *new-fangled crapper* had become a necessity. I'd used enough gas station restrooms in the past to perfect the art of peeing without one inch of my flesh ever touching the toilet seat, and I would have to utilize that talent again now.

When I was done relieving myself, I'd head home and leave Bo to sleep it off in his chair. There'd be no more conversing with him until he sobered up, and I needed to get home shortly anyway, to avoid worrying Stone.

I found the bathroom behind the second door down the hallway. The restroom was every bit as nasty as I'd imagined, but I'd have to risk untold germ and bacteria exposure, and use it. I locked the door behind me in case Bo woke up and came looking for me. Evaluating the toilet in front of me, I tried to imagine what bell or whistle it had that the old one might not have, and came up with nothing. Unless, I thought, it was the black mold under the lid, or the ring around the bowl a jackhammer couldn't chip off.

After peeing while performing a world-class balancing act, I realized there was no toilet paper on the holder. There was not even an old Sears catalog in the john. Thank God I carried a small pack of Kleenex in my fanny pack just for emergencies such as this one.

After completing the task at hand, I grasped the doorknob only to find it wouldn't unlock. I shook the rusty knob as violently as I could, and then jammed my fingernail file in the key opening, and wiggled it frantically. I began hollering out as loudly as I could, hoping to raise Bo. When those attempts failed, I looked for door hinges to remove the bolts from, but for some odd reason the door opened outward instead of inward, putting the hinges on the other side of the door.

My next thought was to crawl out the window, but was forced to accept the fact that, although I might be able to squeeze my arms and head out the tiny window, the extra junk in my trunk was going nowhere. Even if I busted out the window, and greased the window frame with oily residue off the floor, there was no hope of squeezing my rump and thighs through the opening.

Damn that Wyatt Johnston! If I didn't always have to keep so many fattening treats on hand to satisfy his sweet tooth, and then feel obligated to taste-test them before serving them to him, there might have been a prayer of escaping Bo's utterly disgusting privy.

I tried messing with the doorknob again, while intermittently calling out Bo's name, to no avail. Glancing at my watch, I knew it was Stone calling as soon as my phone rang. I could be evasive, or even downright lie about my situation, but what good would that do me at this point? It wouldn't get me out of the slimy, stinking bathroom anytime soon. I decided to bite the bullet and explain to him what had happened. I knew it would result in a lecture about my appalling disregard for my personal safety, and my lacking the sense God gave a lemming, on Stone's part, and a lot of shameless crying and pleading on mine, but it had to be done.

Apparently, Stone was getting accustomed to my impulsive nature, and the unfortunate and sometimes dangerous, predicaments this bad trait sometimes landed me in. He was angry, disgusted, and bitterly disappointed with me, but he didn't sound at all surprised. He sighed and asked for directions to Bo's place. Before he hung up, he asked, "This dude actually bought your story of being interested in buying his harrow?"

"Well, sure, I was very convincing. He even believed I might want to purchase his old toilet, since he done went and bought himself one of those new fangled crappers."

Stone didn't laugh, comment, or even sigh again. He just rudely hung the phone up in my ear. I could tell it was going to be a long, long night.

CHAPTER 8

After serving a pork roast with all the trimmings to the Spurleys, and two other young couples, who were traveling together from Florida and had checked in late that Friday afternoon, Stone asked me to join him on the back porch for a cup of coffee. The idea of relaxing over a cup of coffee greatly appealed to me, as it always did, but the conversation about my actions that day that was sure to accompany it, did not.

Stone had arrived at Bo's place about twenty minutes after he'd hung up on me. He'd been able to jimmy the lock with a special tool he'd kept from his days as a reserve police officer in Myrtle Beach, South Carolina. He made no comment when he opened the bathroom door, but no words were necessary. The look he gave me spoke volumes.

I followed him silently through the trailer, past Bo, who was snoring loudly on the couch, and out the front door. Stone's pickup was parked behind my car in the driveway. He pointed at the harrow in the yard, and said, "I trust that harrow doesn't belong to you now. I've no doubt you've purchased the damn thing if that's what it took to get Bo to talk to you."

"No, of course I didn't purchase the harrow, but something just occurred to me now as I'm looking at it again. I don't know why I didn't see it before."

"What's that?"

"I could have driven right by this place without stopping and known there was very little chance Bo could have had anything to do with killing his ex-wife, unless he had an accomplice, of course."

"Go on," Stone said.

"Anybody who would display a 'Four Cell' sign in his yard could never have created the suicide note left on Ducky's chair. Nor do I think Bo could have stayed sober long enough to come up with a plan of action like that, and then execute the plan without a hitch," I explained. "After what Quentin Duckworthy told me, I'm more apt to think it's he who might have been behind her death, and he'd definitely be more capable of pulling off such a stunt. I'm still on the fence about Quentin."

"My God, Lexie! You went to the Duckworthy's home too? You never left Rockdale at all today, did you?" Stone asked, not waiting for a reply. "You obviously had no intention of going shopping in Kansas City. You know, I knew what I was getting into when I married you, but I'd hoped that out of respect for me, you'd stop and think about the risks involved before doing something utterly ridiculous like this."

"I'm so sorry, Stone." I watched his light blue eyes darken in anger. The lecture from Stone had commenced, and the crying and pleading by me was about to. "I just feel like Ducky deserves justice if she didn't really take her own life. And there's no one else willing to dig deeper into the situation. I was afraid you'd try to stop me if you knew I was going to do a little investigating on my own."

"You got that part right!"

"I'm very appreciative of your concern for me, but I also feel a sense of obligation to Ducky." I wiped a tear off my cheek, and continued. "Please try to understand how important it is to me that the truth about her death be confirmed, with no lingering doubt by me that she didn't commit suicide. From everything I've seen so far, I just can't accept that she did."

"I understand how you feel, Lexie. I have my doubts too. But I don't feel like you should put your life on the line to avenge hers."

"If I promise to be completely open and honest with you, will you help me look into the matter? I just want to see if I can uncover any evidence substantial enough to force the police department to reopen the case. Wyatt promised me they would if anything came up to indicate a murder may have taken place in the library Tuesday night."

Stone opened my car door for me, and before walking over to his truck to lead me home, said, "We'll talk about it tonight at home."

Now, as I walked out to the back porch, balancing a tray holding two cups of coffee, and a tiny pitcher of creamer for Stone, I was certain I knew how Daniel had felt as he'd entered the lion's den. The lion in my case was already sitting at the new patio table we'd just purchased at Home Depot the previous week. He had a very thoughtful look on his face as he watched me place the tray I was carrying on the table.

Stone poured creamer in his cup and slowly stirred his coffee without saying a word. My anxiety level was going up with every rotation of his spoon. I felt a little queasy, as if the fried chicken I'd eaten for supper was coming back to life and trying desperately to escape my stomach.

Finally, he looked up, straight into my eyes, and spoke. For the umpteenth time since I'd met this man, he surprised me by doing the very last thing I'd imagine he'd do. He apologized.

"Honey, I'm sorry I spoke to you the way I did today. You shouldn't have to be afraid of how I'll respond if you tell me the truth about how you feel, and how you want to react to it. I want you to feel like you can come to me with any concern you might have. I can't change your caring nature, no matter how reckless it might sometimes make you. Nor do I feel like I should. I love you for who you are, and I wouldn't want you any other way."

Wide-eyed from being taken completely off guard, I set my coffee down on the table, and was rendered speechless. Stone reached out and took my hand before continuing to speak.

"I've given it a lot of thought and decided I'd help you in any way I can, as long as you never take any potentially dangerous actions without discussing them with me first. My main concern is your safety, but I also want to be there for you. Sometimes two minds working together can accomplish more than one mind working alone."

"Oh, Stone, I love you so much," I gushed. "I'm the luckiest woman in the world to have a man like you by my side. I know I don't deserve someone like you, but I am very, very grateful to be your wife. Thank you so much for understanding. I promise I'll run anything I plan to do by you if I think it might potentially land me in hot water."

"Thank you, honey. That's all I'm asking."

We held hands for a few minutes while sipping

coffee and discussing everything I'd discovered from my conversations with Quentin and Bo. Stone agreed with me that the next plan of action should be finding a way to speak with both Elroy Traylor, the Rockdale City Manager, and my new boss, Colby Tucker, again. Both men seemed to have an ax to grind with Ducky, and either man may have taken their dissension with her a step further.

Friday evening found me passing out oranges and bananas, and occasionally a half-fermented apple, to some very disappointed trick-or-treaters. I'd been so preoccupied with Ducky's death I'd forgotten it was Halloween. The last bunch of ghosts and goblins had loose change dropped into their bags after the fruit supply dried up. They didn't seem half as disgruntled with money, as the earlier ones had with old fruit. At least they could buy candy with the change I gave them.

I had considered just leaving the porch light off and pretending no one was home at the inn. But it didn't seem very hospitable for our bed and breakfast to completely stiff the neighborhood children. We depended on a good reputation in town to encourage locals to recommend our lodging establishment to visiting friends and relatives.

However, I was beginning to think the kids felt worse than stiffed. They felt as if they'd been duped into making the long trek up our driveway for a worthless piece of health food. What kind of witch would hand out fruit, some that was a bit past its prime, instead of something that would raise their blood sugar levels at least three hundred points?

If looks could actually kill, there was one extremely disgusted Princess Nala, who would have left me in the same condition as Ducky. If you've seen *The Lion*

King, you know this is one bad-ass princess. After all, these kids were on a mission to accumulate as much candy as they could in order to quell their sugar addictions. They could get an orange anytime they wanted one from their mother. But a king-sized Hershey's bar? Not so likely.

"Mom? Where are you?" I heard Wendy hollering from the kitchen early the next morning.

"I'm in the parlor, sweetheart. I'll be right there," I called out. Stone had installed a pellet stove insert in the fireplace because he found it easier and cleaner than burning wood. It was a cool morning, so I was firing it up to take the chill off. The parlor at Alexandria Inn was a popular place for guests to gather, imbibe in a cocktail or two, gather around the grand piano to listen to music, or just enjoy visiting with Stone, me, and other guests of the inn.

We had six guests currently staying at the inn, and I thought they might enjoy their morning coffee in front of the fireplace, while I prepared french toast and sausage links for breakfast. The Spurleys were already sitting on the sofa discussing some political fundraiser the Nebraska Senator and his wife were planning to attend on Sunday. I exchanged a few pleasantries with the couple and then joined my daughter in the kitchen.

"Hey Mom," Wendy said. "Did you know there are three bananas and a rotten apple in the front yard?"

"No, but I'm not surprised. A banana takes up a lot of valuable candy space. But I assure you, the apple was still edible."

"Okay," she said. "Not even going to ask."

While I cracked eggs into a bowl, I listened to Wendy rattle on about the pair of alpaca babies, or crias, as she called them, that Stone's nephew, Andy, had purchased to raise on his ranch near Atchison,

Kansas. The crias were an extremely rare set of twins, Wendy told me. "The female alpaca, called a hembra, almost always has a single cria. Andy is bottle-feeding the crias because they were born prematurely and barely weighed enough at birth to survive. They are the cutest little things I've ever seen."

"How interesting," I said, with a smile. As usual, when Wendy was excited about something, she began talking nonstop, rarely pausing long enough to breathe. I waited for her to nearly turn purple from lack of oxygen before cutting in. "We haven't seen Andy in ages. You two will have to join us for supper one of these nights."

"Or, better yet, you and Stone need to come out to the ranch to see the crias that we named Mork and Mindy. Andy still loves watching old reruns of that show from way, way back, like in the seventies," Wendy said.

I graduated from high school in the seventies, but Wendy made it sound like it was before Thomas Edison had invented the light bulb. She had a way of making me feel like I should stop whatever I was doing and get my affairs in order, just in case my crusty, rickety old body gave up the ghost before sundown. I wanted to flip off my own daughter just then.

Wendy and Andy had recently become an official couple, which pleased Stone and me tremendously. She'd even given up her apartment in St. Joseph and moved in with Andy after he'd finished renovating the old farmhouse on the property he'd purchased almost a year ago. Andy had taken to ranching like he'd been born with a pair of cowboy boots on, even though he'd spent the last decade making a living as a charter pilot on the East Coast. Wendy's commute to the county coroner's office now was a long one, but she seemed to think being with Andy was worth the sacrifice, and I had to agree with her.

Wendy and I chatted over coffee for an hour. It was Saturday morning and she was off for the day, unless she got called in for an emergency autopsy, which rarely happened. Stone and I had decided to keep our investigative efforts to ourselves until we happened upon a break in the case that would warrant us taking the new evidence to the police.

We even thought that keeping Wendy and Detective Johnston in the dark about our efforts was in our best interest. Neither one of them would be happy to hear we were taking it upon ourselves to search for clues proving Ducky's death was no suicide.

So Wendy and I discussed the weather, the price of gas, the hideous hairpiece Senator Spurley was donning, and which brand of vanilla wafers tasted the best with bananas, even if the only ones we had left were scattered out on the lawn. She even embarked on a long-winded recital of the rare parasite involving the gall bladder, called a lancet liver fluke, which had taken the life of the oldest citizen in Rockdale the previous day.

As she described the process of dissecting the old gal's withered body, I tried to determine if the deceased lady actually *was* born before the invention of the light bulb. Then I began to mentally schedule the tasks I hoped to accomplish over the weekend, calculating the amount of lodging tax I would need to pay that quarter, and debating on what to fix for supper. I wanted to keep my mind on something besides what Wendy was talking about. I always attempted to show interest in my daughter's occupation without actually visualizing the gruesome details on which she loved to elaborate.

"We determined the ants she digested were in the

angel food cake we found in her stomach contents," Wendy said. Now she had my attention whether I liked it or not. Was the ingestion of diseased ants a chronic health issue? I wondered.

"It's not normally fatal," she continued. "But because of the victim's age and the ensuing diarrhea, the frail one-hundred-and four year-old lady's C.O.D. was actually dehydration."

"That's very sad, and incredibly gross," I said. "But, as fascinating as this conversation is, I need to get started preparing breakfast for our guests. Hopefully there are no ants in the french toast batter."

Just then, Stone walked in the kitchen with Detective Johnston in his wake. After I poured them each a cup of coffee and refilled Wendy's, I got to hear the entire liver fluke, death-by-ant-ingestion story again, and in even greater detail this time. My mind quickly went back to how I could make the most of my time throughout the weekend, shutting out the disagreeable conversation. When Wendy launched into a description of a two-foot long tapeworm she'd once removed from a cadaver's digestive tract, even Wyatt, who'd surely witnessed unimaginable guts and gore at the scene of car accidents, began to look like he wouldn't be able to finish the fourth doughnut he was busy devouring. Wyatt managed to down it, however.

I quickly interrupted Wendy in mid-sentence and changed the subject. I told Wyatt I'd been contacted by my new boss, Colby Tucker, and in turn, notified the library employees when the library would reopen. He told me he'd known Tom Melvard for years, and often saw him in the evenings, entering and exiting businesses in town where he performed custodial duties.

"The old guy ain't no bigger than a ten year-old,"

Wyatt said. "He made a living as a jockey though, so his size was very beneficial. Tom's kind of a loner and has never been married that I know of, but you couldn't ask for a nicer guy."

"Yes, he seemed very pleasant on the phone." I went on to tell him about Carolyn Aldrich's decision to go back to school to learn the cosmetology trade, and how I'd been fortunate to discover my other part-time employee was interested in full-time employment.

"I know Paul Miller too," Wyatt said. "He belongs to the same gym I do. He's training in martial arts for cage-fighting competition. Quiet guy, but very driven. Paul's been involved in body-building since I've known him."

"Quiet is an understatement, but he's definitely built like a tank," I said. "Are there any new developments on the case regarding the string of burglaries?"

"The pawn shop on Main Street got hit last night. Several guns, a *Rolex Submariner* watch, and about a grand in cash got lifted from there. Same M.O. as the prior burglaries, which was disabling the security system and cameras, and breaking in through the rear doors that face the alley. It also appears as if a crowbar was used to open up the cash register in each incidence. We've been following some leads from the tip line, but none of them have resulted in finding a perp, or perps, as we suspect might be the case."

"Wow, Wyatt," Stone said. "Kind of brazen, aren't they?"

"Yeah," Wyatt replied. "We're hoping their lack of fear and defiant behavior will cause them to slip up and do something rash that leads us right to them. It could be just a lone perp, but a pair, or team of suspects, fits the profile better."

I could understand why the police department was preoccupied with this case, because crimes of this nature were a rarity in this small community. Murders in Rockdale were uncommon too, although the quaint little town had been plagued by several of them in the two years since the Alexandria Inn had opened for business. And, like the potential slaying of Bertha Duckworthy, I'd somehow found myself in the middle of every single one of them!

CHAPTER 9

After sprucing up our guests' rooms, and putting new linens on their beds, I went outside and found Stone raking leaves on the front lawn. He was filling large black trash bags with the leaves to put out on the curb with the trashcans on Monday morning.

"What's up?" He asked.

"I'm going to run to the post office to buy stamps this morning, because it's Saturday and the post office closes at noon. I want to get a birthday card off to Sheila today. Her birthday's on Monday." Sheila had been my best friend since Junior High, and would no doubt still be my best friend when the preacher read me my last rites. Actually, unless I converted to Catholicism, I probably wasn't going to be read any rites. But the point is, Sheila and I were as tight as my blue jeans were becoming, and would be best friends forever. The last thing I wanted to do was forget her on her birthday. I also had some bills I'd like to forget, but it would be best to keep the electricity on at the inn for our guests.

"Okay. Are you going to the store this week? I need

some aftershave. Like maybe Brut 33 if they have it," Stone said.

"Sure," I answered, knowing there was no way I was buying Brut 33 for Stone. I didn't have the heart to tell him it went out of style in the seventies, somewhere between mood rings and lava lamps. I'd pick him up some Prada or Polo, or something else from this century, and he'd never know the difference.

Speaking of last rites, there was someone out there I wanted to have their rights read to. "*You have the right to remain silent,*" and "*You have the right to an attorney,*" to name a couple. I'd better grab a cup of coffee to go, and get cranking if I had any hope of helping make that happen.

"Say, Stone, when are you planning to talk to Elroy Traylor?"

"I thought I'd see if I could get in to see Traylor one day this week."

"On what pretenses do you need to speak to the city manager?"

"Well, no pretenses really, because I really do want to discuss the city's budget allocation for tourism this year," Stone said. "It's the driving force behind the economy of this town, and I think more resources need to be pumped in to it. While I'm there, I'll bring up the library and the rumor I heard about it being relocated. Then I will segue into a discussion about the tragic death of our local librarian, and see where it goes from there."

"Good plan, Stone! Thanks so much for helping me. I thought I might call and invite my new boss, Colby Tucker, to supper tonight, or tomorrow night, whichever suits him."

"Think there's a chance in hell he'll accept your offer?"

"No," I replied honestly. "But I didn't think it'd hurt

to be gracious and friendly, and show a desire to meet my new boss. I will have to report to the man, you know. And miracles do happen occasionally."

There was a long line when I walked into the post office to buy stamps. I waved at a gal toward the front of the line that worked as a stylist at the Klip Joint where I had my hair done. When I looked up at the clerk behind the counter, my jaw fell open. I was almost certain she was the woman whose photo I'd seen on Quentin's phone, Barbara Wells. When I got up to the counter, I'd have to find out for sure without taking too much time because I didn't want to hold up the line.

If the postal clerk was Barbara Wells, the lady who called Quentin while I was at his house, and Quentin had told me it was his brother, my first assumption was they were having an affair. The woman behind the counter was decades younger than Quentin, and tremendously better looking than his late wife, Ducky. I could understand why he'd be attracted to her, and even why he'd want Ducky out of the picture so he could pursue a closer relationship with this buxom blonde, with the gorgeous blue eyes and straight white teeth.

But would Quentin kill for her, when divorce was always a less gruesome, and at least, a legal, option? He hadn't really seemed the type to exert cruel and unusual punishment on his spouse, just because she didn't have the good fortune of looking like she'd just stepped off the front page of *Glamour* magazine.

Quentin was attractive in his own way, but certainly not *GQ* material. He for sure wouldn't be taking David Beckham's place in an underwear advertisement any time soon. How would he even manage to catch this woman's eye? There had to be a different connection between these two. It was my intention to find out what it was.

As I waited in line, I turned ideas over in my mind, trying to think of some clever way of finding out, in what form or fashion this woman was involved with Quentin Duckworthy. Finally, I decided the best tactic was a direct approach. I'd ask the clerk, if she indeed turned out to be Ms. Wells, flat-out how she knew Quentin. Hopefully, I'd catch her off guard enough that she'd answer me without having time to realize it was none of my damn business, and that I shouldn't have even had the audacity to ask her such a personal question.

This course of action might have been successful had Ms. Wells not gone on break, and been replaced by a male clerk, just as I was walking up to the counter. I noticed she was blotting her eyes with a tissue as she walked away from her post. And I heard her blow her nose as she exited the room. Was she upset, suffering with allergies, or what? I wondered.

I bought four stamps, just enough to mail Sheila's card, and three utility bills. I knew I'd be back on Monday to buy more stamps, perhaps two or three times, before I was waited on by the gorgeous woman I thought might be Barbara Wells.

Walking up and down the aisles at Pete's Pantry, twenty minutes later, I tried to think of something special to prepare for supper. I'd been bowled over by Colby Tucker's acceptance to my invitation to dine with us at the Alexandria Inn that evening. He'd even seemed delighted, stating he needed to have me fill out and sign a W-9 and several other forms, to take over as interim head librarian. He had a busy week ahead, and this would be the perfect opportunity to meet me and take care of required business at the same time, he told me.

I was almost too stunned to respond. Not to mention, I was practically doing handsprings down the hallway. He asked permission to bring along his wife, and I replied affirmatively, assuring him that I was anxious to meet the both of them.

Now I was thinking about my repertoire of savory recipes and finding it a pitifully short list. I debated the likelihood of me pulling off a Rack of Lamb Persillade recipe I'd recently cut out of a magazine, and decided it was wedged right between meager and hopeless. I could screw up a bowl of Raisin Bran given half a chance.

I settled on a menu of roasted chicken, asparagus, potatoes au gratin, and rolls. I could surely handle that menu without any difficulty. I'd make enough to serve the Tuckers, Stone, and I, in the kitchen, and our four remaining guests in the dining room. The Spurleys had left early that morning to return home to Nebraska, and only the two young couples from Florida remained at the Alexandria Inn.

Then, due to a lack of time to prepare something special, I'd serve a store-bought Dutch apple pie and ice cream for dessert. I still had to stop and purchase some aftershave for Stone if I could squeeze it into my schedule, because the Tuckers were due to arrive at six o'clock.

As I drove home, I felt queasiness in my stomach, and had a sudden premonition the evening would turn out to be something I'd regret. My intuitions were seldom without merit. Was it too late to withdraw my invitation to the Tuckers? Of course it was, I decided. But I would try desperately to ensure the evening would turn out to be a fruitful and informative meeting over a delicious meal, accompanied perhaps with a tearful, and remorseful, admission of guilt.

* * *

The Tuckers arrived promptly at six o'clock. So promptly, in fact, that I wondered if they'd waited at the end of the driveway to pull in just as the cuckoo bird emerged from the clock hanging on our kitchen wall. I admit, I liked to arrive on time at events, as well, but I wasn't anal about it. Within ten minutes of the scheduled time was close enough for me.

I hadn't gotten the chicken in the oven to roast as early as I'd anticipated, but assumed it would be done enough by the time everyone sat down to eat. Everything else would be ready by then too. As it turned out, we'd be eating in the formal dining room, because the four guests at the inn were going out on the town for dinner and a movie. They'd be taking advantage of a nice Saturday evening in an unfamiliar town, and just enjoying the opportunity to be out and about. I'd suggested a fun restaurant downtown called The Hallowed Hog, because the Kansas City area was known for its fantastic barbecue, and I thought it'd be something they'd find fun, and delicious, as well.

Colby Tucker didn't look anything like I'd pictured him. Not very tall, and very rotund, he looked as wide as he was tall. His wife, on the other hand, looked like she'd given up eating for Lent and had never started up again. She was a little wisp of a thing. Both of the Tuckers were dressed very dapperly, making me glad I'd at least changed out of my blue jeans with the ragged, but now stylish, rips in them. Fortunately, I'd chosen to wear black slacks and a black and red sweater. Black was thinning, so hopefully I didn't look too much like a linebacker compared to Mrs. Tucker, who practically disappeared standing next to her husband.

After introductions were made, I led our guests into the parlor, and Stone fixed them a cocktail at the rustic wet bar that looked like it was straight off the set of a John Wayne movie. Stone and the Tuckers visited in front of the roaring fireplace, while I readied the table for supper. Mrs. Tucker offered to assist me, but I turned her down, telling her I didn't have much to do and I'd rather she relax in the parlor. Actually, I didn't want her to see the horrific mess I'd made of the kitchen, or watch me rush around it like a kitten who had overdosed on catnip.

"Is something burning?" Stone hollered.

"Oh crap!" I said, with one hand over my mouth.

I sprinted to the kitchen from the dining room, like O. J. Simpson running through an airport. Smoke was escaping around the top door of the double oven. Grabbing a potholder, I flung open the door to release a cloud of black smoke. The rolls looked like something that had been belched out of the Mt. St. Helens volcano. I set them aside to toss in the trash once they'd quit smoldering. Thankfully, I had an extra package of rolls, because, when I was grocery shopping earlier in the day I'd been expecting to also feed the four Floridians.

I'd already set the table, so I pulled the potatoes au gratin out of the top oven to cool, and replaced them with the new rolls. I left the chicken in the bottom oven to give it as much roasting time as possible. The rolls would be ready about the same time as the asparagus. I set the timer on the stove to make sure I wouldn't forget them again.

Dinner turned out to be an interesting experience. Colby pulled a chair out for his wife before sitting down at the table. As he plopped down, I could hear the ominous sounds of a wooden chair trying to hold up more weight than it was designed to handle.

"Should we begin by blessing the food?" I asked, as I always did when entertaining guests. It wouldn't hurt to tack on a prayer that God please keep Colby's chair intact, so it didn't dump an estimated four hundred pounds of pure lard onto the hardwood floor. That would put such a damper on the evening.

"No," Colby replied to my question regarding a prayer before supper. "Let's just eat! My stomach's beginning to think my throat's been cut. I haven't had a bite to eat since lunch."

With that, he began filling his plate with enough food to feed a family of five. His wife put one tiny slice of chicken, a spoonful of potatoes, and 2 asparagus spears on her plate, and said, "I usually wouldn't eat this much, but I just love asparagus."

I was further amazed when she tore a roll in two and put half of it on her husband's plate alongside the other two he'd already removed from the wicker basket. I put less on my plate than I normally would have, had we been dining with normal people. For one thing, I didn't want to look glutinous sitting next to someone who didn't have enough on her plate to keep a baby sparrow alive. For another, I was suddenly concerned there wouldn't be enough food on the table to satisfy Colby's massive appetite. I noticed Stone restricted himself to much less than usual, too.

The conversation at the dinner table was minimal. Mrs. Tucker seemed to be just naturally introverted, and Colby never stopped chewing long enough to form a sentence. To fill the awkward silence, Stone and I discussed normal, everyday things like the delicate floral pattern on the china I'd chosen to serve supper on, the upcoming mayoral election, the rising price of beef, and what kind of toothpaste Stone should buy to brighten his teeth. When we grew weary of searching for topics to make small talk about, I got up, turned the radio on, and tuned in a country music station. I'd rather listen to someone singing about a love affair gone wrong, than to a sound reminiscent of a starving hog bellied up to a trough. Listening to Colby's incessant chewing was grating on my nerves.

"I believe that was the best chicken I've had in weeks," Colby said after he'd polished off everything on the table.

"Did you get enough?" I asked, already thinking about what else I could pull out of the pantry to fill this bottomless pit.

"Oh, sure, thank you. I can grab a couple hotdogs when we get home, and that should tide me over until my evening snack. I like to have a little something to satisfy my sweet tooth while we watch the evening news," Colby said. What in the world would this man have for an evening snack? I wondered. A two-pound box of Russell Stover's chocolates?

"Speaking of sweets," Stone cut in. "Didn't I see a delicious-looking apple pie in the kitchen? Are you two ready for dessert?"

"Of course," Colby replied.

"I'll pass," his wife said. "I've already eaten so much my stomach hurts, but thank you for the offer."

Her stomach probably hurt, I thought, because there was nothing in it to stick to her ribs. But I merely smiled, turned to Colby, and asked, "Would you like vanilla ice cream with your pie?"

"You bet!" He said, enthusiastically. Of course he wants ice cream. What a stupid question. That's like asking someone who'd been floating in a life raft on the Pacific Ocean for a week if they'd like some fresh water to drink. Or maybe a large boat to climb aboard.

Grouped around the fireplace after supper, the four of us chatted about inconsequential things. I signed several documents, establishing my employment.

Colby Tucker was relaxed and friendly, and was gradually changing my first impression of him as being a rude jerk with an over-inflated ego, to something slightly less repugnant. His wife sat quietly, sipping at her cup of coffee.

Before I forgot, I asked Mr. Tucker about letting Tom take on a full-time position, instead of replacing Carolyn Aldrich with another untrained, part-time employee. I was greatly relieved, for both my and Paul Miller's sakes, when he had no problem with my solution to both dilemmas.

When I felt the time was right, and everyone was relaxing with a cup of after-supper coffee, I asked, "How well did you know Ducky, Mr. Tucker?"

"Call me Colby, please," he said. "I've known her for about fourteen years. She was already working at the Rockdale Public Library when I took over the job as the county library system director."

"What was your impression of her?" I asked.

"Ducky was unique. She was very headstrong and opinionated, and could be very hard to reason with occasionally." So far, Colby had said nothing I didn't already know. "Ducky could be a bit cantankerous at times, and I never knew what kind of mood she'd be in when I called her."

"Go on," I prompted, when he'd stopped speaking. I was thinking I'd just heard the pot calling the kettle black, knowing Tucker wasn't always the friendliest soul in the world either, especially on the phone. But silently I listened to his response.

"I was starting to get some complaints from patrons of the library. They thought she was quick to lose her temper, often over small, insignificant matters," he said. "She was at an age she could retire and not lose her pension. So I suggested she do exactly that, and make room for some younger person to take over the reins of the library. I was really trying to replace her, while still letting her save face, so to speak."

"I take it that didn't go over well?" Stone asked Colby.

"Not well at all. But we'd argued about every little thing for years, so her contempt for me 'forcing' her out, as she put it, was not unexpected. We couldn't seem to agree on anything. If I told her broccoli was good for her health, she'd flat out refuse to touch the perilous stuff. She was that hardheaded. But the idea of retirement seemed to grow on her, and I actually think she was looking forward to it as the time grew nearer."

"Oh, I couldn't agree more. She told me she was excited to finally have the time to do things on her bucket list," I said. "By the way, was there any particular reason you never filled her request for a new keyboard? It really is defective."

"Oh, I'm sure it is, but the cranky old broad got on my nerves sometimes, always trying to tell me how to run the entire county library system. I basically just put off replacing the keyboard to put a fox in Ducky's chicken coop—you know—ruffle her feathers just to amuse myself. Given the circumstances, it sounds a little juvenile now, I'll admit."

"So, Colby, were you as surprised as I was when her death was ruled a suicide?" I asked. I didn't want to agree or refute his admission of acting childish. I found it best to avoid insulting my dinner guest, who was also my soon-to-be new boss.

"Yes and no. She was incredibly unpredictable, and so terribly moody. But, yet, she also seemed to have a zest for life, and, like she told you, she had things she was anxious to do during her retirement."

"Yes, she even went into detail about a few of them. Some were expected, some not, but all of them showed a desire to live and enjoy life. I still don't believe it was a suicide, and I told the detectives so."

"Really?" Colby asked. "What was their response?"

"They said there wasn't enough concrete evidence to prove otherwise, but if anything came to light that pointed to murder, they'd take another look at the case. So, I'm trying to uncover the truth about what happened Tuesday night in the library after I left to go home."

"I don't think it's wise for you to get involved in something of that nature. Probably best to leave well enough alone, and spend your time and efforts concentrating on working at the library." He looked a bit agitated, but I didn't really take his suggestion as a threat. It was said more in a fatherly fashion, as if trying to steer one's child down the right path, and protect them from some unforeseen danger. "Besides, it's pretty apparent she actually did kill herself, and I guess no one ever really knows what goes on in other people's minds."

I merely nodded, not agreeing or disagreeing with his remarks. I watched Colby swipe the back of his hand across his forehead, and thought he looked a little flushed. His wife was yawning on the couch next to him. I was not surprised when they rose in unison, thanked us for a wonderful supper, and said it was time for them to head home.

We walked them out to their car, and waited while they drove down the driveway. I asked Stone for his opinion of Colby Tucker, and if he thought he might have anything to do with Ducky's death.

"I'm not really sure how to take him, but I got the impression that, although he and Ducky had their differences, none of them were significant enough to kill her over. He did seem a little uncomfortable when he left, however," Stone said. "Oh, well, at least he doesn't seem as disagreeable as I thought he might. Sometimes people under a lot of stress at work can be short-tempered, or incredibly unpleasant, and nice as can be in a more relaxed setting. And I think that might just be the case with Colby Tucker."

"Probably so," I said. "Guess I'd better get the kitchen cleaned up and get ready for bed. Something tells me tomorrow might be a long day."

CHAPTER 10

Sunday morning was bright and sunny, but I felt a bit unsteady as I descended the stairs and entered the kitchen. I nearly tripped over the throw rug at the bottom of the staircase.

Stone was leaned up against the sink, holding his right hand against his belly. I'd seen the look on his face before, and it was not a good omen.

"Wow, my stomach is sure churning. Something must not be agreeing with me."

By the time we got settled into chairs at the table, I was feeling a bit nauseated myself. When I realized a cup of coffee did not sound appealing, I knew something wasn't quite right. I couldn't remember the last time coffee had sounded unappetizing to me. In fact, before that moment, I didn't even know if it was possible.

However, being a creature of habit and somewhat insane, I poured myself a cup of coffee anyway. Then another, and another, and then one more, even though none of it tasted even remotely good. I sipped at the strong brew while I struggled through the motions of fixing bacon and eggs for our guests, who would be checking out shortly after breakfast. Neither Stone nor I felt up to eating breakfast, and I found the smell of bacon frying unsettling to my stomach. Now I knew something was dreadfully wrong. If there were bacon-scented candles, I'd have one burning in the kitchen all the time.

An hour later, I joined Stone on the back porch with another cup of unsavory coffee, which I felt obligated to drink whether I was enjoying it, or not. Stone's complexion was a ghastly shade of green, his face appearing completely drained of blood. Before we knew it, Stone and I were both throwing up what little we had on our stomachs, which in my case was nothing but coffee. It tasted even worse coming up then it had going down.

"My goodness, Lexie, what could be affecting us this badly? Was it something we ate?" Stone asked, as he staggered back into the kitchen, where I was resting with my head on the table. I was experiencing severe stomach cramps, and puking up a full carafe's worth of coffee had zapped my energy. I very slowly lifted my head off the table to answer Stone's question, trying to prevent the room from spinning in circles and making me dizzy as a loon.

"Well, I'm starting to wonder if the chicken was thoroughly cooked. I did leave it in the oven at least an hour less than the recipe called for, but I figured it was long enough to kill any bacteria that might have been in it."

"That doesn't sound very promising," Stone said, bending over to alleviate the severe stomach cramping as much as possible.

"Oh, Lord," I mumbled, as I rushed for the restroom. "I think I'm getting diarrhea now. And I might need to throw up lunch, which I haven't even eaten yet."

"I'll use another john upstairs," Stone said, holding his hand tightly over his mouth as he fled the room.

I was lying on a hospital bed, completely enveloped by a floor-length drape, which ran along a metal track attached to the ceiling. Stone was in the cubicle next to me, stretched out on another hospital bed. After blood cultures and stool samples were evaluated, we were informed we each had a mild case of salmonellosis. I asked for crackers, or at least something to stop the nausea and diarrhea, and was told it was best to let it run its course and get out of my system, or it would just prolong the infection and symptoms of salmonella poisoning.

It suddenly occurred to me I had fed the contaminated chicken to the Tuckers too, and Colby had eaten a mind-numbing amount of it. I whispered Stone's name to get his attention. "Oh, Stone, you don't think I've killed my new boss, do you? We need to contact the Tuckers, I'm afraid."

Just as I finished my comments, an emergency room nurse, one who recognized me from my numerous former visits to the E.R., walked in, and said, "Hey! Lexie, did you just mention the name Tucker?"

"Yeah, why?" I asked, with a bad feeling that I wouldn't like his answer.

"We just admitted a Colby Tucker and put him in a room upstairs. He came into the E.R. terribly ill, and very dehydrated. We had to put him on intravenous fluids." The nurse frowned and gently patted my hand. "Like you and your husband, he also had food poisoning."

"Oh, dear God! Was Mrs. Tucker with him? Is she ill too?"

"She's with him, but she seems just fine. In fact, she

drove him to the hospital. Why do you ask?"

"I'm pretty certain I'm the one who poisoned the Tuckers, with a bacteria-laden raw chicken last night. Fortunately, Mrs. Tucker didn't eat very much, so she wasn't affected like Colby, Stone, and I. Colby ate the bulk of it though, so I'm also not surprised he's now hooked up to an I.V. and getting fluids."

I was relieved to hear that Colby's wife was fine, but not totally surprised. There was little room for bacteria to hide on the minuscule piece of chicken she'd placed on her plate. And after scooting everything around, making it appear as if she'd eaten more than she had, not much of anything was actually ingested.

"Well, there you have it, Stone!" I said, loud enough for him to hear. "I've gone and poisoned my new boss. Should I go up to his room right now and submit my resignation, or wait until he's up and about and able to have the satisfaction of firing me himself? I'll be lucky if he doesn't opt to sue me for assault and battery, using poultry as my weapon."

"He'll be all right, now that's he's here being taken care of by medical professionals. The salmonella poisoning was not premeditated, Lexie. A bit foolish, perhaps, but certainly not intentional. The nurse said we would both be able to go home soon. The worst of it is over, considering neither of us ate much of the chicken last night. But I guess we really should go up to Colby's room and see how he's doing," Stone said.

"Yes, and I need to fall all over myself apologizing. I feel absolutely awful about what's happened. He has every right to fire me for being stupid enough to not test the chicken with a food thermometer. I was just a bit frazzled from burning the rolls, and felt rushed to get the food on the table. Colby had been making comments about being on the verge of passing out from lack of nourishment, you know. And, after all, he hadn't eaten since lunch."

"I understand why you felt pressed for time, and undercooking the chicken could have happened to anyone, Lexie," Stone said, reminding me of why I loved him so much. "I think Colby will be understanding too, at least once this is all behind him, and I doubt he'll fire you. He needs you. I'm sure he knows you're the best person around to handle the librarian job while he searches for a full-time replacement for Ducky."

"I hope so, but I'm almost too embarrassed to even speak to him now, much less work for him. I'd wanted to make a good first impression on him, and this dinner party fiasco was certainly not apt to impress him much. This is not a very promising beginning to a good working relationship."

"Colby may be more forgiving than you think. Try to relax, and don't fret over it," Stone advised.

Easy for him to say, I thought. He wasn't the poor sucker who had just poisoned his new boss, the person he'd have to report to for the next several months. And Colby was a man who'd already proved to me on the phone he didn't handle stress well. I most certainly would be going to Wal-Mart to purchase a new keyboard in the near future. I hardly wanted to start my job off by requesting one, because Colby might now have a hankering to put a fox in my chicken coop too. And the last image I wanted to help Colby Tucker conjure up was a chicken!

When I called the Wheatfield Memorial Hospital the next morning, I was glad to hear I hadn't killed Colby. Using a contaminated chicken as a murder weapon would be a hard thing to live down with my fellow inmates, while I wasted away in a maximum-security women's prison.

His wife did tell me, however, they were keeping him in the hospital another day because his symptoms had not abated much. As a matter of fact, Colby was currently experiencing projectile vomiting, she told me, just from having taken a few sips of water to moisten his dry mouth.

She told me she appreciated my concern, and my call to inquire about his condition, but she needed to get off the phone so she could help Colby put in a meal order for lunch. The man couldn't keep down water, was in fact spraying the room with it as we spoke, and yet he wanted a tray of food delivered to him? The way I felt, just the smell of food would be enough to drive me over the edge. I'd be spewing all over the poor soul who brought the tray into my room before she'd even placed it on my bedside table.

Well, at least it didn't sound as if Mrs. Tucker was angry with me. She appeared to have a "shit happens" attitude about the incident. Of course, she wasn't the one cramping, puking, and pooping nonstop either. Colby's opinion of me was obviously still in question. When we hadn't been allowed to visit him in his room Sunday, I didn't know whether to be disappointed or relieved, but relieved beat out disappointed after the nurse told me he couldn't get off the pot, anyway.

So after we'd been released from the emergency room, we'd gone home and spent the rest of the day lying around the house, thanking our lucky stars we'd let Colby Tucker eat the bulk of the foul fowl the evening before. We had gradually begun to feel like we could tolerate a little food, so I made us each some toast. I'd gone to bed dreading the phone call I felt obligated to make to Colby's hospital room the next day.

Now I hung up the phone and retreated back to the

couch, glad there were no longer any guests currently staying over at the inn. They might have been a little disappointed in the toast and cold cereal I would have fed them for supper. And, although the risk of poisoning someone with Cheerios had to be slim, if anyone could do it, it was me.

Monday was spent lounging around the inn, accomplishing very little. Stone and I both felt much better, but the affects of the food poisoning had made us weak and lethargic. I was distressed to discover Mr. Tucker was spending yet another day in the hospital. He'd probably not realized yet, that continuing to eat large amounts of food, even as he was regurgitating it all back up, was not allowing the salmonella poisoning to run its course, and he was only prolonging his agony, as the E.R. nurse had explained to me.

Knowing there was nothing I could do about it, I tried to keep my mind on other things. And as much as I'd have rather been doing something proactive about discovering the truth behind Ducky's death, it was all I could do to walk from the kitchen to the back porch without needing a walker to lean on.

I vowed to throw myself back into the investigation the following day. The number of days before the library reopened was getting smaller with each passing hour spent accomplishing nothing.

CHAPTER 11

By the time I got out of bed Tuesday morning and had showered, dressed, and gone downstairs, Detective Wyatt Johnston was sitting at the kitchen table having coffee with Stone. I was happy to discover that coffee sounded very appealing to me, and I felt almost completely like my old self again. Stone was laughing, and appeared as if he too, was completely back to normal.

"Good morning, Wyatt," I greeted the snickering detective. With my hands on my hips, I continued, "I can tell by that silly grin on your face, Stone has already told you about my cooking catastrophe . You can quit laughing at me now."

"Yes, he did, but I'm not laughing *at* you, Lexie, I'm laughing *with* you."

"I'm not laughing, Wyatt. Don't I need to be laughing for you to be laughing *with* me?" I asked. "I don't find it at all funny. When I tell the story to my grandkids, maybe ten years from now, I'll probably find it mildly amusing, but for now I just feel like the biggest nincompoop in the world."

"Hey, don't feel badly. People expect that kind of thing from you," Wyatt said, in a lousy effort to console me.

Watching Stone try to contain his laughter, I said, "Swell. Thanks, Wyatt! I feel so much better now that I know everyone *expects* me to behave like a ninny."

"I'm sorry. You know what I mean," Wyatt said, looking toward Stone for help.

"Go on, Wyatt," Stone said. "I'm anxious to see how you try to climb out of this hole you've dug for yourself."

"Okay, guys," I said. "Enough amusing yourselves at my expense. I know it was a senseless thing to do, and also that I have a tendency to do idiotic things on occasion, but this is the first time I've actually harmed someone else, and not just myself. And hurting an innocent bystander, who has the misfortune of stepping in the deep doo-doo I've created, really upsets me."

After Wyatt and Stone both tried to placate me, and convince me everything would work out okay, I apologized to Wyatt for not having any Danishes, tarts, cookies, or other treats, to offer him to enjoy with his coffee. I'd been too ill to cook anything on Sunday. He assured me he wasn't at all hungry, and probably wouldn't have eaten any even if there were some available. This was as believable as the beefed-up eating machine telling me he was giving up police work to become a ballet dancer.

Wyatt's obvious lie led me to believe he was now scared spitless of eating anything I prepared. Most of the pastries I baked contained eggs, and eggs were another common cause of salmonella poisoning. Apparently, the detective was not anxious to be occupying the empty bed in Colby Tucker's room at the hospital.

"I do have a bag of Keebler's Chips Deluxe cookies I bought at Pete's Pantry a couple days ago, if you'd like to have some to dip in your coffee," I offered.

"Well, yeah, I could probably handle a few of those," Wyatt said, with his eyes lighting up. Sure, I thought, he wants nothing to do with anything I've slaved over, but he'll jump all over cookies baked by a bunch of blasted elves!

Right before Wyatt left to report to work, he asked me, "Remember Clint Travis, the detective that questioned you at the library and rubbed you the wrong way?"

"Yeah. What about him?" I asked. "He's been fired, I hope."

"No, that's not it. Last night there was another robbery in town. This time it was at the Jazzy Jigger Liquor Mart over on Elm Street. Mostly cash stolen again, plus three cartons of Marlboro Lights, and a couple bottles of Three Olives Vodka off a display shelf near the cash register."

"Any suspects in this string of robberies yet?" I asked.

"No, and few leads. But Detective Travis was the first one on the scene. In fact, he noticed the back door kicked in while on his beat, and called it in to the station. I heard the transmission on the radio, and was in the area, so I joined Clint in scrutinizing the crime scene. Same M.O. as the others, back door kicked in, crowbar used to open the cash register, and the alarm system and security cameras disabled."

"Wow, somebody's on a real spree, aren't they? I thought you always worked the day shift?" Stone asked his friend. "What were you doing on duty last night?"

"I've been picking up an extra shift here and there. I

can use the overtime income to upgrade to that Ranger bass boat with the Mercury one-fifty horsepower motor. You know, the one I had my eye on at the boat show."

"Yeah, I don't blame you. That one's a dandy!" Stone said. "Wouldn't that be nice to take walleye fishing next spring?"

"Yeah," Wyatt said with a nod. "I thought if we could troll the flats and—"

"Hey," I cut in. I might be viewed as having a one-track mind, but once the men got off the subject about the rude detective, and more involved in talking about crank baits, and drift fishing with a windsock, Wyatt might never get back to his story. "You two can discuss boats and walleye fishing later. Go on with what you were saying about Detective Travis."

"Oh yeah, sorry," Wyatt said, sheepishly. "Anyway, Clint's been very withdrawn, and kind of short and snappy with other officers, ever since he's joined the force. He really hasn't bonded with any of us much. But, last night after I asked him if something was wrong, he opened up to me some while we swept the liquor store for trace evidence, fingerprints, and all. The sweep was completed with little success, I might add."

"Go on," I prompted Wyatt. The detective had piqued my interest and I wanted to hear the whole scoop. If I was tempted to pass on any gossip at the Klip Joint hair salon next week, I wanted it to be as accurate and detailed as possible.

"Officer Travis is going through a rough spell right now and I feel for him," Wyatt said. "He recently caught his wife of ten years cheating on him with his best friend, and now he's involved in a bitter divorce, and fighting for custody of his four kids. Apparently his ex-best friend is an attorney, known for his underhanded tactics, and ability to sway judges, usually with payoffs, Clint believes. He's pretty sure between his cheating ex-wife, and the back-stabbing attorney, he's going to get a royal screwing."

"Hmmm. Can I get this attorney's name and number, just in case?" I said, with a wink at Stone, and a quick kiss on his cheek to assure him I was only teasing.

"Nope!" Stone and Wyatt said in unison.

"Well, it was worth a try," I said. "Go on with your story, Wyatt."

"Clint is pretty torn up about the whole situation, naturally, and I think it has a lot to do with his moodiness and inability to concentrate on anything else at the moment. While we surveyed the crime scene, he sat on the floor and talked while I did most of the work. I didn't mind, of course, and I was happy to get to know Clint a little better. I feel sorry for him losing his wife and best friend at the same time, plus being worried about losing the bulk of his property, and that he might not even be able to spend much time with his kids. At one point, as he spoke about missing his kids, he was actually sobbing."

"That is a sad story," I agreed. "I can understand now why he was so insensitive and snippy at the library the other day. Poor guy. Well, I hope it turns out okay for him, even if it doesn't sound very promising."

"Yeah, I feel for him too," Stone said.

Wyatt nodded, and said, "Me too. I just hope it works out all right for him. I think he probably really is a good guy, and a competent police officer."

"Oh, I almost forgot to tell you, Wyatt," Stone said. "Wendy called this morning and invited us, you, and Veronica, to supper tomorrow night. She and Andy would like to show off the improvements and renovations they've made to the ranch house. And Wendy can't wait to introduce us all to Mork and Mindy. She's so enthralled with the baby alpacas, you'd think she'd given birth to them herself."

"It's good practice for when the time comes she'll need to care for my grandchildren. Miscarrying the baby she conceived with her first husband was sad, but I hope she'll be able to have healthy babies in the future." Both men agreed with my sentiments, and then Stone walked Wyatt out to his car. I poured myself another refill of coffee, and sat down at the table to read the daily *Rockdale Gazette.*

When Stone rejoined me in the kitchen, he sat down at the table as I refilled his coffee cup. I sat down across from him with my own cup. He thanked me and said, "I didn't want to mention this while Wyatt was here, but I was able to make an appointment to talk to Elroy Traylor today at two. It will be in his office at city hall."

"Oh, cool, do you have in mind what you're going to say to him, and the questions you want to ask him?"

"I'm not going to interrogate him, as you're probably hoping, Lexie. I'm just going to bring up the issue about this year's budget for tourism, and see where it goes from there. I will follow my instincts and play it by ear," he said.

"That's good. I didn't really expect you to 'interrogate' him, Stone. I just hope you get a chance to ask Traylor a few questions pertaining to Ducky's death. Things like 'Where were you last Tuesday night, and do you have anyone who can validate your alibi?' Or maybe something a little less vague, like, 'How, exactly, were you involved with the murder of Bertha Duckworthy? Are you, by nature, the quintessence of evil, or what?' Ask a few questions along that line. Just to kind of feel him out and see how he reacts."

"Yeah, I certainly wouldn't want to be vague," Stone replied, with a chuckle. "I'm not sure I even know what *quintessence* means, but even if I did, that's the very last thing I'd ask the city manager. And I'm pretty sure I can already tell you how he'd react. He'd probably throw me out of his office on my ass, and then have security escort me out of the building. Honey, just let me handle it my own way, okay? I promise you I'm not a complete idiot and I know what I'm doing."

"I'm sorry," I said. "I didn't mean to infer you were an idiot, or didn't know what you're doing. I trust you, and I appreciate you doing this for me. I just have a feeling he could be behind her death. He seems awfully determined to build an apartment complex on the library property, and was not happy at all about her standing in his way, according to Ducky, herself. It may have been a combination of retribution, and a way to eliminate the barricade that was blocking his path."

"Seems a little extreme to me," Stone said. "I can't see him resorting to murder over plans for an apartment complex. But, if you insist, I will go talk to him and see what I can deduce from our conversation."

"Thanks, Stone," I said, sincerely. "And in the meantime, I'm going to be buying stamps until I get a chance to meet, and speak with the person I felt sure was Quentin's mysterious caller, Barbara Wells."

"I'm sure she'll be extremely delighted to make your acquaintance. I quintessentially feel for her."

"Nice try using that word in a sentence," I said, with a smile.

I then asked Stone if Wendy had mentioned wanting me to bring anything to the supper the following evening. He told me she'd specifically told him to let me know I didn't need to bring anything, because she had everything covered. Obviously, Stone had told my daughter I'd poisoned my boss Saturday night, and the poor fellow was still in the hospital waiting to be released this morning. I guess I wouldn't want me to add anything to the dinner menu either.

But, I was thrilled with the invitation to go out to the ranch and see what the kids had done with the place, and meet the baby alpacas, otherwise known as my new grand-crias, which for now was the closest thing I had to grandchildren.

I was also anxious to see Wyatt's girlfriend, Veronica, who we'd first met when her father was killed in the nicest suite at Alexandria Inn, on the inn's opening night. We now had the bad habit of referring to that suite as the "crypt" but we never discussed the death that had occurred in the suite with our paying guests. What they didn't know wouldn't hurt us, we decided.

I truly had been concerned about what the ghastly murder of Horatio Prescott would do for the reputation of the bed and breakfast, but it hadn't seem to hurt business any. Nor had the death of the young man, Walter Sneed, who was later killed in the parlor, after we'd hired him to work for us when we held a haunted house at the inn just over a year ago.

The only really good thing that had resulted from the death of Horatio Prescott, was that his daughter, Veronica, had reconnected with her high school admirer, Detective Johnston, and they'd been an item ever since. Although we saw Wyatt on an almost daily basis, we hadn't had the opportunity to visit with Veronica since the Labor Day picnic we'd held on the back patio, where we ate grilled hamburgers and hotdogs in the gazebo Stone and I had been married in the previous spring.

But, the thing I was the happiest about with the invitation to the kid's place for supper Wednesday night, was that I didn't have to tempt fate again by doing any of the cooking myself. I wasn't ready to climb back up on that horse again quite yet. In fact, with no guests currently lodging at the inn, I'd be talking Stone into going out to eat tonight at the Hallowed Hog restaurant in town. Barbecue sounded nice to me, and I was sure I could convince Stone he'd been craving it, too.

CHAPTER 12

I was beginning to hope Stone would have better luck on his assignment than I was having on mine. When I finally got up to the counter the first time, after waiting in line twenty minutes, there was an older man who waited on me. I bought a book of stamps, and asked him if Ms. Wells was expected to work that day. He wasn't certain, but told me she'd be in at twelve if she were on the schedule. It was eleven-fifteen at the time.

I didn't want to wait in the parking lot for forty-five minutes, so I drove down to the coffee shop I'd stopped at Friday afternoon. I ordered a large espresso to go. I then drove back to the post office and sipped on my coffee while I listened to a golden oldies radio station until a couple minutes after noon.

When I got in line again, there was a pretty, black woman at the counter. The only way I was going to find out if Barbara Wells would be working at any time during the afternoon was to stand in line *another* twenty minutes, purchase *another* book of stamps, and ask *another* clerk if Ms. Wells was scheduled to work during the afternoon. And as feared, it was *another* waste of time. This clerk didn't know Barbara's schedule either, but offered to leave her a message.

Sure, I'll leave a message. How's this?

Tell Ms. Wells if she killed Bertha Duckworthy, or has any information on who did, please call me at this number, 555-1022. I'd also be curious to know if she's been sleeping with Ms. Duckworthy's husband. I'll anxiously await her call.

"Maybe it'd be best if I try to catch her at another time," I said instead.

"Okay, ma'am," the clerk replied. "If she does come in, it will probably be at two."

I thanked her, but had no intention of sitting in the parking lot another two hours. Instead, I ran a few errands I needed to take care of anyway. I stopped at Casey's General Market to fill up with gas, pulled through the drive-thru at Rockdale Savings and Loan to make a deposit, and finally went to Wal-Mart to pick up a few things on my list. I still needed to pick up a bottle of aftershave for Stone. I'd been too busy to go there earlier for just one item. At two o'clock, I drove back to the post office, bought another book of stamps, and was told by the same older gentleman who'd waited on me earlier in the day that Barbara was sorting mail in the back, where customers were not allowed per postal regulations, but she would definitely be working the counter at four, replacing him when he clocked out.

"Have you already used up all the stamps you bought earlier?" The clerk asked.

"Umm, well, yes. I'm working on my Christmas cards today, you see. I wanted to get them done early so I can concentrate on decorating the house and buying gifts during the Christmas rush. I have so many gifts to buy I was afraid I'd run short on time, so I decided today would be a good day to work on all the many cards I need to send, and get that monumental task out of the way. But, unfortunately, I'd miscalculated and needed a few more stamps than I'd realized because I'd forgotten about my cousins on my mother's side, and I didn't want to cause a rift in the family, you know. Oh dear—listen to me go on and on when there's ten people in line behind me."

Before I began babbling about what kind of Christmas cookies I planned to bake and distribute, providing the stigma of me poisoning people had worn off, I quickly thanked him and rushed out of the post office. I was sure my face was as red as the depiction of Santa Claus on the Christmas stamps the clerk had swapped my "Forever" stamps out for after my rambling story about making out Christmas cards.

I had actually preferred the "Forever" stamps since the price of postage went up regularly, and I'd soon have a year's worth of stamps at the rate I was purchasing them. I felt a bit guilty about my Christmas card story because I usually sent out about a dozen cards, often two or three days after the actual holiday. Still, I was a little proud of my ability to make up believable excuses at the drop of a hat in situations like this.

Now I had another two hours to fill, and since Stone's appointment with Elroy Traylor at city hall was scheduled to have just commenced, there was little left to do but swing by Quentin Duckworthy's house, one more time, and see how he was faring. Just a friendly gesture, on my part, of course. Maybe I could assuage his grief a bit with my words of comfort and concern.

When he answered the door after my second attempt of raising him, he didn't look as if he needed a great deal of consoling. The TV was tuned to an old war movie, *Patton*, I think, and was so loud I could understand how he hadn't heard my rapping on his door the first time I'd knocked.

He had a roll of packing tape in his hand and there were cardboard boxes stacked up against the back wall.

"I'm sorry. Did I catch you at a bad time?" I asked.

"No, I needed a break anyway. It's nice to see you again, Lexie. Come on in and join me for a soda, cup of coffee, or even a beer, if you'd prefer," Quentin said.

"Coffee, please, if it's not too much trouble."

"No trouble at all. I just brewed a fresh pot. Let's sit in the kitchen. Was there something I could do for you?" He asked.

"No, I just had some spare time and thought I'd drop in on you and see how you were faring."

"I'm doing okay, considering the circumstances. I've kept my mind off Ducky's death by boxing up a bunch of her old books. I'm going to use the room she used as a personal library, of sorts, as a room for assembling my woodworking projects. I like to construct little wooden toys and pass them out to kids at Children's Mercy Hospital every Christmas. I enjoy making them, and they enjoy receiving them, so it's a win-win situation," Quentin explained.

"What an incredibly sweet and thoughtful thing to do," I said, sincerely. And what an unlikely thing for a cold-blooded killer to do in his spare time, I thought. Perhaps I'd misjudged this man entirely.

As we drank coffee, Quentin told me a few humorous antidotes about Ducky that made me realize she was even more eccentric than I'd given her credit for. He didn't say or do anything I felt was inappropriate for a man who'd just lost his spouse. I couldn't quite picture this congenial man having an illicit affair with a much younger woman, and I didn't think it was the time or place to inquire about it.

I enjoyed conversing with him so much, I almost lost track of the time. When I heard his grandfather clock signal it was four o'clock, I stood up and told Quentin I had to get to an appointment. I was surprised when he leaned into me with a heartfelt hug, and said, "Thank you so much for taking the time to come see how I was doing. It's support from people like you that are helping me handle my grief and get through this horrific ordeal."

"I greatly enjoyed our conversation too, Quentin, and, like I said, if you need anything at all, don't hesitate to call. I wrote my name and number on a post-it note and left it on the table. I can be reached at the library too, of course. I'm sure you already have that number memorized."

"Thank you," he said, with a great deal of emotion in his voice. I was thankful he didn't know I'd come to his house hoping to find evidence substantial enough to pin the murder of his wife on him. When I'd walked into his house, I'd wanted to see him arrested, convicted, and crucified. Now I only hoped he'd find happiness again, even if it was with a buxom blonde half his age.

Without taking a second to think it over, I pointed to a small box on the fireplace mantel and, wanting to lighten the mood, said, "Those must be some tiny books to fit in a box that size."

"That's my Ducky, not her books," Quentin said, with a bittersweet laugh. I'd wanted to brighten his spirits, but not in the manner I'd chosen. I should have realized she'd already been cremated. They don't delay the funeral, or cremation, of the bodies of people who weren't considered to be the victim of a crime.

For the second time in two hours, I'd left a building with my face crimson with embarrassment. Humiliating myself was not a hobby I wanted to pursue.

I finally hit pay dirt at the post office at ten after four. After waiting in line only a couple minutes this time, I walked up to the counter to be waited on by Barbara Wells. I'd had her identity confirmed earlier in the day by the older male clerk who'd had to listen to my recital about my holiday season rituals. I hadn't wanted to spend an entire day waiting to talk to someone who only resembled the photo I'd seen on Quentin's phone.

After visiting with Ducky's husband for nearly two hours, I wasn't sure I even needed to speak with this woman. I was fairly convinced the association between Quentin and this lovely woman was innocent and aboveboard. But I was here, and I never liked to leave a stone unturned, so after purchasing yet another book of stamps, I said, "You look very familiar to me. Do I know you from somewhere?"

"Not that I'm aware of," she answered politely.

"Oh, say, I know where I've seen you! I was talking to an acquaintance of mine, named Quentin Duckworthy, when his phone rang and your face popped up on his caller identification screen. I knew I'd seen you somewhere," I said, as I casually put my stamps and change into my fanny pack. "You must be his daughter."

I said this just hoping to encourage her to explain her actual association to Quentin, so I was taken aback when she nodded and said, "Well, actually that no-good, gold-digging bastard is just my stepfather. Please excuse my French, but I would never claim him as my father, not that my biological father is any prize either."

Just then, it occurred to me that this gorgeous and statuesque young woman was the offspring of Bertha Duckworthy and Bo Reliford. I knew she had come by her ample breast size naturally, but wondered where, in the combined gene pool of Ducky and Bo, the rest of her assets came from. I was tempted to ask her if her parents had utilized a sperm bank in order to create a beauty like her. Instead, I chose to offer my condolences.

"Oh, sweetheart, I am so sorry for your loss. Ducky, your mother, I mean, had just hired me to temporarily replace her at the library until a permanent replacement could be found. I didn't know her long, but found her to be a very intriguing woman."

Barbara had the grace to smile and say, "That's the understatement of the year. But thank you for your kind words."

People in line behind me were beginning to sigh, cough, and make themselves known in any way they could. One even whispered to the customer in front of her, "Will we still get waited on if that woman is still yacking when they lock the doors?"

Embarrassed once again, I said, "I guess I better keep the line moving."

"Yes," Barbara said. "We close in ten minutes."

I was really curious why Barbara Wells referred to Quentin as a "no-good, gold-digging bastard." There must be more to Quentin than meets the eye, I thought. Knowing Barbara would be clocking out shortly, I decided to wait in the parking lot for her to exit the post office. I parked my car where I could keep an eye on both doors. I hoped she didn't think I was stalking her when I approached her as she left the building. I'd had a stalker before, while investigating a previous murder, and I knew how scary it could be. I didn't want to frighten Ducky's daughter, just gently pump her for more information.

As it turned out, she didn't seem at all surprised to see me waiting for her as she came out the back door. "Hello again," she greeted me with a friendly tone.

"Hello. I don't mean to pry, but I am involved with the investigation of your mother's death—"

"There's an investigation going on?" She stopped and quickly interrupted me. "I was under the impression it'd been ruled a suicide and no investigation was deemed necessary."

"Yes, you're correct," I agreed. "But I have reason to doubt Ducky would take her own life, and I've taken it upon myself to look for evidence to prove otherwise. What do you think? Do you think your mother could honestly have killed herself?"

"Well, I know she'd been on a lot of anti-depression medication, and was upset about having to retire, so I never questioned the official cause of death notated on her death certificate. It was pretty cut and dried, so I'm not sure you taking on such an uphill battle is warranted, or worth your time and effort," Barbara said. I couldn't read her eyes through her sunglasses, but I got the impression she wasn't interested in helping me with my mission to prove her mother was murdered. Maybe the possibility of that conclusion would be too much for her to bear.

"You're probably right," I said. "Do you mind me asking why you don't like your stepfather?"

"Quentin was only interested in my mom for one reason. He wanted her for her money."

"Money?" I asked. The Duckworthy house was nice, but very modest, and I'd seen nothing there that indicated Ducky had any substantial wealth. I doubted a small town librarian cashed huge paychecks.

"Well actually, it's her investments. She had a very impressive collection of first-edition books, worth well over a million dollars. Instead of taking vacations, buying expensive cars or nice clothes, she spent her spare money on old books."

I could certainly agree Ducky didn't waste a lot of money on nice clothes. I smiled at Barbara, and encouraged her to continue with her story.

"Mom owned most of these books before she even met my stepfather, but, now that she's passed, he thinks he should inherit everything she owned. As her only child, I feel like I deserve the biggest chunk of her wealth. I don't know where the bastard gets off thinking everything Mom owned and worked for should now belong to him after just a couple years of marriage to her!"

Barbara's demeanor had gone from being soft-spoken and cordial to being so angry she was nearly shouting. People on the sidewalk across the street were staring at us. I hoped no one thought she and I were in the midst of an argument.

I calmed her down as best I could, and told her I'd look into the matter if at all possible. I didn't tell her, however, that her no-good gold-digging stepfather was already busy boxing up her mother's book collection, as if in a hurry to dispose of the valuable items. I wondered if he already had a buyer, someone anxious to purchase the entire first-edition collection. As an assistant librarian for a number of years, I was aware there were first-edition copies of some of the classics worth many thousands of dollars.

I walked Barbara to her Ford Taurus and helped her get in it, telling her I'd probably be in touch, and then hurried over to my own car. I was anxious to get home and find out what Stone had learned in his meeting with the city manager, and tell him what I'd learned about Ducky and her daughter.

CHAPTER 13

Stone was out in one of the flowerbeds digging up bulbs when I pulled down the driveway. We'd had a frost the night before, and he'd mentioned that morning he needed to get the lily, gladiola, and elephant ear bulbs dug up and put away in a cool, dark corner of the basement until spring. He said they were too tender to withstand a harsh winter, as our local weatherman had predicted we might have this year.

I took my two Wal-Mart bags inside, and by the time I'd put my purchases where they needed to go, Stone had joined me in the kitchen. After he washed and dried his hands at the sink, we both grabbed a cup of coffee and went out on the back porch to chat.

I told him about my day first, keeping my accounting very brief because I was anxious to hear what he had to say about his meeting with the Rockdale City Manager. He nodded, knowingly, as I told him about Ducky's valuable book collection.

"So, what did Elroy Traylor have to say?" I asked, impatiently. "Did you discover anything incriminating?"

"Incriminating? No. But I did come to the conclusion he had no part in Ducky's death."

"How did you come to that decision?" I asked.

"First, we talked about the tourism budget for next year. He agreed tourism was crucial to the economy of Rockdale, since most people come here to visit all our antique stores, and unique specialty shops downtown. They also tour the numerous historic homes in the area, and in the process, they stay in hotels and bed and breakfast establishments like ours. A lot of money in our city's coffers originates with visitors."

"Very true. I'm glad he's aware of how much money tourism brings to this town. So, what are his plans?"

"Traylor told me he's increasing the tourism budget by thirty percent next year, which is even more than I'd hoped for. He wants to put some of the money into increasing the promotion of our annual Rockdale Days festivities, and the nightly country music concerts in particular. They're planning on bringing in some pretty big names, like JoDee Messina, and a popular Black Sabbath tribute band. There's going to be something from just about every genre of music."

"Will the front man of the Black Sabbath tribute band bite the head off a bat like Ozzie did?" I asked, with a dramatic shudder.

"Ugh, don't count on it. But we do have a popular jazz band lined up for opening night. They're from New Orleans originally, and feature a first-class saxophone player performing some awesome solos."

"Cool. I'd like to go to the jazz concert! It sounds terrific," I said.

"Me too. Jazz is my favorite kind of music."

"Really?" I asked. "I learn something new about you every day."

"Same here. I just discovered you like to horde

stamps and send out your 'multitudes' of Christmas cards around Halloween."

"Yeah, right. The few people I send cards to are lucky to get them by Valentine's Day. So, is Snoopy coming to Rockdale Days to represent the rap genre?" I asked, in jest.

"I think you mean Snoop Dog, and no, that's one genre that won't be represented. According to local demographics, Rockdale's median age is about forty-five, so the interest in rap music is limited. Most of our young people move to the city to find better-paying jobs after they get through with their schooling. In fact, if it weren't for our small community college, our median age would probably be pushing sixty."

"No doubt. So, what was your impression of our city manager?"

"As a businessman and public employee, I believe he's very competent. As a person, I think he's high-strung and doesn't lack in the ego department, but I found him friendly and engaging. He had his secretary bring me a cup of coffee after I joined him in his office. Very robust coffee, I might add, with a terrific flavor. I think you'd really like it too. Do you think you could call his office and see what kind of coffee they use?"

"I'm sure I can, and I promise I will, but get back to your conversation with Traylor."

"After we discussed the tourism budget, we spoke mostly about the sports teams in Kansas City. He was happy the Chiefs look strong this year and that the Royals should have a number one draft pick due to their poor record this last season."

"Go on," I prompted, hoping he'd soon get to the part about why he didn't suspect Traylor had any involvement in Ducky's death.

"Traylor told me he caught a ten-pound largemouth bass this weekend in a farm pond just south of town," Stone said, with a lot more enthusiasm than I felt about the city manager's trophy catch. "Oh, and did you know he's related by marriage to Rosalinda Swift from the Rockdale Historical Society? His wife is Rosalinda's niece."

"Stone, I don't really care if he's related to the Pope. What did he say about Ducky? You could have just gone to the local greasy spoon to listen to a bunch of old crows tell fish stories and discuss sports teams, while you drank one buck-fifty cup of coffee, and fourteen free refills. Didn't you get around to discussing Elroy's plans to buy the library property and build an apartment complex, at all? Did you mention the dead librarian that he just happened to be at odds with? Ducky had told me her dislike for Traylor went far beyond the fate of the library."

"I'm getting to that part. Have patience, my dear," Stone said. "Traylor told me he's now considering purchasing a plot of land next to the theatre that's vacant and offered at a ridiculously low price. He said the location is not quite as ideal as the library and Subway area, but big enough to build twice as many apartments."

"Did he say anything about Ducky or how she died?" I felt like I was beating a dead horse to death again.

"Yes, he seemed somewhat distressed at the notion she had killed herself. But when I mentioned her being upset at the idea he'd demolish the library and build apartments there, he told me he got a kick out of their ongoing debate, but there was no way she could have prevented him from getting what he wanted."

"Yeah, I'll bet," I said.

"You know, Lexie, Elroy Traylor's a powerful man

with a domineering, almost arrogant, personality. He didn't seem nearly as emotionally involved in his and Ducky's dispute as she did. Kind of like he considered her nothing more than an annoying gnat he could brush off his shoulder anytime he felt like it. He's not the type to let his plans be thwarted by a ninety pound senior citizen, and certainly not the type to risk losing his empire by killing a librarian he didn't even view as a threat."

"You're probably right, and I trust your judgment, so I'll cross him off my suspect list for now."

"But he did tell me something about Ducky that you were just mentioning. I remember you telling me Ducky argued with a woman with a dark complexion, long raven hair, and bangs on the morning of Ducky's death. Traylor had a photo of his family on his desk. It was Traylor with three sons, two teenaged boys and one about college-age, and a mixed race woman matching the description of the one Ducky quarreled with. When he left the room to speak with his secretary, I snapped a picture of his framed family photo with my cell phone to show you."

When Stone brought up the photo of the black-haired woman, I said, "That's her! That's the woman I saw argue with Ducky and then storm out of the library. I recognize Elroy's oldest son too, from the library parking lot when he was helping his father survey the property. But what really puzzles me is, why would Traylor's wife have a spat with Ducky?"

"Her name is Tina, and I was almost sure she was the one you saw arguing with Ducky, after Elroy told me his wife also collected first-edition books, although her collection paled in comparison to Ducky's, he told me. Mrs. Traylor is from a wealthy family, Elroy said, and his wife was interested in purchasing two books from Ducky, which were J.D.

Salinger's *Catcher in the Rye*, and *The Adventures of Tom Sawyer,* by Mark Twain of course. The second one alone is a signed, mint- condition copy from 1885, and worth about a hundred-grand, according to Traylor. Tina offered Ducky a very substantial amount for the pair, and Ducky wouldn't even consider it."

"Maybe she didn't want to break up her collection," I said.

"No, it wasn't that at all. In fact, she had collected the books over the years as a sort of retirement account, and was now going to sell them to help finance their retirement plans. Mostly she wanted to purchase a home with some acreage to put in a horse arena for her daughter and grandkids, all who compete in equestrian events, and a large garden for herself to putter around in," Stone explained.

"I could not have imagined Ducky 'puttering' anywhere. 'Tromping' through a garden, maybe. But if selling her collection was Ducky's plan, why wouldn't she consider Tina Traylor's offer?"

"Elroy told me his wife went to see Ducky Tuesday morning, which would be the encounter you witnessed at the library, and raised her offer for the two books a significant amount. Ducky declined the offer, saying she wouldn't sell *anything* to a Traylor, even if it meant living in her car for the rest of her life. I take it Ducky had a strong stubborn streak," Stone said with a smile.

"Yes, I think that's a fair assumption. I'd imagine she was ridiculously headstrong, and the type to stick to her principles, no matter what! Well, that does fit with what Ducky's daughter told me today, but now I'm wondering if Quentin knew about Tina's desire to buy the books from Ducky. The fact that he was boxing up the books makes me think he could have already arranged to sell her those two, or perhaps the entire collection. He has no qualms with either of the Traylors, most likely, and according to his stepdaughter, Barbara, he's anxious to sell the books and keep all the proceeds to himself."

"It's possible he's made some kind of deal with Elroy's wife," Stone said. "But Traylor didn't mention it. He could well have thought it was none of my business, and he may just not know yet about any arrangement made between his wife and Quentin Duckworthy."

"Tina's a striking woman with that long black hair, and she has a very fit-looking body from what I could see," I said. "She pretty much towered over Ducky, and yet Ducky seemed to have the upper hand in their quarrel. But, I know from my own experience with her, she could be very intimidating, despite her size."

"Elroy is tall too, and has a well-toned body, as you no doubt noticed when you met him in the library parking lot. He told me both he and his wife work out at Gino's Gym, rarely skipping a day. She usually gets there as soon as it opens, and Elroy works out in the evenings after work."

"Where's Gino's Gym?" I asked. "I'm not real up-to-date with the exercise facilities in town. I know every single place in Rockdale a person could buy a cup of coffee in a caffeine emergency, but not one place where you actually pay people to let you sweat all over their property while pushing your body to its absolute limit. It just sounds like pure craziness to me!"

"I know, it sounds dreadful to me, too. But Gino's Gym is right next to the high school. They took over the school's old gymnasium when the school district enlarged the school and built a newer, more modern gym with more capacity. The school's athletics department has a contract with the gym too, and use it as a training facility for the athletes," Stone said. I was always amazed at how Stone seemed to amass knowledge, as if through osmosis, and was always able to spit out facts and statistics about any given subject at the appropriate time. I couldn't remember what I read on the front page of the *Rockdale Gazette* by the time I got to the third page of the paper.

"I wish I had that kind of ambition and commitment to an exercise regimen. In fact, if Gino's Gym or the Traylors are interested in them, I'd be happy to donate our treadmill and elliptical machines to them. We've used them approximately twice since we bought them, and they're taking up valuable storage space."

"Good idea, Lexie. I think our good intentions and desire for better-toned bodies flew out the window as soon as we remembered why we never used the exercise equipment we've each owned in the past. It's hard work, and it's not a hell of a lot of fun. Not nearly as enjoyable as lying in the recliner eating chocolate swirl ice cream. So, sure, I'll ask Elroy if he and Tina would like them," Stone said. "I think you and I can stay in reasonably good shape by continuing to go on long walks after supper, like we've done pretty much ever since we met."

"Yeah, I agree. And fortunately, we both love to walk. I'm not sure about even asking the Traylors, now that I think about it. They are wealthy and probably already own their own machines, or would if they wanted them. I'd rather ask Gino's Gym first, since the high school uses the equipment so often, and I always like to support educational pursuits as much as possible."

Actually, the extent of my support for the local schools had been buying a couple raffle tickets from the Future Business Leaders of America club. I won the red and white quilt with the appliquéd hearts we now use in the "Honeymoon Suite." They'd raffled the handmade quilt off when they set up a booth at the fair, in order to earn money to attend the state competition in Jefferson City. Buying two raffle tickets hardly made me a prime candidate for the "Philanthropist of the Year" award, but Stone didn't question my dedication to education, and agreed with my idea to donate the equipment to the local gym.

My real purpose for visiting the gym was the hope of running into Tina Traylor and conversing with her about Ducky's death. I wondered how angry she'd been at Ducky's refusal to sell her the books she desired for her collection. Was it enough to seek revenge? It seemed far-fetched as far as motives go, but I didn't want to overlook any little conceivable possibility. The argument she'd had with Ducky on the morning of the librarian's death had appeared to be heated, and could have centered around something even more potent than Ducky's refusal to sell Tina the books. If nothing else, Tina might have some insight into Ducky's death that I hadn't heard about yet.

"I'll run by the gym the next chance I get," I told Stone. "By the way, did Traylor happen to say anything about being surprised Ducky would commit suicide?"

"No, not really, because Elroy inferred he thought she was pretty off-balanced, or 'one flounder short of a fish fry,' as he put it. I told him you didn't believe she'd commit suicide and were busy looking in to it. I didn't tell him I was involved, or that it was my principle purpose for arranging a meeting with him."

"It sounds to me like we both garnered some interesting information today, and I really appreciate your help. It's so nice to have company in my quest for the truth about Ducky's death."

"Happy to be of assistance, my dear. By the way, Elroy took tomorrow off because he has a dental appointment in the morning. He asked me to go bass fishing with him in the afternoon at the farm pond he caught the ten-pounder in this last weekend. You don't mind, do you?" Stone asked.

"Not at all, and you don't have to ask my permission to do anything you want to do. Just make sure you're home and cleaned up by six, because we need to be at the ranch by seven for supper tomorrow night. And hey, who knows, fishing with Elroy Traylor all day, you might just learn something else of importance to aid in our investigation."

Stone groaned, and replied, "Probably nothing any more significant than what lure's best to use for top-water bass fishing. But that's extremely important too, you know."

I laughed and told Stone to get back to what he was doing until it was time to get cleaned up and dressed to go to the Hallowed Hog for supper. He had heartily endorsed my suggestion to eat out and leave the cooking to a professional.

When I woke up Wednesday morning, I could hear Stone's baritone voice crooning in the master bathroom while he was drying off after his shower. I recognized the theme song of "The Sportsman's Friend," Harold Ensley's old fishing show. *Gone fishin', instead of just a' wishin'.* I heard this verse reverberating inside the bathroom walls several times, and had to grin at Stone's youthful exuberance. His energy and unbridled zest for life always brought a smile to my face. It was just one of the many things I found so attractive about my new husband.

"You must be excited about your fishing trip with Traylor this afternoon, Bing," I said in jest, as he walked through the bedroom door.

"Oh, I'm sorry," he said. "I didn't mean to wake you."

"You didn't wake me. I was already stirring, but I would not have wanted to miss hearing your lovely singing voice this morning. Crosby had nothing on you, my dear. On the contrary, listening to me sing could seriously make your ears bleed, so I promise never to put you through that agony," I said.

"Oh, come on, your singing can't be all that bad."

"Trust me, it is that bad! So horrendous, in fact, my Sunday school choir director once asked me if I wouldn't rather stand off to the side by the manger scene, silently, in a costume depicting a shepherd, throughout the entire Christmas program. I felt honored to be singled out, but thought the choir desperately needed my contribution to the harmony of the carols we were going to perform. But, when I told the choir director my concerns, and also that I really didn't want to draw attention to myself as a shepherd and have people staring at me during the recital, she said, 'Then perhaps you ought to just pretend you're singing, sweetheart, or hum quietly to yourself.' Well, as it turned out, I was a very convincing mute shepherd, if I have to say so myself."

Stone laughed at my anecdote, and asked, "Is that why you never belt out the National Anthem at sporting events?"

"Yes, it's very fortunate for you and others around me that I learned to lip-sync early on in life."

Stone chuckled and grabbed my foot, which was resting at the end of the bed. He began pulling on my toes one by one, because he knew it drove me nuts and made me emit high-pitched screams. When he got to the little one, he asked, "Is this squealing little piggy going to stay in bed all day? If not, get dressed, and by the time you get downstairs I'll have a cup of coffee waiting for you."

"That's the best offer I've had all day!" I said. I jumped out of bed, kissed Stone briefly, and headed to the bathroom. I was ready to face a new day, and praying we could put the true nature of Ducky's death to rest by sundown. In retrospect, it might have been better to have just prayed that my toes really would morph into piglets while I stood on stage, at the Super Bowl, holding a microphone and torturing the millions of people in the viewing audience with my rendition of the Star Spangled Banner.

I thought it was a good time to box up all of Ducky's personal items at the library and drop them off at her house with her husband. There probably wasn't anything of monetary value in the paraphernalia she kept at the library, but I was sure there'd be some sentimental aspect to a few of the items as far as Quentin was concerned. He deserved to have her stuff, and I needed to make space in the drawers for my own worthless, but necessary, crap.

I informed Stone of my plans, and he volunteered to accompany me to carry the boxes since he wasn't due to meet up with Traylor until eleven. I figured I could carry the one box I anticipated would hold everything that belonged to Ducky, which probably would weigh no more than five or ten pounds, but I'd welcome Stone's company, and it'd be a good opportunity to give him a tour of the building I'd be in charge of, starting on Monday. He would, no doubt find it as scintillating as watching a slug cross the road, but I felt confident he'd at least feign interest in my new working environment. Just as I had feigned interest in his long-winded and very animated description of the best way to "present" your bait to a bass earlier, as we ate store-bought cinnamon rolls for breakfast.

Using my key, I let us into the building, locking the door behind me so the library didn't fill up with patrons wanting to check out books. We decided to take care of the chore of cleaning out the desk first. For such a stern, task-oriented person, Ducky kept her desk drawers in a very messy and disorganized fashion, almost exactly like I kept mine.

The top drawer on the right side of the desk contained typical office supplies, such as pens, scotch tape, stapler, a roll of stamps, and things of that nature, along with dozens of tootsie rolls and empty candy wrappers. I was amused to find a half-full Daffy Duck Pez dispenser among the conglomeration of items, knowing it'd probably been a gag gift because of its association with her nickname.

The middle drawer had several notebooks, including the one in which I had previously found the employee's W-9's, contact information, and time sheets. There were unused plastic library cards scattered throughout, a couple of McDonald's french fry containers, a half-eaten Subway sandwich, now green and furry, and a crumpled up Valentine's Day card signed by Tom Melvard. I was somewhat surprised to see a first-generation Kindle. What did it say about the future of local libraries when even their head librarians preferred to read their books on an electronic device?

The object I found most unexpected was in the bottom drawer; a first-edition copy of Truman Capote's *Breakfast at Tiffany's*. I opened the book to the copyright page, and handed it to Stone. "This is obviously from Ducky's collection, and worth thousands of dollars, I'm certain. It's really old, copyrighted in 1958."

"Indeed," Stone said. "Even more ancient than you,

if I'm not mistaken."

I closed the book and whacked him on the head with it, probably not the recommended way to handle a valuable first-edition copy of a classic novel.

"Ouch!" He hollered, in mock pain. He took the book from me and opened it. "Check out the title page. It's even signed by the author. Why in the world would Ducky keep something like this in her desk at work?"

"Could she have had some kind of arrangement to show it, or sell it to a potential buyer, and then brought it here to execute the transaction?" I asked.

"Possibly," he replied. As Stone continued to sort through the drawer, I took my phone out of my fanny pack and googled the book title.

"If the information on the website is accurate, this book is worth in the neighborhood of seventy-five-hundred dollars if in great condition, which I think this copy would qualify as. It's in quite good condition, at the very least. Well, let's put it in the box and then I'll show you around the library," I said.

I started my tour in the hearth room with the floor-to-ceiling rock fireplace, and the worn leather couches. "Isn't this cozy? The furniture in this little nook needs to be replaced, but I love the rustic lodge feel of the old building. It's so inviting, or at least it was before I found Ducky hanging from the rafters in here."

After I'd shown him the entire main floor, I asked, "Would you like to see the basement?"

"Sure," he said. I expected him to decline the offer, but figured he was playing the "feigned interest" card to the hilt, so I switched on the lights, which didn't amount to much, and led him down the stairs. There wasn't much to see, and you couldn't see what little there was to see very clearly due to the dim lighting.

We stopped at the shelving unit containing the mops, brooms, and cleaning solutions first.

"Tom's janitorial supplies, obviously, and the stacks of boxes are old library books, no doubt," Stone said. Then he pointed to the far corner. "What's that over there?"

As Stone headed toward the weight-lifting contraption, he said, "Oh, yeah, I remember you saying Paul worked out down here during library hours when he wasn't on the clock. I think Wyatt told me he was training to be a cage-fighter."

"Yes, that's right. He's so quiet that I can't imagine him fighting in a cage. Why would anyone submit himself to such a brutal sport? Staying fit is wonderful, sure, but having one's head repeatedly slammed against a wire cage? No, thank you. That's as gruesome and disgusting as dog or chicken fighting. But why would Paul need to train to compete in what seems like nothing more structured than a common bar brawl?"

"There's a lot of skill and finesse involved," Stone said. "It's not just a matter of brute strength. It requires a lot of training and practice. There are karate, judo, and jujitsu techniques involved, as well as wrestling and other technical maneuvers."

"If you say so," I said with a shudder, thinking about the pain the cage fighters must endure on a regular basis.

"I actually enjoy watching it," Stone said.

"Oh jeez, there's something about you I could have gone without learning."

"It's one of those man things, Lexie, that you'd never understand. No more than I'll ever understand how you can stand to watch more than thirty seconds of *The Housewives of 'Anywhere.'* And how about the catfights those women get involved in? Talk about brutal!"

"Touché," I said, just as we were both startled by repetitive sounds over our heads. "What was that?"

"I don't know, but it sounded like footsteps. Didn't you lock the door behind us when we came in?"

"Yes, I'm positive I did."

The sound started up again, and there was most definitely someone upstairs in the library. I hurried over to the bottom of the steps, and hollered up the stairwell. "Hello?"

I heard the footsteps coming closer to the door at the top of the stairs, so I hollered again, louder this time. "Hello. Who's up there? We're down here in the basement and we'll be right up!"

Stone was by my side now. When there was again no response, he gently pushed me back with his right arm, and whispered, "Stay here while I go upstairs and see who's there. I know they heard you that time, and aren't responding for some reason. My guess is that whoever's upstairs is up to no good."

"Wait! Do you have a weapon?" When Stone grabbed a broom, I felt a sense of panic. "Really? You're going to sweep them to death if they threaten you? What if they have a gun? Will that broom stop bullets? Let's just call 9-1-1."

"Okay, you'll have to call, because I left my phone in the car," he said.

"Oh no! I must have left mine upstairs on the desk when I took it out to google the value of that book."

"Swell. Then I don't see any other choice but for me to go up there and see what's going on, while you remain here."

I was going to try to convince him it wasn't worth the risk. There'd already been one corpse in the library just a week ago. I didn't want the love of my life being the second one. But it became a moot point when we heard the door at the top of the stairs shut, and the deadbolt being slammed home.

"Oh crap!" I whispered. "What do we do now?"

Stone did a quick appraisal of our surroundings. The locked door was the only exit. There were no windows in the basement, and we had no way to contact anyone for help. We listened carefully as we heard what sounded like one set of footsteps cross the entire expanse of the library and exit through the front door.

"Okay, let's not panic," Stone said. "Let's concentrate on what resources we have at our disposal."

"Which isn't much, unless we're going to clean our way out of here," I added, with a slight wavering of my voice.

"Well, we've got one thing going for us. Elroy is expecting me to show up at his office at eleven to go fishing. When I don't arrive, he might get concerned about my whereabouts."

"Concerned enough to call the police?" I asked.

"No, I doubt it," Stone replied, with a long drawn-out sigh. "He'll probably just think I've changed my mind, or forgotten about our plans to go fishing. He'll most likely just head on out to the pond and go fishing by himself."

"Well, it might mean spending a long, boring day down here, but when we don't show up at the ranch for supper, Andy and Wendy will try to contact us at the inn, and when that fails, they'll try both our cell phones. I'm sure they'll be concerned when they can't contact us, and alert Wyatt, if no one else," I reasoned.

"That's true. Guess we might as well try to get comfortable on the concrete floor and wait it out, while we try to come up with a better plan."

Stone had me sit on the padded weight-lifting

bench, as he wadded up some cleaning rags to make a semi-comfortable cushion for sitting on the floor. We chatted about who could have locked us in the basement of the library, and other matters of our self-imposed investigation, before switching to other mundane topics of conversation, for what seemed like hours. I was disappointed when I looked at my watch and only forty-five minutes had passed.

We decided to try to relax and rest, and both ended up drifting off to sleep for several hours. We woke up and chatted some more, played the game called twenty questions, and wiled away the long, boring hours as creatively as we could.

It had been chilly in the library with the thermostat lowered while it was closed, but the temperature seemed to be dropping even more. I was shivering and wishing I hadn't left my windbreaker draped across the back of the chair upstairs. Stone hadn't even worn a jacket, so I asked him if he felt the temperature dropping too.

"I was just thinking about that," he said. "I can hear the furnace running, but it sounds like its starving for air and struggling to operate properly. Do you know where the maintenance room is located, with the furnace, water heater, and all?"

"Yes, across the hall from the restroom upstairs."

"Dang it! I was afraid of that, since I didn't see any place down here it could be. Why don't you come down here and sit by me. If I can hold you next to my body, I can help keep you warm."

I moved down to the floor, where Stone wrapped an arm around me, and I found it did help significantly having his body heat radiating warmth to me. We began to talk about Stone's projects at the inn, and what else might need to be updated. I found myself trying hard to concentrate and finding it difficult to do so. His comments were really confusing me for some reason.

"Why would we want to put a new toilet in the kitchen?" I asked. "Isn't the one we got in there already good enough? Do we need a new one in the pantry, too?"

Stone turned my face towards his with his free hand, "Are you all right, Lexie? Suddenly you're not making any sense."

"I'm sorry. I'm beginning to feel light-headed."

"I'm starting to get a headache, myself. I'm beginning to wonder if someone has done something to the furnace to affect the flow of oxygen to it, and allow carbon monoxide to build up in the building," Stone said. "Confusion, light-headedness, and headache are all symptoms of carbon monoxide poisoning."

"I don't smell any gas. Can't it be extremely harmful?" I felt as if I were about to pass out.

"Yes, even deadly. Carbon monoxide has no scent, which is why we didn't notice it," he replied. "Did you know a scent is intentionally added to natural gas so it can be detected? I recall seeing an old furnace back in that little storeroom on the other side of this basement. I'll go check it out. Even though it looked antiquated, maybe it's the one we hear running."

"No, that furnace isn't functional anymore. When it shot craps, they built the new maintenance room across from the restroom upstairs, and put the new one in there. I remember Ducky told me about it when she took me through the library."

"We can't stay down here breathing this toxic gas until later on this evening. We've got to come up with a way to get help. With the furnace upstairs, I can't check it out, or turn it off. Oh, hey! There's the fuse box on the far wall! Thank God! I can turn the power off to the furnace. We'll just have to deal with the colder temperatures, which is better than being asphyxiated."

"I'm not sure about that, Stone," I said. "I think Ducky also told me they installed a newer, second fuse box in the new maintenance room to run power to the new furnace, water heater, and water softener. I might be thinking about the inn, though. Or maybe Wal-Mart."

"What? Oh dear God! I need to get you out of here. Let me think," Stone said. "There's got to be a way to alert somebody."

I saw him look up at the decrepit old door covering the fuse box, and was knew he was wondering if the door had rusted shut. I was also wondering if I'd fed our pet muskrat before we left the inn, and whether or not I should take banjo lessons. I couldn't quite follow my own line of thought, but then nothing going through my head was making any sense to me, anyway. My mind was flitting from one thought to another, not stopping to focus on any of them for more than a few seconds. For a moment I couldn't remember where I was, fearing I might be under-dressed for the occasion and wishing I'd taken the time to put on my best dress and new black heels. I really wasn't completely aware of much of anything, other than the fact my butt was so cold it was beginning to feel numb.

I watched Stone walk toward me across a dark expanse. Then I felt him put one hand on either side of my face, and I tried to remember where we were. I recalled being locked in somebody's nasty bathroom, but I didn't remember being chilled to the bone at the time, like the way I felt now. Stone's lips were moving and I concentrated as hard as I could to make out what he was saying.

"Don't worry, honey. I've got an idea I think will get us out of here. Think hard. Are the lights on the front porch of the library on a timer?"

I closed my eyes tight, trying to get my bearings, and picture the front of the library. "I'm pretty sure Ducky told me they are on a sensor and automatically come on at dusk."

"Good, I think my idea might work then. Fortunately, the breakers in the fuse box are marked. One is labeled 'outside lights.' I learned Morse code when I was a boy scout earning my 'signaling' badge. Flipping the breaker off and on will make the porch lights flash. I'll use Morse code to send out an S.O.S. signal, and hope somebody sees it, realizes something's wrong, and notifies the police. And just in case, I can use the code to say 'call cops' occasionally too, hoping somebody sees it and recognizes the code. It just might possibly work. It's our best bet at this point anyway."

"You're so smart," I think I said, maybe even out loud.

"At the very least, somebody might notify the cops about the lights flashing, knowing Ducky was found dead in the library just a week ago." Stone was basically verbalizing his thoughts to come up with a workable plan, knowing I was finding it difficult to even stay awake. "But I need to hurry before both of us are overtaken by the gas, and I'm unable to even remember where I am."

"Don't worry, darling. You're at the *Pink Floyd* concert with me. Hey! Did you say you were a boy scout? I think I was one too," I said, mystified as to why Stone was looking at me with such an expression of concern on his face. Looking back, I'm sure he was wondering what I'd been smoking at that concert years ago to make me think I was there again. I was now seeing psychedelic hallucinations as my thoughts faded in and out.

The next thing I remember was a big, burly firefighter carrying me up the stairs and out onto the front lawn of the library. Somebody strapped an oxygen mask on my face and instructed me to take long, deep breaths. I looked up and saw Stone, wearing his own oxygen mask, staring down at me and tenderly stroking my arm.

"Erg, hey, crung, spoot, Stone, mally," I croaked, trying to put two words together that made sense.

"Don't try to talk, honey. Just take deep breaths. We're safe now, and you're going to be just fine."

Twenty minutes later, Stone was talking to Wyatt, and another detective I didn't recognize. The rookie officer, Clint Travis, was walking from the side of the library toward the other two cops with a balled up piece of material. When he held the wadded-up item up to show it to them, I realized it was my light blue windbreaker. I could hear the men talking. "This was stuffed in the exhaust pipe of the furnace which protrudes from the east side of the building. It was clogging the pipe, making the carbon monoxide back up inside. Since it's heavier than oxygen, it would sink and pool in the basement first."

"Damn, I should have thought of that," Stone said. "I could have taken Lexie up to sit on the top stair, where the air would have been the freshest and had the highest content of CO_2."

Wyatt put his arm around his friend, and said, "Don't beat yourself up, Stone. Coming up with the ideas of flashing the porch light on and off was brilliant, and probably saved both of your lives."

"Who saw my signal and called it in?" Stone asked Wyatt.

"Tom Melvard, the janitor, was waxing the floor in

the pharmacy across the street and noticed the lights flashing. Since he also does janitorial work at the library, he knew something wasn't right and got concerned. He doesn't know Morse code, per se, but like most adults, he recognizes the S.O.S. code. He called 9-1-1 and we came right over. We used Tom's key to get in, and quickly searched the building for whoever was sending out the help signal. Thank God Tom saw the flashing lights before you both were overcome by the fumes, Stone."

I felt much better by then, and removed my mask so they could hear me clearly, "Remind me to thank Mr. Melvard when I see him next Tuesday, Stone. Could someone please drive me to Casey's so I can use their restroom? I've had to go since the very moment I heard the dead bolt slide shut. I've never in my whole life regretted my addiction to coffee as much as I have today."

Thirty minutes later, we were on our way to the ranch to join Wendy and Andy for dinner. I had retrieved my cell phone, along with the box of Ducky's personal items to take to Quentin, and called the kids to let them know we were going to be a little late. I explained only briefly what had delayed us, because I had a feeling the events of our day would be the main topic of conversation at the supper table that evening.

Stone used his phone to call Elroy Traylor and explain why he hadn't met him at eleven to go fishing. As Stone had expected, Elroy just assumed he'd changed his mind, and headed out to the pond alone after waiting twenty minutes for Stone to show up. I guess we all have our priorities, and apparently, concern for Stone's well-being wasn't currently on Traylor's list.

* * *

As I'd anticipated, our supper conversation Wednesday evening was primarily about the events of our long, trying day, and included the obligatory sermon from Wendy about the foolishness of our actions. I was accustomed to being preached to by my daughter, but I saw Stone blanch when she said, "You two need to grow up and leave all detective work to the police department. What part of 'to protect and to serve' don't you guys understand? That's what cops are paid to do. All anyone expects *you* to do in the community is to live peacefully amongst your neighbors, respect others, treat them like you'd like them to treat you, and donate half your stinking income to the tax roll."

I hate when Wendy treats me like I'm her unruly child, with a noticeable lack of respect, and a great deal of impatience. When she was growing up, I was expected to lecture her when she did dangerous, irresponsible things that could potentially harm her, but I was not expected to accept having our roles reversed later in life. When she brought up the subject of paying taxes, I saw an opportunity to change the topic of discussion. She was ticked off about a letter she'd received from the IRS, so it didn't take much to get her off the subject of our childish behavior, and up on her soapbox about the audacity of the government auditing an honest, hard-working taxpayer like herself.

After supper, Wendy and Andy took Wyatt, Veronica, Stone, and me, to the barn to meet our new grand-chias, and I had to agree baby alpacas were the cutest little critters I'd ever seen. All in all it was an enjoyable evening. But I was anxious to get home, take a hot bath, and a Percocet for my throbbing headache, and call it a day. With any luck, I wouldn't dream about passing out at a *Pink Floyd* concert.

CHAPTER 14

Thursday was a quiet day at the inn. We had paying guests that checked in early that morning, but none that required special attention. I knew the days were ticking off rapidly, and the library would be opening back up before I knew it.

I don't normally act like a lazy slug, but I found myself worn to a frazzle from the events of the week. The day was overcast and drizzly, and our guests spent most of the day in front of the fireplace in the parlor, curled up and reading books they'd borrowed from the inn's small library.

I was so bummed out by the lack of progress we'd made in our investigation into Ducky's death that the last thing I felt like doing was cooking. So I declared it an official pizza party type of night, and had Domino's deliver supper for us and our guests. I vowed to snap out of my blue funk and get cracking on the case the following morning. With any luck at all, clues would begin to pour in, and all the hens would soon be coming home to roost.

* * *

I woke up Friday morning with a sense of foreboding, and a need for speed. I was aware I only had a few days left before I took over my head librarian position at the library, and felt no closer to proving to the police department someone had killed Ducky. If I was going to accomplish my goal of obtaining justice for her, Stone and I would have to speed up our search for the truth. But hanging over my head, like a bad haircut, was the feeling that justice would not be served without sacrifice on my part. Nothing worth having ever came easily, and I felt sure this time would be no exception.

As I stood at the sink peeling carrots for a big pot of vegetable soup I was preparing, it occurred to me that Stone and I had not been locked in the library basement for no reason. I hadn't hidden the fact from anybody that I suspected Ducky's death wasn't a suicide, and that someone out there was responsible for maliciously hanging her from the rafters, and purposely making it appear as if it was of Ducky's own doing.

I'd made it clear to everyone I'd spoken to that I was trying to ferret out the true circumstances of that fateful evening. Could that knowledge be making the killer feel threatened, and maybe even thinking I'm closer to the truth than I am? Are they making an effort now to silence me? Or did getting locked in the basement have no relevance to Ducky's death at all?

Could Ducky's killer really be responsible for what had occurred in the library basement Wednesday night? I asked myself. If so, Stone and I could be in danger and our lives in jeopardy. For example, had the killer been hoping to do away with Stone and me with the carbon monoxide poisoning, before we stumbled on to the truth? Could the detectives not see the two events were related to each other, and be proof enough Ducky might have been murdered to warrant a closer look?

I placed the peeler on the counter and called Detective Johnston. He picked up the phone on about the seventh ring, just as I was thinking about what I needed to say to him in a voice mail message.

He told me he was tied up, working on yet another burglary in town. According to Wyatt, Tom Melvard had called 9-1-1 for the second time Wednesday evening at about ten p.m. to report that when he arrived at Joe's Gun and Ammo on Birch Street, he found two men in blue jeans and black hoodies robbing the store. When Tom unlocked the front door to the gun store for its scheduled Wednesday night janitorial service, he witnessed the perpetrators grab a handgun and several long arms off the shelf, and quickly exit out the back door, which they'd kicked in earlier in order to enter the shop. He was unable to see their faces or give any descriptions of the robbers, other than the fact that they were both of medium height and weight, but he did state the cash register was open and had been emptied out.

"This at least confirms our suspicions there are two individuals involved, and gives us a vague description of the pair. It wasn't much of a description, but it's a start," Wyatt told me. "What I thought would be a routine extra shift last night turned out to be very interesting. I'm discovering I kind of like working nights. The day shift can be pretty uneventful. Sometimes I give people a warning for jaywalking in downtown Rockdale just to break up a long boring day."

I laughed, but I knew he was busy, so I quickly told Wyatt my thoughts about the unlikely coincidence of Ducky's death, and Stone and I being locked in the library's basement just days later. I knew the police department would not be pleased to know we were doing a little investigating on our own, so I left that part out.

"I don't know if it will do any good, but I'll run it by the Chief this afternoon," Wyatt promised me. "It may be associated with the string of burglaries, and not Ducky's death. But in the meantime, be vigilant and extra cautious, and don't do anything stupid."

"Okay, Wyatt. Good luck with the investigation you're working on." I was a bit insulted by being told not to do anything stupid. But I also knew telling me to be extra cautious was like telling Ted Bundy to be extra angelic. In neither case did the two things belong in the same sentence. I would be vigilant to a degree, but I could only be extra cautious if it didn't stand in the way of me getting to the truth of the matter.

Stone planned to spend the morning finishing up the restroom in the suite we were going to use for the couple checking in later that afternoon. They would be celebrating their tenth anniversary, so we had assigned them what we called our "Honeymoon Suite." It was designed for honeymooners but also worked well for occasions such as this one. The bed featured a red and white quilt with appliquéd hearts, the one I'd won in the raffle at the county fair the previous year.

I had the box of Ducky's personal items in the back seat of my car, and thought it'd be a good opportunity to take the box over to give to Quentin. If he wasn't home when I got there, I didn't feel safe leaving it on the front porch, even though it was hidden from view by a row of untrimmed knockout rose bushes. The first-edition Capote book was too valuable to leave unattended, where even a boy scout selling rolls of trash bags could pick it up and take it home with him. More likely, the kid would pilfer through the box for the tootsie rolls and Pez dispenser, and throw the book and school supplies in a nearby dumpster.

If Quentin was home, I'd ask him if he knew anybody else with even a remote motive to murder his late wife, even if he wasn't convinced Ducky didn't take her own life. I'd eliminated most of the suspects on my list, and wasn't sure it was worth the time and effort to revisit those individuals. But I wasn't sure where to turn next, and I wasn't ready to give up on my desire to find her killer.

When I pulled in his driveway, Quentin was tacking a "For Sale" sign on the side window of Ducky's Volkswagen Beetle, which was parked in the front yard. I unrolled my window to speak to him. "Have you got a minute, Mr. Duckworthy?"

"Of course. I'll always have time for you, Ms. Starr. Why don't you come in and join me for a glass of lemonade in the kitchen?" I wondered if he'd still *always have time for me* if he knew I was still a bit suspicious of his involvement in the death of his wife. I'm not sure if it was a reflection of my personality, or not, but in times such as these, few people seemed as genuinely happy to see me as this man did right now, and that departure from normal bothered me somewhat.

As soon as that thought flitted through my mind, another more sinister thought flitted right past it in its haste to bring itself to my attention. It was very possible the perpetrator in Ducky's death, was also keen on perpetrating mine. Could that be why this fellow was so happy to see me this morning? Had I been drawn right into his trap, like a mosquito to a bug zapper?

Had I been practicing my "extra cautious" skills, I

would have made up an excuse about not having the time, handed him the box of Ducky's stuff, and high-tailed it out of there like a purse snatcher running away from an angry old lady with a cane. However, we all know my skills in the extra cautious department need a great deal of work, particularly when my curiosity antenna is picking up a signal that piques my interest.

New Year's Eve was rapidly approaching and I made my decision for this year's resolution as I walked through Quentin's front door. I was signing up for a "conceal and carry" class, and purchasing my very own handgun. I'd read an article in one of Stone's magazines about a nine-millimeter pistol made by Smith and Wesson called the Ladysmith 3913. It would be easy to conceal, and I could get birdshot ammunition for it. I didn't really want to ever have to live with the fact that I'd killed another human being. But it would sure be nice to be able stop someone in their tracks if they were approaching me with a knife, or a rope tied into a hangman's noose, some evening as I was locking up the library.

Stone had a "conceal and carry" license but rarely packed a weapon. After I'd nearly been killed while investigating the murder of Walter Sneed in our parlor almost exactly a year ago, Stone had suggested the idea of my taking shooting lessons and pursuing the same license for myself. At the time, I thought it was unnecessary, but I was beginning to realize his suggestion had merit. An added bonus - the little gun was incredibly cute!.

I soon realized I hadn't been lured into Quentin's lair on false pretensions. He merely wanted to chat with someone to help him deal with his loneliness. I was beginning to think my earlier impression of the man had been correct. He was genuinely upset about his wife's death, and although he had a few quirks, and who of us doesn't, he was basically a decent human being. He felt comfortable with me too, he told me. In retrospect, it was an affirmation that should have concerned me. He patted my hand affectionately, and said, "You're such a nice lady, and I guess I just needed a shoulder to cry on today."

"Feel free to cry on mine," I offered. "I can only imagine what you're going through with the loss of your spouse."

I had placed the box of stuff I'd collected from Ducky's desk on a vacant kitchen chair. I picked up the box, handed it to him, and said, "It may be too hard to go through this box right now, but eventually you may find comfort in some of the things it contains. I'm sure a few will have sentimental value to you."

"Yes, I'd rather not deal with the emotions a few of the items might evoke right now. I'd rather spend the time visiting with you. You're such a sweet and delightful woman."

I didn't like the look in his eye when he made that comment, but gave it no more thought. I did however, want to draw his attention to the valuable first-edition copy of *Breakfast at Tiffany's* so it didn't get misplaced somehow. After I explained the book had been in her drawer, and was worth in the neighborhood of seventy-five hundred dollars, Quentin couldn't dig into the contents of the box fast enough. So much for the emotions its contents might evoke. I guess greed outweighed his sorrow in this case.

After scouring through the box, tossing the miscellaneous items on the floor like a five-year old opening up a birthday present, and haphazardly flinging the scraps of wrapping paper, he looked up at me in confusion. "I don't see any book in here."

"Oh my! I guess I never thought to look for it after I picked the box up off the desk in the library." I hadn't wanted to mention what had happened to Stone and I the day before, not knowing who was responsible for the incident. But now, with the book missing, obviously pilfered by the intruder at the library who'd locked us in the basement, I felt obligated to tell him what I believed had to have happened to it. I would call Wyatt as soon as I left the Duckyworthy home, and pass on the discovery to him to process. It seems he may have been correct in his assumption that the incident might have been associated with the burglary spree, and not the suspicious death of Ducky.

Having brought up the subject of Ducky's first-edition books, I felt it might not hurt to find out what his intentions were regarding the valuable collection, so I asked him as if I had every right to know. He told me he planned to sell them, for he saw no reason to keep them, and he wanted to use the room they were stored in as a place to do his woodworking projects. He still had a number of toys he wanted to make before the holidays for the sick kids in the children's hospital.

"Do you realize how valuable those books are, Mr. Duckworthy?"

"Please call me Quentin, and yes, of course I do. She's bought a couple of them since we got married a couple years ago. I wasn't wild about her spending so much money on them, but she assured me they'd only go up in value, and we could use the investment to finance much of our retirement. I was hoping you could help me use the computer to look up their individual worth, and then help me list them for sale on craigslist," he said.

"I would be happy to help you, but I don't think

craigslist is the place to sell the books. For one thing, being unfamiliar with the website, and apparently computers in general, you could easily become the victim of a scam, and lose a lot of money in the process. I think you need to find someone with knowledge in this area to broker the collection for you. You'd have to pay a fee for the service, of course, but would probably wind up more ahead of the game than if you were to try to sell them on your own," I said. I could picture this older gentleman packing up books worth many thousands of dollars, shipping them to some postal box in Nigeria, and then waiting patiently for a check that would never arrive.

"Yes, I'm sure you're right, but I wouldn't know where to start to find a broker with the knowledge of first-edition books."

I agreed to help him in any way I could. But I still wanted to know if he intended to keep all the proceeds for himself, or share them with Ducky's only child. I'd almost promised her I'd look into the matter for her. So, again, I asked him point blank. "Are you going to share the proceeds with your stepdaughter? I assume you are planning to do that since she's Ducky's only child, and it sounds like most of the collection was acquired quite a while before you two were married."

"You know Barbara? Is she a friend of yours?" He asked. He had an expression of uncertainty on his face, as if suddenly wondering if I'd been sent to his home to drill him on his stepdaughter's behalf.

"Oh, no. We're barely acquaintances. I just happened to meet Barbara at the post office when I bought some stamps there a couple days ago, and the subject of her mother's death came up. I asked you because I was merely curious. It seemed to me as if that'd be the natural thing for you to do. Either hand the collection over to Ducky's daughter, or sell them and split the proceeds with her," I said, appealing to his sense of fairness.

"She probably told you I was a freeloader."

"No, of course not. She said nothing of the sort, Quentin."

I didn't want to inform him she'd actually referred to him as a "no-good, gold-digging bastard." I didn't think that would help her cause any when it came to convincing her stepfather she deserved at least half of her mother's wealth, which in my opinion was only fair, considering Ducky had amassed the bulk of that wealth before she'd even met Quentin Duckworthy.

"Well, I can tell you think I should split the money with her, and that it'd be wrong of me not to share the proceeds."

"Yes, of course. Don't you?"

"I'm not sure. I haven't decided yet."

"Did Ducky have a legal will?" I asked.

"No, she didn't expect to need one this soon," he said.

"Nobody ever does, Quentin. Nobody can predict if they'll live to be a hundred years old with perfect health, or die unexpectedly in their teens in a tragic accident. Sadly, death is an inevitable part of life. Although, it's probably most people's least favorite part."

"Death must not have been Ducky's least favorite part of life. Apparently, living was her least favorite part," Quentin said, with a quivering voice and tears welling up in his eyes. "I still can't believe she'd leave me like this."

"I can't, and don't believe it either, Quentin. I still think it was premeditated murder, and I'm determined to prove it. I don't believe she willingly left you to suffer her loss this way. She gave me the impression she was looking forward to retiring and spending more time with you, driving across the country on your Harley, taking ballroom dance lessons, and things like that."

"Really?" He asked. His face brightened as an expression of hope and relief fluttered across his face. "I so much want to believe you. I don't know what I'm going to do without her, though. I feel so lost and alone right now."

"I'll help you get through it any way I can," I said, not truly expecting he'd cash in on my offer. "But what about Barbara?"

"What about her?"

"Don't you imagine she's hurting and grieving just as much as you are? It was her mother that died, for God's sake. You knew her for a few years, but Barbara knew her for her entire life. A mother and daughter usually have a very tight bond."

"Yes, I hadn't thought of it that way, but you're right," he agreed. "Although I'm not sure how tight their bond really was."

"Regardless, Quentin, when you stop to think about it, it's Barbara who deserves the majority of the money. However, I think she would be willing to settle for less. If you offered her half, she'd probably accept it and be done with the matter. If not, she's apt to take the matter to probate court, in which case, your step-daughter might end up with every last cent of it."

My last statement stopped Quentin in his tracks even more effectively than a Ladysmith 3913 could have. He looked like a deer in the headlights for a second, before nodding and picking up his phone. While I sat there sipping on lemonade with a self-satisfied expression that probably could have only been described as looking like the cat who ate the canary, Quentin called Barbara Wells and offered her half the proceeds, providing she help him find a brokerage firm who'd help both of them achieve the maximum amount of profit from the sale of the books. Before I could swallow my lemonade, and wipe the cocky smile off my face, they came to a mutually satisfying agreement. I could tell by Quentin's side of the conversation they were mending old fences and willing to meet each other halfway in reconciliation. I was disgustingly proud of myself.

After he'd hung up the phone, Quentin wrapped his arms around me and held me tight a little longer than I was comfortable with, so I broke the clinch as gracefully as I could. I said, "It sounds to me like you two have worked things out, or are at least in the initial stages of doing so."

"Yes, thanks to you! I can't tell you how much I appreciate your advice. I actually look forward to Barbara and me spending time together, dealing with this book collection, and having each other to lean on while we try to work through our grief together." He licked his lips and smiled a bit too dreamily.

"Good. I'm so glad I could help. I'm sure it will work out well and you'll be glad you came to the right decision," I told him. I was surprised when he nodded, took two steps toward me, and put his hand on my shoulder.

"Thank you for offering to do anything you could to help me through this rough patch, and offering to be there for me." Before I could wrench myself away, he grabbed my other shoulder, leaned toward me and planted a big, wet, sloppy kiss on my lips, while lowering his right hand to cup my left cheek and squeeze it roughly. I pulled myself away so violently I tripped and fell flat on the butt Quentin had just been groping. I stood back up, sputtering, as I ignored his outstretched hand, which he had extended to help me up.

"Quentin, stop that right now!" I put my arm out to block him from coming any closer. I didn't remember actually saying I'd be there for him. And I really hadn't thought my offer to help him any way I could sounded all that sincere. It was the kind of thing people you knew said to you when a loved one of yours died, even in a case such as Quentin, a man I barely knew, and had only just met.

"You must have misunderstood my offer, Mr. Duckworthy. When I said 'anything,' I meant 'anything up to a point.' A point that stops well short of any physical contact or affection of any kind. I'm happily and newly married, and you for crying out loud, have barely been widowed a week. You can't seriously be interested in getting involved in anything more than a friendship with another woman already."

"I'm sorry, Lexie. I don't know what I was thinking," he said. He did have the decency to look ashamed of his actions. "I'm just so lonely and out of sorts right now."

"That's all right, this time. Just don't ever let it happen again, to me or any other woman, or you might just get sued for sexual harassment, or even assault. You need to be completely and utterly certain the feeling is mutual before trying a stunt like that again!" I hoped I hadn't just set Barbara up to be groped on by her stepfather when she offered to help him sell the books. She was an incredibly fine looking woman, who had no blood ties to her stepfather, and nothing prevented him from thinking of her as fair game. I needed to set this old man straight, for Barbara's sake more than anything.

"I'll be sure the feeling's mutual in the future, and, again, I'm really sorry. I must have misread the signals you were sending."

"Signals I was sending? Really? I was no more

sending you signals that I wanted to be intimately involved with you than I was asking you if you wanted me to poke your eyes out with a stick. And, in case you read that statement wrong too, I truly will poke your eyes out with a stick if you ever make a move like that toward me again!"

"I won't ever do something like that again, I promise. I'm so grateful for your help regarding Barbara, and the old books, of course. I also appreciate you taking the time to gather up Ducky's personal items and bringing them to me," Quentin said.

"Okay, fine. You're welcome, but I'm leaving now," I said. I was willing to let it go this one time, but I wasn't sticking around to subject myself to another unprovoked and unwanted lip assault. My mouth felt swollen, and my butt was surely bruised from the hard fall I'd taken on the ceramic-tiled floor. "If I hear of a broker who deals in old books, I'll let you know."

I was glad I could help reunite Quentin with his stepdaughter, but I was still a bit shook by the unexpected lip lock, and praying he didn't try a move like that on Barbara, who he'd seemed almost too anxious to get closer to. What happened to Quentin not knowing what he was going to do without Ducky? Had he decided on a course of action, like maybe a plan to attack every woman who walked in his door and hope one of them was open to his advances? Good luck with that was all I could say.

I hobbled out the door and on to the front lawn with my rear end and back aching. As was a habit on cool or cold days, I pulled my key fob out to hit the remote start button on it. When I pressed down on the button, I froze in pure shock as I watched my pretty little blue convertible explode into a zillion pieces. The reverberation of the explosion threw me to the ground, and I landed hard on my already sore ass for the second time in ten minutes.

The concussion of the mighty blast jarred me so badly it took me awhile to realize I had a piece of metal from the car protruding from my thigh, just below the panty line. I had tiny shards of glass in both arms and felt blood running down my face, as well. I knew a head wound could bleed like a stuck hog, so I was more concerned with how deeply the shrapnel from the car bomb was embedded in my leg.

Quentin Duckworthy was kneeling beside me within seconds, having witnessed the explosion while watching me through the front room window. He was instantly on his cell phone speaking to a 9-1-1 operator. After giving them a brief explanation of the emergency, and his address, he pulled a handkerchief out of his back pocket and applied it to the cut on my forehead. Even in severe pain, I couldn't help but wonder how many times he'd blown his nose on the hanky that day.

While waiting for the ambulance, fire truck, and every police department vehicle in town, to arrive, I watched my precious car burn to a crisp. The tires, lined up next to the edge of the ditch, began to burn and melt, and emit black, pungent smoke. I felt a great deal of sadness. It was like watching a good friend suffering a terrible fate. Quentin had drug me off the concrete sidewalk, across the grass, and back toward his house, in case the gas tank had not already exploded in conjunction with the bomb blast. While he was pulling me away from the street, I could feel a painful twitch in my left ankle, as if I'd sprained it when I fell to the ground.

Later, while being attended to by an EMT, I saw Stone pull up in his pickup. He jumped out quickly, not bothering to close the driver's door, and rushed to my side. While Detective Clint Travis was getting a statement from Quentin, Stone cradled my head, holding the handkerchief Quentin had handed him tightly to my head wound. I was so sore and rattled by then, it didn't even bother me that I might have remnants of Quentin's boogers being spread all over my forehead.

Wyatt walked up with deep concern etched on his face, and asked Stone how I was doing. He'd contacted his friend when the call came into the station, and Quentin had mentioned me by name. Stone told him I was faring all right and what little he knew about the situation. I hoped bringing a box of personal items to deliver to the deceased librarian's husband did not implicate me in any way as far as investigating Ducky's death without the official consent of the police department.

As I listened to Stone and all the emergency responders talking around me, I felt confident my involvement in the case was not an issue. But how could I make the detectives see the significance of the car bomb without implicating myself?

"You are one lucky lady," Wyatt said to me.

"Lucky?" I asked. "Why don't I feel lucky, sitting here with blood pouring out of me in numerous places, and a car I dearly loved having just been reduced to ashes? *Lucky* is hitting three seven's on a slot machine and winning a big jackpot!"

Stone and Wyatt exchanged a look that clearly showed they thought my brain might have been adversely affected by the explosion.

"No," Stone said. "Winning a jackpot is a nice surprise. Lucky is when you have, and use, your car's remote start feature, and aren't sitting in the driver's seat being blown to bits when you turn your key in the ignition. That's what *lucky* is, Lexie!"

"Oh my God! You're right! I was almost killed—again!" I said, in horror. Why had that thought never crossed my mind? Somebody wasn't trying to kill my sports car; they were trying to kill me! Narrowly escaping death was getting to be a habit I needed to break. Not the narrowly escaping part, but the part about being put in that position in the first place.

Now the detectives just *had* to reopen the case regarding Ducky's death, if we could explain what had occurred without pissing them off. Wyatt had told us to stay out of it, and do no investigating on our own. They might not take kindly to knowing I was questioning a list of suspects I'd created. Especially after I'd crossed paths with the Chief of Police on a couple of occasions in the past. He hadn't been happy about my overstepping my bounds then, and he'd be even less happy about my intrusion now.

But, despite how the truth affected me, I'd have to come clean and let the chips fall where they may. They would most likely fall right in my lap, but I couldn't help Ducky get justice by keeping quiet. I would try not to include Stone in my explanation. I had dragged him into this situation, and I wasn't going to have Wyatt, and the other detectives, think badly of him because of me. My dear husband had only agreed to help to try to keep something bad from happening to me. Something bad like me nearly being blown up with my car.

I wanted the detectives to see that the car bomb, and even our being locked in the library's basement, were not coincidences. Someone who knew I was probing into Ducky's death had most likely perpetrated it, and they also knew I was damned and determined to prove it wasn't a suicide. That *someone* was obviously afraid I was closing in on the truth, and was trying to stop that from happening. At this point, they had nothing to lose by killing me. They were already looking at a pre-meditated murder charge, along with attempted murder charges on their failed mission to asphyxiate Stone and me. If caught, they'd get life in prison, if not the death penalty, which was legal in Missouri.

Not only did I want the case reopened by the detectives, and a full-on investigation begun on who killed Ducky, and was now trying to kill me, but I also wanted to have no more personal involvement in the situation. I wouldn't even feel safe working at the library until the killer was caught and arrested. In fact, if the killer wasn't in custody by Monday, I would not be working at the library when it reopened. Perhaps Paul Miller, who'd worked there fifteen years, could handle the position until a full-time replacement was found. I'd talk to Colby Tucker about it as soon as I got home from the hospital.

"How did the bomb get in my car?" I asked Stone.

"I'm sure whoever planted it followed you here from the inn. The Duckworthy home is secluded enough from the view of any nearby residents. They could have attached the bomb to your motor while you were inside talking to Quentin and left before you came back outside. Wiring a car bomb is not a particularly lengthy task if you know what you're doing. The person responsible, naturally, had no idea you'd choose to use a remote starter, but thank God you did."

"It was strictly out of habit," I said. "The car wouldn't have had time to even begin to warm up by the time I got in it. But my mind was on other matters at the time."

I didn't want to cause any friction between Stone and Quentin, so I didn't elaborate on why my mind was a million miles away from what I was doing.

With that thought in mind, I glanced over to where Quentin was standing, leaning against the hood of Ducky's VW Bug. It was a pretty pastel yellow in color, and probably no more than a couple years old. With Ducky working five blocks from home, I doubted it could have many miles on the odometer. It was a cute little car that I could see myself driving, now that my convertible was history.

I motioned Quentin over to ask him the price of the car. Stone agreed with me that the amount he offered to sell it to me for was a very good deal. I told Quentin to take the "For Sale" sign down and I'd bring him a check the following day when I came to pick up my new car. I was going to need a new vehicle as soon as possible anyway, and I'd feel proud and a little nostalgic owning Ducky's Beetle.

Stone rode with me in the ambulance. Quentin had told him to leave his truck in his driveway and he'd keep an eye on it until Stone could reclaim it. Wyatt said he'd assist Stone in picking the truck up later on in the evening, and then returning for the Volkswagen the following morning if I was unable to drive.

I couldn't depend on Stone to chauffeur me everywhere like I was Miss Daisy, but with my car in an urn, or wherever they put the ashes of a cremated sports car, I wouldn't have any other option. So, I thought purchasing Ducky's car made perfect sense, and solved my sudden transportation problem.

Not surprisingly, I was greeted warmly by the entire emergency room staff, who had not only heard about the explosion, which was all over the local news, but were also making bets on whether I'd be making my second trip to the emergency room in the same week. Several of the hospital employees looked entirely too happy to see me arrive in the back of an ambulance, so I knew which way their bets had been made.

Fortunately, most of my wounds were superficial, including, as I expected, the laceration on my forehead. The only area that needed more intensive treatment was my thigh. The doctor anesthetized the area before carefully retracting the piece of metal buried deep in my thigh. As the nurse sewed in eighteen stitches to close up the wound, the smiling young doctor said, "This scar shouldn't affect you too much, except during bikini season."

"Don't worry," I replied. "You won't be seeing this body in a bikini until I lose about fifteen pounds and twenty years!"

CHAPTER 15

I woke myself up by groaning Saturday morning, wondering if anyone got the license tag number of the Mack truck that must have run me down while I was sleeping, backed over me, and then run me down again. Every bone, joint, and muscle in my body was stiff and sore. As it had turned out, my ankle hadn't been sprained, only wrenched, and it felt as if I could at least put some weight on it now.

On the nightstand next to my side of the bed, was a whistle on a lanyard. It was the kind an umpire would use to signal a foul had been committed. By the way I felt, I was sure a vast number of fouls had been committed against me. My head was throbbing, my arms were itching from all the tiny abrasions, and the pain in my stitched up thigh was almost enough to make me holler out in agony. Even my eyelashes had developed a tic, not in a painful way, but just the type of incessant twitching that could drive a person absolutely batty.

Stone had placed the whistle on the table the evening before, after Wyatt had carried me up to bed.

I'd felt like a rag doll in the detective's arms. Stone had made me promise I'd blow the whistle when I was awake and ready for a cup of coffee, or if, at any other time, I needed his assistance. I felt like a royal pain in the tush when I did exactly as he'd requested. I wasn't sure I could make it down the stairs quite yet, but I wanted a cup of coffee bad enough to attempt walking a tightrope across the Grand Canyon to get one.

But first, I needed to do something to dull the pain I was experiencing. Next to the whistle, there was a small glass of water and a bottle of pain pills. I swallowed a Percocet with a gulp of water, and then blew just hard enough into the whistle to produce a pitiful-sounding screech.

Within a minute or two, Stone was kissing me on the top of my head and handing me a steaming cup of my favorite brew. He'd come upstairs instinctively knowing what I wanted. He asked how I was feeling, helped me change the dressing on my thigh, and checked for any bruising or swelling in my ankle.

"You're not getting out of this bed today, Lexie, except to use the restroom. I'll be finishing up the remodeling project on the *Honeymoon Suite* so it will be ready for our weekend guests. You can whistle any time you need something, even if it's just help to get to the bathroom, or for a refill on your coffee. Okay?" He asked. After I nodded my head, he continued, "I'm going to bring you up some toast, and a bowl of oatmeal for breakfast. Is there anything else you'd like?"

"No, that sounds great. I am a little hungry. Thanks for taking care of me the way you do. I appreciate you more than I can say. You're always so good to me, honey."

"That's what I get for promising to take care of you in our wedding vows. I'm just happy the 'until death do we part' clause didn't come into effect yesterday. And I hope you aren't planning on bringing the 'sickness and in health' thing into play very often either," Stone said, as he massaged my aching back.

I knew he was kidding, but I also knew he would always take care of me, no matter what the future brought. His tenderness only made me love him even more than I already did. And I'd thought we'd already crossed the love threshold, maxing out its potential. Now I wasn't sure there was even a limit to the love between this wonderful man and myself.

"I love you, Stone, and I'm sorry this happened. I really didn't mean to provoke a reaction like that from the killer."

"Alleged killer, you mean. We have no proof the car bomb was rigged by the same person who killed Ducky. But someone obviously meant to do you harm, and he or she is still out there. So, promise me you won't leave the Alexandria Inn without me until there's a suspect in custody."

"I promise. Did Wyatt say the police department was reopening the case now?" I asked.

"He hasn't said, but he called this morning and said he's coming over in an hour or so to talk with us. He wants to get a detailed statement from you and go from there. When he arrives, I'll bring him up here so you don't have to use the stairs. In the meantime, I want you to eat your breakfast, and then rest, watch television, read a book, or do something else that's relaxing. I'm sure that somewhere amongst the hundreds of cable channels, you'll find an episode of *The Housewives of Some-damn-where*."

Stone propped the pillows up behind my back, handed me the remote control, tucked the blankets around my legs, and kissed me before leaving the room. As he had stood up, he'd given me the 'I'm watching you' gesture with his index and middle fingers pointed at his eyes, and then at mine. I laughed and threw a throw pillow at him, making sure to use the pink and purple frilly one he found completely emasculating.

"May I speak with Mr. Tucker, please?" I asked the receptionist who answered the phone. I could hear lively talking and laughing in the background. I wished I was in the mood to laugh and had something amusing to laugh about, because at the moment I could think of nothing at all humorous about my situation.

"Yes, ma'am, if you don't mind holding for a moment. He's just finishing up with another caller."

I had decided it was a good opportunity to bite the bullet and call my new boss. I knew I probably wasn't his favorite person at the moment, but I had to speak to him about the possibility I wouldn't be filling the head librarian job on Monday when the library reopened. I waited a good five minutes before Colby Tucker finally came on the line. I had grown weary of listening to people enjoying themselves. It was the first time I could remember wishing I had elevator music to entertain me while I waited.

"Hello, Colby Tucker speaking," he said.

"Good morning, Mr. Tucker. This is Lexie Starr. I hope you're feeling better than you were the last time I saw you. I can't apologize enough for my chicken fiasco. I had no idea it would make anyone sick. I am so, so sorry!"

"No worries, Ms. Starr. I've completely recovered and feel wonderful this morning. I read the article in the *Rockdale Gazette* a few minutes ago about your car being blown up yesterday. I hope you're doing okay. What an awful thing to happen. It sounds like someone was trying to kill you. You know, kind of like you were trying to kill me Saturday night."

"Oh, Mr. Tucker, Again, I'm so sorry. You surely know I had no intention of—"

"Relax, Lexie, I was just pulling your leg. I realize it was an accident, and I hold no animosity toward you whatsoever. God knows it wasn't the first time I've had salmonellosis, and I'm sure it won't be the last. For some reason, I tend to fall victim to food poisoning quite often. But I feel fine now, so don't give it another thought."

I wasn't surprised to hear that Colby got food poisoning frequently, the way he ate everything in sight. I imagined if you'd put salt and pepper, and a fork, next to a bucket of night crawlers, he'd eat them too. But if he didn't want me to give it another thought, I was more than happy to change the subject.

"Well, I'm relieved to hear you feel all right now. I've been worried about you. Now with this car-bombing incident, I'm worried about me, as well. I'm not sure it would be safe for me to be out in public until the suspect is apprehended. I'm pretty sure the same person who killed Ducky also rigged the bomb to my car. I think they're aware of my desire to prove she was murdered, and they obviously feel threatened by that fact."

"I recall you saying you didn't believe she'd taken her own life at supper the other night, but I personally think you're barking up the wrong tree. I feel certain whoever planted a bomb in your car had nothing to do with Ducky's death. The investigators ruled her death a suicide, and I'd leave it at that. There's no sense in wasting your time trying to prove otherwise. And if the car-bombing was related to her death, why would you want to put yourself in that kind of peril when, no matter how she died, nothing is going to bring her back? It's just not worth the effort, or the risk you'd be taking by pursuing the matter."

I didn't care at all for his dispassionate demeanor, but arguing with him wasn't going to get me anywhere. I decided to try another tactic in explaining why I most likely would not be showing up to work at the Rockdale Public Library on Monday morning.

"Well, not only do I feel threatened by an unknown perpetrator, and do not want to put myself in any unnecessary danger, I'm also in pretty rough shape from injuries I sustained yesterday when my car exploded no more than thirty or forty feet from where I was standing," I explained. "I'm not sure I'll even be able to walk by Monday. I suffered a nasty laceration to one leg, and tweaked the ankle on my other one. Not to mention the headache I have from the gash in my forehead."

"I'm terribly sorry to hear about the severity of your injuries, Lexie, but I don't know who I can get to fill your shoes with such short notice," Mr. Tucker said. "I wish I'd known sooner."

Apparently, I was expected to schedule the car bombing incident at a more opportune time for him, or at least let him know a week ago that it was going to happen. Where were my manners, anyway?

"I'm sorry. I know this is an inconvenience, Mr. Tucker, but it came as a surprise to me too, and there's little I can do about it. How about Paul Miller? He's worked at the library for years, and I'm sure he could handle things until a permanent replacement can be found or a suspect is apprehended."

"I was under the impression Mr. Miller was not much of a people person. You have to be at least a little sociable, a little personable, and be able to deal with the public to fulfill the duties of head librarian," he said.

"Yes, it's true, Paul doesn't talk much, but I think he could handle the job effectively enough until this predicament is rectified. He appeared to me to be a hardworking and reliable employee who I'm sure would step up to the plate if called upon to do so. These are unusual circumstances, which may call for a less than ideal solution," I told him.

"Yes, of course. You're right, Lexie. Just having a warm body behind the counter will have to suffice if it comes down to that. But let's wait until tomorrow afternoon to make a decision. The bombing suspect could be in custody by then, and you could be feeling well enough to report for duty. If that's the case, we won't have to call on Paul Miller to take the position. If not, I'll speak with Mr. Miller tomorrow evening and arrange for him to pick up your key to the library and reopen it on Monday morning. Does that sound fair enough to you?" He asked.

"Yes, all right. I guess I'll go along with that plan for now. I'll be in touch with you Sunday afternoon."

The pain pill I'd taken was beginning to take affect, and I couldn't muster up the strength to debate the matter any further. Besides, I felt as if I owed Colby Tucker that much, having put him in the hospital the previous weekend. And if a suspect were indeed in custody, I would somehow manage to drag myself down to the library and be the warm, but battered, body behind the counter. In the meantime, I would rest and recuperate as much as possible, and pray the investigators would reopen the case and arrest the guilty party by tomorrow afternoon.

"Thank you, Ms. Starr. Take care and get better soon. I'll look forward to hearing from you tomorrow."

I laid the phone down and the next thing I knew, Stone was patting me on the shoulder to wake me up for lunch. He explained that Wyatt was downstairs having a cup of coffee and visiting with him, as he was warming up a pot of leftover vegetable soup for the three of us.

I felt remarkably better already. Not better enough to partake in a rambunctious game of racquetball, but good enough to go downstairs and join the two men at the kitchen table for lunch. I could tell my caffeine level was dipping well below the recommended level, and I was anxious to speak with Detective Johnston and give him my complete and honest statement. I wanted the detectives to hit the floor running on their way to tracking down Ducky's killer, and my would-be assassin!

CHAPTER 16

I related almost the entire story of my activities since Ducky's death, to Wyatt, over lunch, and all the while, he was shaking his head in disbelief. His condescending attitude is what prompted me to leave out a few minor details, such as my getting locked in Ducky's first husband's bacteria-ridden bathroom, being groped by her second husband, and stalking a postal clerk. Unfortunately, he was already aware I'd nearly killed my new boss with my less than stellar cooking skills, and now he knew why I'd invited the Tuckers over for supper to begin with. I had lured them into my web to interrogate them.

I tried not to catch Stone's eye, since he was aware I was being somewhat evasive, as I rambled on. I told Wyatt that Ducky had been suspicious of her ex-husband, Bo Reliford's, intentions when she caught him following her in traffic two separate times. But I also explained why I was certain Bo couldn't have constructed the suicide note when he couldn't even spell simple words like 'for' and 'sale.'

"How do you know Bo didn't have someone else

type the note for him?" Wyatt asked. "You have to look at all the possibilities, no matter how remote they may seem."

"Well, I don't know anything for sure about who wrote the note. But wouldn't it be pretty stupid to involve a second party who could end up being a hostile, or worse yet, a willing witness at his murder trial if he were to be arrested for the death of his former wife? If the person who penned the note for Bo was charged with being an accessory to the murder, isn't it likely he'd be persuaded to turn state's evidence in hopes of getting a lighter sentence? Why would he, or anyone else, even take the chance of getting himself in that position? His accomplice would have to be operating on one brain cell to do something that idiotic."

I was proud of my ability to come up with a reasonable answer to the detective's question. Unfortunately, the detective was not quite as impressed as I'd been.

"It happens all the time. And who said the killer, if there is one, mind you, was smart?" Wyatt countered.

"Well, um…."

"What if Bo was unable to create a legible suicide note, but felt it was crucial to make the death look like it was self-inflicted, and made someone who was as much of a moron as himself, an offer he couldn't refuse?"

"Yeah, but…"

"We already know Bo is practically illiterate, just by his 'for sale' sign," Wyatt continued. "So it stands to reason he could have drug someone else into the situation to assist him, but yet carried out the murder on his own, or perhaps with his accomplice's help."

"Yes, that's true." Why did I suddenly feel as if I was rapidly losing my stake in this debate? Maybe the detective was right. It was obvious from Wyatt's questions that I hadn't looked at the possibility of Bo Reliford's involvement in this crime from every angle. He probably did merit more scrutiny than just basing his innocence on two misspelled words. I usually was not so quick to let a suspect off the hook. Maybe the noxious fumes in Bo's bathroom, that I was trapped in at the time, had muddled my reasoning in some way.

"Who said he didn't have a co-conspirator? Maybe even one who was a writer by trade?" Wyatt asked. It was clear he was fully invested in this dispute now. "Ducky did work at a library, you know. She could have known lots of writers, and tons of readers for that matter. And with her sometimes less than amicable personality, she could have easily pissed somebody off. For that matter, his co-conspirator could have wanted Ducky dead as much as Bo did."

"Pissed them both off to the point of murder?" I asked.

"Who knows? I've seen people murdered for more unimaginable reasons than anger. And why would Bo Reliford move back to Rockdale in the first place?"

"Maybe to be closer to his daughter, Barbara Wells, who lives here in town. I wouldn't want to live too far away from Wendy, or even Andy now," I replied. I was desperately trying to regain my footing in the argument of Bo's guilt or innocence, but knew it was a losing battle.

"Barbara's been interviewed this morning, along with several other potential suspects. Ms. Wells said she hasn't seen him or even spoken to him since he moved back here from Lee's Summit, so I doubt his daughter had any bearing on Bo's change of residency," Wyatt said. He took several additional ladles of soup out of the pot, and refilled his bowl before continuing to speak. I was tempted to slap the spoon out of his hand. Where was just a wee bit of salmonella when you needed it?

"Could be, I guess," I said, in resignation.

"And, why was Bo following his ex-wife? The man has a rap sheet that includes assault and battery, spousal abuse, resisting arrest, and public intoxication. You wouldn't believe how many times we responded to domestic disturbance calls to his and Ducky's house in the last few years of their marriage."

"Yeah, I remember you telling us that before," I said. Throughout my conversation with Wyatt, Stone had sat stoically, sipping on spoonfuls of soup, and listening without commenting. I wondered what he was thinking. Probably that it was painful to watch his wife continually being knocked off her high horse, and pitifully attempting to get back on it.

"And I think I also told you about Bo's tussle with my partner, Clayton, one night, where he ended up slicing his own leg open with a broken beer bottle. He's not exactly the pick of the litter, Lexie."

"Well, I guess that's true enough," I said, just before a light bulb came on. "Hey, back up the bus! Did you just say the police department was interviewing potential suspects? Does this mean Ducky's death is now being considered a murder—?"

"—*potential* murder!"

"—and the case has been reopened?" I continued. It had just occurred to me I'd accomplished my primary goal of getting the police department involved in investigating Ducky's death as a homicide, and I was thrilled by the realization.

"After discussing the situation with the Chief this morning, I got him to consent to putting a couple of us on this case, at least long enough to determine who rigged your car with an explosive device. Hopefully, if we can find the bomber, we'll also find the killer in the process," Wyatt said.

"Does that mean you agree with me the two incidents are related, and most likely, the same perp is responsible for both crimes?" I asked.

"I agree with you that it's a high probability. And now, even Chief Smith believes there's more to Ducky's death than meets the eye. Enough so that he's willing to assign Clint Travis and me to the case, temporarily anyway."

"Oh, Wyatt, I can't tell you how much of a relief it is to hear her death is finally being investigated. It's so important to me that justice is served for her death. She'd worked hard her whole life, and was just getting set to enjoy her retirement when her life was cut short. I know the police department doesn't appreciate my assistance, but I swear I'm only trying to help you solve a case that I feel shouldn't go unpunished."

"I know, Lexie. Actually, you've been a big help in a few past cases and Chief Smith has reluctantly said as much. This murder investigation with Ducky would have never come to light without your interference—"

"—assistance." I corrected.

"Sorry, I meant *assistance*, as well as perseverance, because your involvement has, on occasion, been invaluable to the entire Rockdale police force," Wyatt said, apologizing, but not without a gleam in his eye and a smirk on his face.

I knew Detective Johnston's apology wasn't totally sincere, and a tad sarcastic, but I wasn't going to let him get by with referring to my aid in helping the cops close murder cases as "interference." The cases had consumed a lot of my time and energy and placed me in risky situations in my efforts to track down the killer in each instance. And, but for the grace of God, I'd be dead now for my efforts. My successful investigative techniques, which I admit included risky pranks and often bordered on being illegal, in at least some instances, deserved more credit than the police department had ever extended me, and Wyatt should know that better than anybody.

"Well, whatever. At least now I can sit back, relax, and let you guys handle the case, and hopefully you'll nail the bastard quickly!" I said, emphatically. "Thank you, Wyatt! Stone and I will help you in any way we can."

I ignored the groans echoing throughout the kitchen, and Wyatt shaking his head slowly back and forth. I hadn't won the battle, but I'd definitely won the war! I was thrilled with the outcome, and appreciated Wyatt's efforts to convince Chief Smith of the potential of murder being the cause of Ducky's death. I even felt a bit remorseful for having momentarily wished a little food poisoning on my favorite detective.

CHAPTER 17

The rest of the day I lounged around, relaxing, recuperating, and watching *The Love Boat* reruns I'd taped on our DVR. To celebrate their tenth anniversary, our guests had made reservations at the *Golden Ox*, one of Kansas City's premier steakhouses, and would be heading out as soon as they got freshened up. It was quite a drive from Rockdale to downtown Kansas City, and they had early reservations so they could go to an event at the Performing Arts Center afterward.

On Monday, the visitors would be attending a family reunion in Chillicothe, so I got out of preparing supper for our guests both evenings. I felt like I'd hit the culinary jackpot. I didn't particularly enjoy cooking under the best of circumstances, but considering the injuries liberally scattered all over my body, I was happy to be going out for supper both nights. We'd been wanting to try a new seafood restaurant in Atchison, so we agreed to pick up Wendy and Andy on our way and treat them to platters of all-you-can-eat snow crab legs.

Just as we were walking out the door, the phone rang. Wyatt wanted to let me know Bo Reliford had been apprehended and arrested on first-degree murder charges. He was sitting in the county jail as we spoke, the detective assured me.

"I hope you didn't arrest him just to have someone to hold responsible for Ducky's death so you could close the case quickly," I said. "Were all of the potential suspects interrogated before pinning the murder on Bo?"

"We didn't really 'interrogate' anyone, but we did question several people we thought might have a motive to want Ducky dead. All but Bo had a verifiable alibi for their whereabouts the night of her death."

"Could Quentin prove he was elk hunting in Wyoming? Where did Bo say he was at the time of her death?" I asked.

"Quentin wasn't even questioned, and Bo couldn't remember his whereabouts. He'd been out on a bender that night and couldn't honestly recall where he'd been or what he'd done."

"So, Bo having blacked out in a drunken stupor the night of Ducky's death, automatically makes him the killer? Is that all his arrest is based on?" I was a little incensed by the news. I couldn't prove Bo hadn't killed his ex-wife, but the police department couldn't rightfully prove he did, either. I'd seen better investigative work from a couple of ten-year-olds playing the board game called *Clue.* I wanted the case closed, but I wanted the person punished to be, without a shadow of a doubt, guilty of the crime, not just accused of it because of the lack of a verifiable alibi.

"No, there's much more to it than that. Bo has a strong motive and a weak alibi," Wyatt said, a little too defensively, I thought. "It's the combination of the two that make him such a solid suspect."

"And just what is his strong motive?" I asked.

"He told us he was cheated out of his half of the first-edition book collection, most of which was obtained during the course of his marriage to Ducky. The books were purchased with a combination of his and his ex-wife's income. Therefore, he told us that he feels he should have received his fair share of the value of the books in the divorce settlement. It was a bitterly fought and contested divorce, and Bo made the statement that, 'if not for that freaking broad,' he'd be comfortably settled in a nice home, not renting an old trailer and living in squalor. Actually, his description of Ducky was a lot more vulgar than 'freaking broad,' but I don't speak that way in front of ladies. He also said she should rot in hell for how she screwed him over in the divorce settlement. Doesn't that sound a bit vindictive to you?"

"Well, yes, and Bo's right about the squalor. But I'd say he drank up his half of their combined wealth and is lucky Ducky never pressed charges on him, or he'd already be serving time in prison for assault and battery at the very least," I said. "Bo Reliford's a loser, I'll admit. And I can assure you, I don't have any more respect or affection for him than you, or the other detectives do, but that doesn't necessarily make him a killer."

"There'll be more investigation done on the case, I promise, but Bo was considered a flight risk, so we've got him where we can keep him from fleeing, and not so inebriated he doesn't know right from wrong. He'll probably wake up in his jail cell wondering how and when he'd gotten there."

"Well, I hope you'll keep digging for more evidence and not just hang your hats on Bo being the killer. If it turns out he is guilty, then hallelujah. But if not, then Ducky's killer is still out there walking the streets among us, when he should be wasting away in a jail cell," I told Wyatt. "We'll talk more about this later. Stone, the kids, and I, have reservations for supper in Atchison. There are a whole lot of crab legs calling my name."

"Sounds great! Enjoy your dinner and I'll stop by the inn tomorrow or Monday."

"Good, I'll have coffee and doughnuts waiting for you."

I woke up Sunday morning still feeling like I'd run the Boston Marathon in record time the day before. The soreness in my legs and back reminded me of the two times I'd used the elliptical machine and treadmill we'd purchased on the one day of the year we felt passionate about our health and fitness.

Buying exercise equipment was one of those spur-of-the-moment decisions we should have slept on and given more thought to, kind of like buying a bread machine. In the case of a bread machine, you spend twice as much for the ingredients as it would cost you to buy a loaf of bread at the grocery store. You add too much yeast to the mix and watch the dough pour out of the machine like lava erupting from a volcano. You magically turn the homemade delicacy into a pile of smoldering embers, and then you spend four hours cleaning the machine up afterward. And, finally, the hundred-dollar bread machine gets pushed to the back of the cabinet above the stove, where you store things you can't reach because you know they'll sit there and gather dust until your next garage sale. Been there, done that, and it's never safe to say I won't do it again someday.

If nothing else, the soreness I was experiencing

reminded me I wanted to stop by the gym and offer them our like-new exercise equipment. If I hurried up and dressed in a loose fitting, but comfortable sweat suit, did a fly-by job of brushing my teeth and combing my hair, and, of course, grabbed a to-go cup of coffee, I could possibly still catch Tina at the gym, assuming she worked out on Sunday mornings.

Stone had agreed to get up at the crack of dawn and sneak up on some bass at the farm pond with Elroy Traylor, so I knew his wife, Tina, wouldn't be occupied with him, and might find it an opportune time to work out at the gym. Particularly if she was as dedicated to keeping fit as her husband had told Stone she was.

I'd promised Stone I wouldn't leave the house without him until a suspect was in custody. Well, a suspect *was* in custody, and despite the fact I didn't believe it was the real killer they'd arrested, I would still, technically, not be breaking my promise to my husband. I felt the mission was worth the risk.

I arrived at Gino's Gym at 8:30, hoping Tina had not already come and gone, since the sign on the front door read that the gym opened at 6:00 on weekends. I asked the girl at the front door if I could speak to the owner about donating some equipment because we needed the extra space the exercise equipment was taking up. She took a long swallow of her super-sized soda, finished the text she'd been typing on her cell phone, pulled the right ear bud out that was attached to her iPod, and asked me to repeat myself. I rolled my eyes, and did as she'd requested.

The owner was out of town, the twenty-some year-old girl told me. I'd have to come back and speak to her boss because she didn't have the authority to make that kind of decision. As she was talking, I was scanning the gym for a statuesque, raven-haired woman, who needed to put her rock-hard body through an intense daily workout like I needed to dig a hole in the backyard to bury Mason jars full of money. When I failed to spot Tina, I asked the young girl if she knew if a Mrs. Traylor was currently working out at the gym.

"Oh, Tina's here every day, but I think she goes to mass on Sunday mornings, because she usually shows up around ten o'clock on weekends," she said. I glanced at my watch. Tina wasn't due here for an hour and a half if this young gal was correct. I noticed a sign posted on the wall behind her offering a limited-time, one-week free trial membership at the gym.

"No big deal," I said. "But I would like to sign up for a free one-week trial while I'm here. Today would be a great day to work out and see what I think about the facility."

After filling out a trial membership application, a consent form, a liability waiver, a medical release document, and enough other forms to feel like I was purchasing a new home, I walked over to a stationary bicycle. I had absolutely no desire to walk, in my current physical condition, much less ride a bike, but I had to appear as if I were trying out the gym equipment. I couldn't just stand there like a pillar of salt until ten.

The wheels on the bike turned so slowly an observer would barely be able to tell if they were spinning. At the rate I was pedaling, if I'd been on a real bike it would take me three weeks to get back to the inn. But the young lady at the desk had tuned me out and was focused entirely on the music streaming out of her iPod, so I felt no need to impress her or anyone else with my overwhelming zeal to get in shape.

"New here?" The bare-chested man on the bike next to me, who was proudly baring his six-pack abs, asked me. "There's more than one speed on these bicycles, and I'd be happy to help you adjust yours to a more practical speed."

"Oh, thank you," I said. "But I'm really working on endurance rather than speed right now."

When the young man, who I'd instantly dubbed *Mr. Olympus*, looked at me as if I were Grandma Moses trying to work up a heart rate, I felt I needed to come up with a viable reason for my sluggishness. As often happened with my compulsive nature, I figured a lie would sound more convincing than the truth. Telling him that I was sore from nearly being killed by a bomb that was planted in my car made me sound like someone who'd escaped from a home for the mentally insane. So, instead, I mumbled, "First day of cardio rehab, you see."

"Oh, well, I'm sorry to hear you have heart issues, ma'am, and I wish you a speedy recovery," he replied politely. It was nice to see young people today who respected their elders. Maybe when I got off this contraption, he'd help this old woman across the street to her car, so I could go home and let this body gradually get flabby and deteriorate like it was designed to do. I'd already been put through the wringer once, through no fault of my own, so it hardly made sense to willingly do it again.

I held my hand over my heart as I thanked him, wanting to look like I was experiencing a little fibrillation or pressure as I slowly pedaled. Once again I felt like Pinocchio. If I weren't careful, I'd be banging my protracting nose on the handlebars.

When my legs began to feel like they might fall off, I switched to the weight-lifting machine. Before long Mr. Olympus came over to inform me that pumping iron was probably not the best type of exercise for a cardio rehab patient. By the look on his face, he was expecting the unexposed long scar down my chest, where'd my ribs had been pried apart for a bypass operation, to spring open and spurt blood at any second. The muscular young man pointed to his left, and said, "That's probably the recommended piece of apparatus for cardio rehab."

"Oh, thanks, I'm sure you're right. I wasn't thinking. The treadmill is probably more my speed, until I heal anyway," I said. I had ignored it on my way to the barbells for the same reason I was donating my own treadmill to the gym. It is boring as hell to walk for thirty minutes, where the scenery never changes and you don't move a foot from where you started.

I absolutely loved going for long walks with Stone around the neighborhood, but treadmills took more fitness enthusiasm than I possessed. Now I had little choice but to start walking nowhere on the "recommended piece of apparatus" that I usually avoided like the plague.

By the time the clock struck ten, which, judging by the way I felt, took a guestimated fourteen hours, every perspiring inch of my body was screaming silently in agony. I moved like a dying sloth toward a bench to sit down and wait another twenty minutes or so for Tina Traylor to show up for her morning workout. If she didn't arrive by ten-thirty I was dragging my worn-out carcass home. I felt like a *wake* of buzzards had been picking my bones clean since I'd arrived at Gino's Gym. "Wake" was the perfect name for a group of feeding buzzards, I thought, and I felt like someone should throw a wake right then, with me as the guest of honor.

To rub salt in my wounds, Mr. Olympus walked by me as I was heading to the bench to rest my weary bones, and asked me if I was all right, or if I needed assistance in walking the remainder of the way, which was all of ten feet. I told him I was fine, just cooling down from my work out. He actually choked as he tried to hold back laughter. Cooling down from what? I'm sure he wondered. I guess he thought if I had worked out any slower on the treadmill, I'd have been walking backward. I was happy when my phone rang so I could turn my attention away from the young man who was amused by my suffering.

"Lexie?" I recognized Colby Tucker's voice on the other end of the line.

"Yes, Mr. Tucker. Can I help you?"

"I certainly hope so. I'm in kind of a pickle. Do you have time to run over to the library to accept and sign for a shipment of new books? I didn't expect them to be delivered on a Sunday, but the driver just called and told me he'll be there in an hour and a half, or so. I'm in Gardner, Kansas, at my nephew's baptism, and you're the only other person with a key to the library," Tucker told me.

"Would I have to unpack them? I'm in no shape to do anything strenuous right now. At present I can barely put one foot in front of the other."

"No, you can just have them stack the boxes in the store room and Paul Miller can deal with them tomorrow. That's part of his duties, anyway."

I was a little tentative about returning to the library alone, but felt like I owed it to Colby Tucker to help him out of a jam. And, if Wyatt and Detective Travis were correct, they already had the suspect in custody, so my safety was not in jeopardy. That is, if Bo Reliford actually was the person guilty of killing Ducky, and attempting to kill me as well, which I doubted.

So, I told Mr. Tucker I'd go take care of the book delivery, and also that a suspect had been arrested for the murder of Bertha Duckworthy. So, against my better judgment, unless things changed between then and tomorrow morning, I'd be reporting to work as scheduled in order to start my job as the interim head librarian, I assured him. Hopefully, with a few hours of rest, and a lot of soaking in a tub of hot lavender and Epsom salt scented water, I'd feel up to it by then.

In the meantime, it was closing in on ten-thirty and I was anxious to get the heck out of this torture chamber they called a gym. Maybe Tina Traylor was late because it took her extra time in the confessional booth to ask forgiveness for all the sins she'd committed recently. I wondered what the penance was for stringing up a ninety-pound librarian.

With over an hour to waste until the delivery truck was due to arrive at the library, I thought it might be a good time to run by *Joe's Guns and Ammo* to see if I could buy a Ladysmith 3913. I'd have Stone teach me how to shoot it one day soon, so I'd have it for emergencies, after I'd qualified for my conceal and carry permit. I'd never even held a gun in my hand, much less shot one, so I was excited about learning how to handle a firearm. I decided I might even join the NRA after I became comfortable with my new "piece."

I ended up purchasing the Sig Sauer P238, a single-action .380 caliber pistol, because Joe's didn't have a Ladysmith in stock. The salesman told me it was light and easy to conceal, and it had an easy-to-move stainless-steel slide, minimal recoil, and a scalloped side and finger relief under the trigger guard.

As he described all the benefits of the gun, he might as well have been talking to the cockroach I saw climbing up the wall behind him. All I cared about was the fact that it was a cool-looking weapon, with pretty pink handgrips. It was like having the car salesman telling me all the intricate details about the turbo-charged, high performance, six-cylinder motor, MacPherson struts, and rack and pinion steering features of my recently incinerated sports car. I didn't have the heart to tell him I bought the car strictly because it was a sky blue convertible with a kick-ass stereo system. And if the car actually moved after you turned the key in the ignition, well, that was merely an added bonus.

There was no waiting time requirement to purchase a gun in Missouri, so I bought a box of birdshot, which I carried out to my new VW Beetle in a sack, and the small pistol, which I stuffed into my fanny pack. I'd remove it when I got home, and store it in Stone's gun safe until I had a license to carry it.

Now that I was officially packing, I felt invincible, like an Annie Oakley, pistol-packing mama who could barely walk under her own power at the moment.

CHAPTER 18

I didn't spend much time at the gun shop, so I stopped to pick up a large cup of french roast coffee to go, at the convenience store a block west of the library. I'd been craving a caffeine boost since I'd left Gino's Gym.

When I pulled the Volkswagen into the library parking lot, I felt a sense of melancholy. It should have been Ducky parking this cute little car in the lot on her way into the building she spent so much of her life in.

I grabbed my Styrofoam coffee cup out of the cup holder, put my iPhone in the pocket of my baggy sweatpants, locked the car doors, and slowly crossed the parking lot to the library. I was having so much trouble lifting my feet off the ground I nearly stumbled twice over cracks in the concrete. And I'm pretty sure one of the cracks was just drawn on the sidewalk with chalk.

I saw a car full of college-aged kids drive by in a passenger van. They were all staring out their windows at me, probably betting with each other on whether or not I'd make it to the library steps without doing a face-plant in the rose bushes first. They probably thought I'd wandered away from home and couldn't find my way back.

The way I was feeling, I would have bet 'yes' on the face-plant thing if I'd been watching myself from the van. But I surprised myself by making it to the top of the steps without incident. The front door was unlocked, which surprised me, but without stopping to consider the ramifications of that oddity, I walked on in and appeared to startle Paul Miller and a much smaller, older man.

"Hello gentleman. What's going on?" I asked, as I approached the leather couch the men were lounging on. For several awkward seconds the two men stared at me in silence.

"You must be Lexie Starr," said the older man finally, as he stood and walked toward me with an outstretched hand. "I'm Tom Melvard, and it's so nice to make your acquaintance. I thought I should stop by and spend a few minutes sprucing up the place since the library will be reopening tomorrow, and it hasn't been cleaned for almost two weeks."

"Good idea, Tom. It's nice to meet you, as well, and I thank you for thinking about giving the place a quick going over. Are you here to help him, Paul?"

"No," he replied.

Since Paul was a man of few words, Tom stepped in and filled in the details. "Paul and I have known each other for years. Often, when I'd be clocking in to do my custodial work, Paul would just be finishing his weight training session on his Nautilus machine downstairs. He'd leave the library at the same time as Ducky and escort her to her car. So when Paul saw me walking into the library a few minutes ago, he decided to stop in and visit with me."

"Oh, how nice. I'm actually very glad to see you here today, Paul. I'm here to sign for a shipment of books coming in on a delivery truck. I imagine you're accustomed to dealing with these deliveries, since Colby Tucker informed me you'd be the one taking care of sorting them out anyway."

"Yeah," he said.

"I'm also glad it worked out for you to move up to a full time position here, in lieu of having to hire another part-time employee to fill Carolyn's shoes. It will work out splendidly for both of us. You'll get the extra hours you wanted, and I'll have someone working by my side who knows this library inside and out. I'm quite certain I'll be coming to you with a lot of questions concerning this facility," I said.

"Sure," he said with a sullen nod.

"With your years of experience here, I'm surprised you weren't immediately hired to take Ducky's place as the head librarian, without the need for a temporary replacement like me."

"I applied, but Ducky didn't think I had the social skills necessary for the job. I guess you have to be a blabbermouth to be considered competent enough to qualify for the librarian position. I know as much about running this library as Ducky did, even if I'm not a big yacker."

It was the most I'd ever heard Paul say, and the way he said it sounded bitter and resentful. I wasn't sure how to respond, but I tried to be diplomatic. "Well, you are a very quiet and soft-spoken man, but I still would have—"

I was interrupted by the sound of a loud honking noise in the back of the building. With more gestures than words, Paul indicated the delivery truck had pulled around behind the building to unload the boxes on the loading dock, where they'd be brought in through the back door and stacked in the storeroom. I followed Paul and Tom to the rear of the building.

As Paul and the deliveryman unloaded the boxes, Tom and I chatted for a few minutes while I blew on my cup of coffee. I had just removed the lid and it was still too hot to take more than a sip. I remembered Ducky telling me Tom had made his living as a jockey in Kentucky. Now that I'd met the man, I could understand how his diminutive stature would have made him the ideal size for his chosen profession.

Tom Melvard seemed like a very kind gentleman, and as we discussed Ducky's death, I could see he had actually cared deeply for her before she'd fallen in love and married Quentin Duckworthy. When I told him Ducky's ex-husband, Bo Reliford, had been charged with her death, Tom was visibly relieved.

"I'm so glad that monster's been arrested. I knew all along he was the one who killed her. He was so abusive to her throughout their marriage. I tried to talk her into leaving him way before she finally did," Tom said. He yelled out to Paul, who was picking up the last box on the pallet. "Did you hear that, Paul? Bo Reliford has been charged with Ducky's murder!"

"That's great," Paul replied.

"So you felt Bo was the guilty party all along, Tom? Hmm, I was under the impression you felt sure Ducky had committed suicide. I'm surprised to hear you suspected her ex-husband after you told me how unhappy Ducky seemed to you, and that you didn't feel it was beyond her to kill herself."

"Yeah, well, I guess I had a change of heart about it after I gave it more thought. I started thinking about Bo's violent nature and realized it was no small wonder he didn't kill her long before now. The main thing is that I'm happy Bo will be held responsible for her death, and justice will be served. I'm sure it will help bring closure to her family, too," Tom said.

"Yes, that is so true. Having the true nature of a loved one's death up in the air, particularly if suicide is suspected, has to be very hard to accept and deal with. I know her death has been very tough on Quentin," I said.

"Yeah, whatever," Tom grimaced and said. He was obviously not at all concerned about Ducky's current husband's emotional status. He seemed to dislike Quentin as much as he did Bo. I was beginning to think maybe he'd had more than just a crush on the librarian.

After I signed the manifest and we went back inside the library, Paul locked the back door, and asked, "So it's true? Bo's in jail?"

"Yes, but I'm still not convinced he's the one who killed Ducky," I told both men. "It doesn't seem to me as if Bo would be clever enough to carry off a well-planned execution in such a way to make everyone think her death was at her own hands. I'm not even sure he could stay sober long enough to commit the murder."

When neither Paul nor Tom responded, I continued, "And as you might have heard already, my husband and I were nearly asphyxiated in the basement here the other day, by who we're convinced was the same person who hung Ducky. Another scheme I doubt Bo Reliford would have the wherewithal to pull off."

After a few seconds of silence, Tom asked, "What made you so sure from the start that Ducky was murdered?"

"She told me all about the things she was looking forward to doing during her retirement. She seemed excited about a number of things she'd planned to do, and new interests she wanted to get involved in, like ballroom dancing and gardening. She was also anxious to spend more time with her grandkids."

"I doubt that would have happened," Tom said.

"Why not?" I asked.

"Quentin had a contentious relationship with her daughter, Barbara, so Ducky didn't get to see Barbara and the grandkids very often," Tom replied.

"Where Barbara didn't go, neither did Marissa and Bernie," added Paul.

"Paul's right. Not spending time with her grandkids had nothing to do with her work taking up all her spare time," Tom said. "But Ducky did tell me she wanted to buy a farm and put in a horse arena for Barbara and her kids to practice their equestrian events. Barbara was a champion barrel racer when she was younger. I think Ducky hoped it would help entice her daughter and grandkids to visit more often. I offered to sell her a couple of my finest horses for her grandkids to ride and practice their riding skills."

"So you still own horses?"

"Yeah, a whole stable of them."

"Did Ducky agree to purchase some horses?" I asked.

"No, she scoffed at the offer, saying my best stallions were not nearly good enough for her grandkids," Tom replied. Tom was getting so wrapped up in his story, he was beginning to get antsy. His voice was getting louder, and beads of sweat were forming across his forehead. I glanced at Paul, who looked nervous and was staring at his friend with his eyebrows raised.

I wasn't sure where the conversation was headed, but I was beginning to smell a skunk in the woodpile.

"Wow, that's kind of harsh of her to say. As a successful jockey, and someone with a vast knowledge about horses, that had to be difficult to accept." I was going out of my way to needle him, trying to jam a burr under this jockey's saddle. I recalled Wendy telling me there had been a hair off a horse discovered on the noose. Tom probably spent a great deal of time with his horses. Could there be a connection there?

"You're damn right it was difficult to accept!" Now Tom was getting agitated. I casually took a small sip of coffee, which was just beginning to cool down enough to drink. I had a hunch Tom might say something I'd want to have Wyatt listen to later, so I acted like I'd felt my phone vibrate. I fiddled with it, pretending I wasn't sure what I was doing. While I was fiddling with it, I opened the voice recorder app I had downloaded on the device and turned it on.

"Oh, well, I'll just turn the silly thing off, and whoever was calling can call me back later. I just got this phone a couple days ago, and I'd have better luck sending and receiving smoke signals than I'm having sending and receiving texts and phone calls," I said, as I placed the phone in the pouch of my sweatshirt, and looked up at Tom.

"I'm sorry, Mr. Melvard, now what were you saying?" I asked the tiny man, who was still obviously fuming.

Before Tom could respond, Paul spoke up, "We need to get going, Tom, and let Ms. Starr get back to what she was doing so she doesn't get stuck here all day. I've got to meet my girlfriend for lunch, and you probably need to go too, before you talk Ms. Starr's ear off."

Tom nodded, his face flushing at Paul's last comment. Paul had suddenly turned in to Chatty Cathy in his haste to get Tom to shut up and get both of them out of the library as quickly as possible. Thinking about Paul's sudden ability to form full sentences, out loud even, made me think about something he'd said earlier in the conversation.

"Tom, I thought you were here to clean?" I asked. Tom just looked down at the floor. "And, say, Paul, did you happen to get a chance to read the suicide note Ducky supposedly wrote?"

"No, of course not. How could I have read it? I'm sure the detectives took it with them when they left the scene," Paul said.

"Yeah, that's what I assumed too. But, it's odd how you just got Ducky's grandkids names wrong, and, even more curiously, wrong in exactly the same way the person that really wrote the suicide note did, because we all know Ducky didn't write it." I had both men's full attention now. Paul looked like he'd been beaned with a fastball thrown by Nolan Ryan.

"Huh?" He said, with a baffled expression on his face.

"Her grandkids are named Melissa and Barney. You just called them Marissa and Bernie, as they were mistakenly referred to in the suicide note. Which, incidentally, was one of the primary reasons I was convinced Ducky didn't write the note. She would know her grandchildren's names, even if she only saw them on rare occasions. And I'm relatively sure that Ducky did not have Alzheimer's."

"Well, I, I, I, um—" Paul managed to say, stuttering as he tried to come up with a response.

"And, Tom, I'm fascinated with that gorgeous Rolex watch on your wrist," I said with a fake sweetness. I knew I was treading in dangerous water, but it had never stopped me before, and unfortunately, it didn't stop me this time either. "Is it new?"

"Uh, yeah," he said.

"It wouldn't be the Submariner model, would it?"

"Um, maybe. Why?" He asked.

"Just curious. It's such an odd coincidence that your

new watch is the exact same model as the Rolex stolen from the jewelry store the other night. I noticed it when we were chatting outside as Paul was unloading the boxes of books."

"I've also noticed you limping, Tom, and rubbing your back. Do you have lingering injuries from a bad fall off a horse?"

"Well, yeah, several bad falls, but—"

"—and I'll bet you have to take a lot of pills to control the pain, like Percocet, and the other narcotics taken from the pharmacy a week or so ago."

"What's your point, Ms. Starr?" Paul asked, with a threatening tone to his voice.

"Nothing, I just find it interesting," I said, as innocently as I could muster. But I obviously didn't muster up enough, because the looks on both men's faces had turned menacing.

It had become obvious to both Paul and Tom that I was now putting two and two together, and coming up with twenty-five to life. The fact they were feeling the pressure did not bode well for me. They had nothing to lose at this point, and everything to gain. Tom stepped in front of me, pointing his finger right at my face. He was livid as he spoke to me.

"Listen, lady! I don't know what you think you know, but I do know your luck is about to run out. You escaped death twice this week, but the third time is definitely not going to be a charm. Sit down in the chair, and don't even try to make a move for your phone," Tom said. "It's off and it's going to stay off while we figure out what we're going to do with you. I knew you were not going to quit snooping around until you figured out what really happened to that old bitch. That's why we've tried all week to shut you up for good."

Only I knew my phone was actually still turned on

and I hoped it would stay on long enough to catch as much of the conversation as possible. Because, if nothing else, when they discovered my body, no doubt hanging from the rafters, with any luck at all, I'd have proof of who killed me, and Ducky, in my pocket, recorded on my iPhone.

"If you try to carry me up the ladder to hang me from the rafters, I have to warn you, I'm younger and heavier than Ducky, and I'll be kicking and screaming for all I'm worth, so I wouldn't even consider it if I were you guys!"

"You won't be kicking and screaming after I knock you out like I did Ducky," Paul said.

"Oh, well, it was just a thought. So, how did you knock her out?" I wasn't sure I wanted to know the answer, but I felt I had to ask to get it on tape, if nothing else.

"I'm trained in several forms of martial arts as a competitor in cage fighting," he answered, boastfully. "And as good of a boxer as I am, I'm even better in the ground and pound game. My guillotine choke has even the best of them tapping out within seconds."

"Oh, that's nice," I said, sarcastically. "How proud you must be. And I'm sure your mother is just as proud, and when she finds out you've killed me too, she'll be even prouder. Trust me, Paul, she will find out! Even after you disable me with your choke hold, to make it obvious I was still alive when I hung myself, you'll still have to carry a heavier body than Ducky's up the ladder."

"Lady, I can bench press four-hundred and twenty-five pounds. That's just a few pounds short of the Missouri state record in my age and weight class. So, me carrying you up a ladder would be like you carrying a dead puppy up it. No big fricking deal."

I didn't like his reference to the dead puppy. I would

never hurt anyone or anything, especially not a puppy. But it didn't encourage me any to know he could lift three-and-a-half people my size.

"I don't understand, Paul. Why would you want to kill Ducky to begin with?" I asked.

"It was Tom's idea at first. He was still bitter about her rejecting him, and not ever even giving him a chance by agreeing to go out on one date with him. She ridiculed him, and called him 'pipsqueak,' saying she'd never consider dating someone tinier than herself," Paul explained.

"Hey! I was a good inch taller than Ducky, and I know I had to have outweighed her too," Tom rebutted, in defense of his size. "And besides, have you ever seen a jockey Paul's size? The filly I rode, *Outspoken*, would have died of a heart attack trying to race other horses around the track if she'd had a three-hundred-pound behemoth on her back. So what Ducky found as unattractive, was very beneficial in the horse-racing world."

"I'm sure it was, Tom. I can understand why you were angry with her. But what about you, Paul, why would you agree to help Tom kill her? What could you have against her that was so bad you wouldn't mind seeing her dead?" I asked. Now that I had apparently pulled their chains, they didn't want to shut up, including Paul, who rarely strung two sentences together during a conversation. I thought if I could keep them talking, I could use it as a stall tactic while I tried to think of a way out of my predicament.

"You said it yourself just a little while ago. Why wasn't I considered for the head librarian position? I know the duties of the position as well as Ducky did, but she said I didn't have the social skills I needed to interact with the library patrons. She had the gall to tell me she could hire a trained monkey to fulfill the duties of a librarian, but if they couldn't talk and communicate with the patrons, what good would it do? How would you like be compared to a trained monkey? And I really needed the extra money the head librarian position would have paid me. First of all, I'd like to enter a cage-fighting competition where the entry fee is ten grand, but the winner claims a hundred thousand dollar purse. Plus, I'm tired of living with my girlfriend's parents. We need a place of our own. And as much as I'd like to get engaged, I couldn't ask her to marry me without an engagement ring. So I got her a really nice one the other night when Tom stole his Rolex, while we were robbing the jewelry store," Paul explained.

I'd just discovered that once you got this man to speak, he was more than happy to spill his guts. Or, at least he was willing to boast about his crimes to someone he planned to do away with so they couldn't repeat anything he said to the authorities. Little did he know his rambling speech was being recorded, and hopefully, even with me gone, his detailed admission would be preserved, and detected, on my phone.

I'd also figured out that not only did these two work in tandem to kill Ducky but they were also a team committing the burglaries all over town. The recording on my cell phone could incriminate these two men in both crimes, if my phone was still at the scene, intact and functioning, when they discovered my body. Surely, neither of these fellows would want my phone, if they even thought to take it out of the pouch in my sweatshirt in the first place. The way the small pouch was sewn on, the phone would probably not fall out, even if I were hanging upside down from the rafters.

"So, tell me if I've got this right," I said. "You, Tom, have a key to all of the businesses you broke into because you do janitorial service for all of them, plus enough other businesses in town to not draw suspicion to yourself And, because you have to enter these businesses at night after closing hours, you already knew how to disable their security systems."

"That's right," he said, puffing out his chest in pride. "I have all the pass codes to turn the systems off."

"So, you came in the front door of the business using your key, and then you quickly keyed in the code to turn off the alarm. Meanwhile, Paul kicked the rear door in so no one would even suspect someone with a key to the store was involved." I was now puffing my chest out a little too, proud I could accurately put all the pieces into place. I continued to surmise the details of their burglary spree as Tom nodded frequently, while listening intently, and Paul sat quietly in deep thought.

"Knowing the complete layout of the store, and much of its contents, made you privy to the information on what to take and where it was located. You knew which businesses kept cash in their cash registers, which ones had safes, and so forth. And then the two of you split the haul after each break-in," I said. "So, how am I doing so far?"

"Pretty damn good!" Tom replied. Paul just sat on the corner of the couch and shook his head as the discussion between Tom and I went on. Tom seemed to be enjoying the game we were playing, and was beaming like a new father, proud of the clever plan he'd devised. I got the impression Tom didn't partner up with Paul because he needed the money the way Paul did, as far as the burglary spree was concerned. I don't think he minded the extra cash, but he appeared to enjoy the challenge more than anything.

So far, the stall tactic was working, and I was gathering important information for the detectives, but

I could tell Paul was getting irritated and impatient with Tom. My time for coming up with an exit strategy was slowly running out. They'd confessed to their parts in both crimes, and there was no way they could allow me to live at this stage of the game. I was toast if I didn't pull off a miracle soon.

"So, tell me, Tom, why did you call in the burglary yourself Wednesday night? You called 9-1-1 to report the crime that you two committed. I don't get the reasoning behind that ploy," I said.

Now Tom was nearly bursting at the seams with pride in his cunningness. "I thought if I called it in, after we robbed the gun shop, of course, it would throw suspicion off of us, just in the event anyone thought we might be involved. I even described the robbers as two medium-sized men to have them on the lookout for two guys with entirely different builds than Paul and I have."

"Jesus Christ, Tom, you freaking motor mouth! We don't have all night," Paul said.

"All right, what should we do with her?" Tom asked. I'd hoped by drawing him into a conversation that I could build just enough rapport with him that he'd hesitate to kill me, but that plan bit the dust when he continued speaking. "I say we stab her. I have a big buck knife in my car."

"Where are your vehicles?" I asked. Even on the precipice of death, I was still curious. The library parking lot had been vacant when I pulled in, and I wanted to keep them talking more about themselves, and less about ways to eliminate me from the picture.

"Down the street, parked in front of the dime store. We didn't want anyone to see our trucks parked at the library since it was supposed to be closed until Monday," Tom said.

"Which one of you drives a black one-ton pickup?"

I asked, knowing that was the other vehicle that'd been parked in the lot with Ducky's VW when I left the library the night Ducky was killed.

"I do. Why?" Paul asked, his interest piqued.

"When I left to go home last Tuesday evening, you were downstairs lifting weights, weren't you? And you were just waiting until Ducky was alone to come upstairs and kill her. Am I right?"

"Yeah," Paul said. "So what?"

"And, Tom, you weren't really here today to do some light housekeeping, were you?" I asked.

"Not hardly. You're a smart lady, aren't you?" Tom's question was meant to be sarcastic, but I felt flattered anyway. Even though it was most likely going to cost me my life, I was getting to the truth of the matter. "Paul told me to come here after he finished his workout on the Nautilus. We were meeting to discuss our final job before we call it quits. We want to make one big final heist, and there's some valuable art in the new antique store across from the coffee shop on Locust Street. I don't clean there, but it has the identical security system as the pharmacy where I do have a cleaning contract. So I know how to disable it, and we can kick in the back door like we always do. We'll have thirty seconds to disarm the alarm, and I can do it in less than twenty, even without a pass code."

"You going to talk all night, or we going to get this done before we get caught red-handed?" Paul asked his partner. He was getting nervous and anxious, and I knew I couldn't put off the inevitable much longer.

"Okay. So you want me to stab her with my buck knife, or what?" Tom asked. "I could also slice her throat, just to make sure she's good and dead."

"No, I think it's best if we hang her the same way we did Ducky," Paul countered. "That worked well, I thought."

Even though I didn't particularly have a preference for being stabbed and my throat sliced over being hung, I couldn't help but point out to them that one small-town librarian hanging herself in the library was an anomaly, but two of them hanging themselves in the same town, in the same library, was a serial killer on the loose who was targeting librarians. Who'd have ever thought being a hooker in Rockdale was a safer occupation than being a librarian, as least as far as serial killers were concerned?

While they discussed the best way to do away with me, who was the only current threat to their freedom, I was trying to think of a way to defend myself. Two men against one female did not put the odds in my favor. I'd barely been able to walk up the stairs to enter the library, but I'd heard of mothers lifting cars off their children after adrenalin had kicked in during a life or death situation. In a fight for my life, I felt sure I could hold my own with the aging jockey until the cows came home, but a cow wouldn't have time to pass gas before Paul would have me in a guillotine choke, leaving me defenseless within seconds. And the big hulk was standing within two or three feet from me, so I tried to start mentally boosting my adrenalin level by visualizing having to lift my new car off my daughter, Wendy. I don't know if it did anything for my adrenaline level, but it did help keep my mind off being carved up like a jack o'lantern with Tom's buck knife.

"She's right, you know," Tom said. "I think we need to think of a less obvious way to whack this broad. I still vote for the buck knife."

"Either way, *whacking* this broad will make it obvious both of them were murdered, not suicidal," Paul said. "But stabbing her would leave a bloody mess where it'd be easier to leave footprints, fingerprints, and other evidence. We weren't prepared for this, so we didn't bring gloves with us like we did when we hung Ducky, and when we robbed the local stores."

"And think about it, Tom. If, by some very slim chance, your prints weren't discovered in the blood bath stabbing me is sure to cause, as the janitor you'd probably be asked to clean up the 'bloody mess' that would result from the brutal slaying," I said dramatically.

"Shut up lady!" Paul said. "I've got to think."

"Okay, fine," I said. "I'll go sit out in my car, so as not to disturb you two, and you can come get me when you've made up your minds. You wouldn't want to make the wrong decision, so take your time, talk it over, and maybe take a vote after you've debated the pros and cons of each method of killing me that's under consideration."

"Lady, what part of 'shut up' didn't you understand? I've made up *our* minds, and we're going to do it my way. Tom, do you have more rope in your truck?"

"Yes, I always carry plenty of it in the back tool chest. It comes in handy for a lot of things," Tom replied.

"Go get the ladder and some rope while I knock her out, and we'll go from there. Try not to draw attention to yourself, because we don't want any witnesses. Wait until the coast is clear before you go outside. At least with these dark-tinted windows in the library no one can see inside from the street."

I knew that to be true. The windows were not only tinted, they also had a reflective finish that reminded me of those one-way mirrors in interrogation rooms. I was getting very frightened now. Paul could overpower me and choke me into unconsciousness within seconds. And whether or not these two buffoons ultimately got away with killing both Ducky and me was really not an issue to me anymore. Saving my ass had taken precedence.

I watched Tom scan the entire street before letting himself out the front door to run to his vehicle, parked in the dime store parking lot down the street. With a determined expression on his face, Paul stepped toward me. I put my hand up, and said, "Wait! Since I don't get a last supper, like most people do who are about to be executed, can I at least have one last swallow of my drink? I deserve that much, at least. My throat is so dry I can't even swallow."

"Being able to swallow won't be an issue in about 10 seconds. But, what the hell, go ahead. Just make it quick. We haven't got much time," Paul replied.

Wrong answer, I thought, as I picked my coffee cup off the table, where I'd sat it down to mess with my phone while I turned on the recorder. I flung my still reasonably warm coffee in Paul's face, scrambling for the new gun in my fanny pack, as he cursed and wiped the tepid liquid away from his eyes. Before he could regain his vision, and reach out for me, I'd taken a couple steps backward with my brand new pink-handled pistol in my hand. I pointed it right between his eyes, with a steely resolve I had no idea I possessed. I was angry, and found I didn't even need to fake the bravado I was exhibiting.

I was almost relieved the gun had no bullets in it, or I might have been tempted to blow the scumbag away, for taking one human being's life, and threatening another, just so he could get revenge on Ducky, and also speed up the process of moving into his own apartment. Well, he'd be moving all right, but he might not like his new eight-by-ten foot home.

"Whoa lady! Be careful or that thing might go off!"

He hollered, his eyes as big and fixed as a hoot owl's. For a moment I thought he might turn his head around a hundred and eighty degrees, looking for a way out of the mess he'd just found himself in.

"Don't get any stupid ideas, Paul. I am very proficient with this weapon and I can guarantee you I won't hesitate to shoot you if you make one sudden move. Get down on your knees with your hands behind your back, right now, before I blow your worthless head off! Try anything stupid and I'll turn your brain into gooey confetti and scatter it all over this room!"

I knew I had to sound tough to have even a remote chance to get away with my little charade of being able to actually shoot the poor dumb bastard. I was pleasantly surprised when he believed I could, and would, and did exactly what I'd told him to do.

I was also thankful he didn't challenge me to prove my shooting proficiency, which is tough to do when the gun is not loaded and you have no clue how to even use the weapon you've owned for less than an hour. I'd actually be more dangerous with an undercooked chicken than I would be with my empty-chambered firearm.

Little did Paul know the only ammunition I had for the gun was in a sack in the front seat of my car, and I wouldn't know how to load the thing even if I had the box of birdshot shells with me.

In fact, I was pretty certain the safety was on, or so the salesman had told me, but I didn't know where it was, or how to release it. With the gun still trained on Paul, I fiddled around with it, without being obvious about it, until I figured out how to take the safety off, for whatever good that would do me with no bullets to fire.

I'd seen actors cock their guns in movies, so I pulled

back the cock thingy on my little Sig P238 right then for a little extra affect, and with hopes of raising the fear factor up a notch.

"Don't shoot me! I promise I won't move! Please be careful and don't accidentally pull the trigger!" Paul said.

"It would be no accident, trust me!"

"Please, put the gun down, or at least point it the other way. I promise I won't move until the police get here to arrest me." Paul was nearly begging me as his eyes were welling up. It looked to me like the big bad, iron-pumping, karate-chopping, cage fighter had turned sissy on me. He'd be lucky if he didn't wet his pants before I could call the cops on him.

Just for my own amusement, I pointed the empty gun just below his belt, and laughed out loud when he immediately fainted and slithered to the ground. This would certainly make keeping control over him much easier, while I called for help.

Without setting the gun down, just in case Paul was faking it and trying to pull a fast one on me, I pulled my cell phone out of my pouch and called 9-1-1, which I had on speed dial. When the dispatcher answered and asked me what my emergency was, I explained briefly I was holding a man at gunpoint in the library who, along with his partner-in-crime, had just threatened to kill me, and had already killed Bertha Duckworthy. I asked them to tell the responding officers to watch for Tom Melvard to be walking up the street with a length of rope he and Paul Miller were planning to hang me with, as they had the librarian the previous week.

As I ended my phone call, I noticed Paul was starting to stir already. I began praying the cops would arrive quickly. Tom would be back any minute, and one of the men might decide to take a chance on taking a bullet in an attempt to overpower me, and disarming me in the process. Of course, if either of them was going to take a bullet, he'd have to go out to my car and get one first. I could feel my palms begin to sweat, and my hold on the gun become shakier. Paul was waking up and becoming more alert with each second that passed.

Fortunately, no more than thirty seconds later, Tom Melvard came through the front door of the library with Detective Travis following closely on his heels. I was never so glad to see a police officer in my life. On first impression, I hadn't been overly fond of Clint Travis, but as of that very moment, he was my new best friend.

Before long the library was as full of police officers, firemen, and other first responders, as it had been the morning I found Ducky strung up from the rafters. Even a reporter for the *Rockdale Gazette* had arrived on the scene, and was trying to pin me down for an interview.

I was getting kind of tired of having my face and name plastered all over the front page of the local newspaper, but I could not have been any happier about being able to announce to the world that even though the Rockdale Police Department had paid no attention to my keen observations and suspicions, I'd been right all along. Ducky had not taken her own life. Instead, it had been taken from her! And now, justice would be served on her behalf.

I'd feel completely safe now when I walked into the Rockdale Public Library tomorrow morning to begin my new job as interim head librarian. It still hurt to breathe, much less move, but I felt upbeat and excited about the next couple of months, even though I'd just lost my only other employee at the library, not to mention the custodian. I'd have to contact Colby

Tucker as soon as I got home to give him the news and see what he wanted me to do about hiring new employees.

In the meantime, I was going to sit back and relax, and enjoy one hot cup of coffee after another on the back porch of the Alexandria Inn, while wallowing in the satisfaction of knowing I'd once again been instrumental in bringing down a killer.

CHAPTER 19

"Congratulations Lexie!" Detective Johnston said to me in greeting, as he walked into the kitchen early Monday morning. We'd long ago given him a spare key to the inn so he could let himself in and out as he pleased. We thought of Wyatt as family now, and he was one of our dearest friends. And who better to give a key to than a police officer who had pulled my feet out of the fire more than once.

"Sit down and join Stone and me for a cup of coffee and some chocolate long johns, and tell me why I'm being congratulated," I said. After an evening of soaking in our whirlpool bath, and nearly overdosing on pain pills, I didn't feel half as sore as I had on Sunday. I could cross the entire kitchen without groaning continuously now, so it was a step in the right direction.

After my long bath Sunday night, I had called and introduced myself to Tina Traylor. After discussing the situation with her, I arranged for her to contact Quentin so she could offer to purchase the books in Ducky's collection she was interested in, and in exchange, help Quentin and Barbara sell the rest of them for a small handler's fee. Tina had a great deal of knowledge and experience in marketing first-edition copies of old classics, and was happy to help them sell the valuable books. She was also excited to get first crack at purchasing a few first-edition books not already in her vast collection.

I'd fallen asleep with a deep feeling of contentment and had awoken at six, well rested, and ready to report to the library at nine o'clock to begin my temporary stint at our local library. I'd dressed in a manner Ducky would have approved of—not quite Goodwill castoffs, but certainly not Rodeo Drive, either. I didn't have to leave for work for at least an hour, and I had questions I wanted answered by the lead detective in the Bertha Duckworthy murder case.

"I'm dying to know something, Wyatt," I said. "I didn't think to ask Paul when I had him gloating over his well-planned scheme, and happily telling me everything I wanted to know. So, how did they lock Stone and me in the basement if Paul didn't have a key to the library, and Tom was the one who called the police when he noticed the flashing porch lights?"

"I'd been curious about that myself," the detective acknowledged. "At first, both men refused to talk, but after we let the two numbskulls listen to the recording you'd taken of your encounter with them, they started chattering like magpies, knowing it would serve no point to lie with their confessions already on tape. At first they turned on each other, as often happens, and tried to pin the entire crime spree on their partner. Both were 'coerced' by the other one, of course. But when they figured out no one was buying their lies, we started getting the entire true story out of them."

"Morons," I muttered, as Wyatt went on talking.

"It seems Tom had made a copy of his library key to

give to Paul, so Paul could go in and use his weight-lifting equipment any time he wanted. With the library closed for a number of days following Ducky's death, Paul didn't want to lose any muscle tone with the cage fighting tournament dates rapidly approaching. And especially now that he'd been able to steal enough money from the burglaries to pay the entry fee."

"Guess he'll be withdrawing from that tournament he's trained so hard for, huh? I've always heard it was the quiet ones you need to watch out for," I said. I refilled Stone's and my coffee cups as Wyatt continued with his recounting.

"Paul went to the library that night to work out and saw your car in the parking lot. When he went inside, he heard your voices in the basement. He knew you'd been snooping around, as he put it, and thought it might be a good opportunity to shut you up for good. So he locked the door to the basement, grabbed your jacket, Lexie, and took it outside to stuff in the exhaust pipe. Then he hightailed it out of there before anyone noticed his truck in the Subway parking lot, where he thought it would be more inconspicuous. Using the copy of the key Tom had made for him, Paul locked the library door behind him, presumably to slow down any rescue attempt, which explains why we later had to use Tom's key to get in."

"Go on," I prompted, when Wyatt paused momentarily.

"Well, having worked around books for so many years, and probably knowing about Ducky's collection, Paul also took the Truman Capote book off the top of the box, where you'd left it when you went downstairs to show the basement to Stone. He didn't know how much it was worth, but he knew it was valuable."

"In retrospect, sweetheart, agreeing to let you show

me the basement was an ill-advised decision," Stone said. "Particularly when I was only pretending to be interested in seeing the dank, dark underbelly of the library, to begin with."

"I was well aware you only agreed to go downstairs with me to score some brownie points. Given the choice, you'd have probably been more enthralled watching me paint my nails," I said.

"Wrong! Checking out the basement would have been an easy choice to make. A short span of moderate boredom, checking out a Nautilus, boxes of old books, and cleaning supplies, is better any day than a long, drawn out period of mind-numbing boredom in your *powder room*."

Stone winked at Wyatt as he teased me. Then he turned to the detective, and asked, "So why did Tom call the cops when he saw the front porch lights flashing?"

"He was waxing the floor at the pharmacy across the street from the library, which was his first stop on his cleaning schedule that evening. He had no idea Paul had locked you two in the basement when he saw the lights flashing, so he called the cops. He thought it was probably just a short in the wiring, until he recognized the S.O.S. signal. Still he didn't know what was going on, so without giving it much thought, he made the 9-1-1 call," Wyatt explained. "I bet Paul was ticked off when he heard it was his partner who alerted the police, and ultimately saved your lives. Together, Paul and Tom are like the *Two Stooges*."

"Serves them right, though," I said. "Ready for a refill, Wyatt?"

"Sure," he replied. "You know, Lexie, I've always wondered if the massive amount of coffee you consume on a daily basis would have any ill effect on your health. Who would have ever believed that one day a cup of coffee would play an instrumental role in saving your life?"

I smiled, as Stone grimaced, and said, "Oh, thanks for bringing that to her attention, pal. Now I'll never get her to cut back on her caffeine consumption."

"Cheer up, honey." I patted Stone's hand in mock consolation. "You would have never gotten me to cut back anyway, even without Wyatt's keen observation. So, Wyatt, what were you congratulating me about earlier? The fact that, against all odds and trying my damnedest, I've somehow managed to not get killed this week?"

"Well, there is that!" Wyatt agreed. "But that wasn't what I was referring to."

As we all sat around enjoying our coffee, Wyatt explained to me that the Chief of Police had decided to present me with a Certificate Of Appreciation for my part in solving two of the most sensationalized crimes in Rockdale's history. I was pleased with Chief Smith's desire to recognize me for my efforts, although the award did come with a reprimand about getting involved in a police matter, and a warning to never do anything like it again.

Wyatt went on to say I'd also be receiving the five thousand dollar reward for being the individual responsible for bringing about the arrest of the burglary suspects. The townsfolk, who had been on edge throughout the crime spree, had set up the fund as a means of helping the police department catch the thieves.

"Will the burglary victims get their merchandise and money back?" I asked.

"Yes, one way or the other. Miller and Melvard will have to pay them all back, and besides, the businesses all carry insurance in the event reimbursement's an issue," Wyatt said.

Stone nodded, and then took the words right out of my mouth when he asked, "Has Bo Reliford been released? I feel a bit bad for him to have been wrongly accused of murder."

"Yes, he was released an hour ago, but it didn't hurt him any to spend a couple nights in the drunk tank at the county jail. It's kind of his home away from home, anyway. Plus, it gave him a chance to sober up before he goes on his next bender, which has probably already commenced. Reliford's just another 9-1-1 call waiting to happen."

"But still, it seems wrong to tarnish his reputation for no reason," I said, in Bo's defense.

"Tarnish his reputation?" Wyatt asked, laughing at the very idea. "His reputation could not be any worse now than it already was before he was thrown in jail, and having been falsely accused will probably actually help his reputation, and maybe even garner him a little sympathy among the older ladies in town. I'm sure he'll be wallowing in the sympathy bestowed on him. Besides, there were a lot of times Bo should have been arrested and wasn't, so this just evens the playing field a little."

"I suppose you're right," I said. "I was just trying to decide who I should donate my reward money to, because there's no way I could accept payment for just doing what I thought was the right thing to do. Do you think I should I give the reward money to her family, Quentin Duckworthy and Barbara Wells?"

Stone shook his head, and said, "They'll both be financially sound after they sell Ducky's book collection. Didn't you tell me it bothered you that the couch and chairs around the fireplace in the library were worn, and the coffee table between them was water-stained? I believe you mentioned they all needed to be replaced. The library was Ducky's passion, so why not spend the reward money to update the furniture you told me made the library so warm and inviting?"

"Great idea," Wyatt said. "That's how Ducky would have wanted you to spend the reward money."

"Yes, that's a wonderful idea!" I said, enthusiastically. I was really intrigued with Stone's suggestion, and ideas began zipping through my head. "I'll get rustic and hardy stuff that anyone can feel free to put their feet up on in order to find a comfortable reading position. I want people to feel at ease and enjoy their time in the library, and maybe even want to visit it more often. And, also, changing the look of the cozy nook completely will help me not visualize the scene I walked in on last Wednesday morning every time I enter the room. Seeing Ducky's lifeless body hanging from the rafters is already a hard enough thing to get out of my head. Thanks for the suggestion, honey."

"My pleasure," he replied. "I can see your mind working a zillion miles an hour already."

"Quentin's favorite hobby is woodworking. I saw a couple of the toys he makes, and he's very talented. I wonder if I could get him to make a sign that reads 'Ducky's Den', or something of that nature. We could mount it over the fireplace mantel, and dedicate the area in Ducky's honor. I think she'd have been really pleased at the gesture."

"For sure, and I've no doubt you could convince Quentin to make a sign to honor his late wife," Stone said. "You could talk an eighty-year-old nun into entering a wet tee shirt contest if you wanted to."

We all laughed when Wyatt said, "Hey, I went to Catholic School, and now I'm seeing a vision of my task-master teacher, Sister Catherine, in a white tank top glued to her wrinkly old skin with cold water.

Like Lexie visualizing Ducky's dead body, that's not a picture I want in my head all day, either. Eww…"

Wyatt's mention of a picture, reminded me of a photo I'd seen hanging on the wall in the Duckworthy's living room, the day I'd gone in to the house with Quentin to drink a glass of lemonade and have my rear end fondled. When I'd commented on the photo, Quentin told me it was taken during a presentation while she was receiving her thirty-year pin from the county library department, which was, ironically, presented to her by Colby Tucker.

"I know what I'm going to do now!" I told Stone and Wyatt. "I'll purchase the new furniture at Nebraska Furniture Mart at the Legends shopping area next weekend. And, there's the perfect photo of Ducky in the Duckworthy home that I'm sure Quentin will let me have enlarged and framed. I'll hang it over the fireplace at the library, with a handcrafted wooden sign above it that simply says, 'Just Ducky'."

THE LEXIE STARR MYSTERIES

Leave No Stone Unturned
The Extinguished Guest
Haunted
With This Ring
Just Ducky
Cozy Camping
The Spirit of the Season (a novella)

Turn the page for an

excerpt from

COZY
CAMPING

A Lexie Starr Mystery
Book Six

Jeanne Glidewell

"Have you lost your mind?"

"Not at all, Lexie. The clean air and beautiful scenery in Wyoming is incredible. And camping will be a lot of fun. You know how much you enjoy new adventures," Stone Van Patten, my husband of one year, replied.

"Adventures, yes! Sleeping on the ground with spiders, and other creepy crawlers, is definitely not my idea of a fun adventure. And I just cringe at the idea of a snake slithering in next to me to curl up in the bottom of my sleeping bag! Sitting next to poison ivy while eating gritty hotdogs, turned into burnt leather over a blazing fire, does not sound all that appealing to me either."

At fifty-one years of age, I had no desire to hone my survival skills in the deep, dark woods, where danger might be lurking around every corner. With the snap of every limb, I'd fear I was about to be mauled by a bear or a mountain lion. I'd run out of pepper spray before we reached our camping site, just reacting to phantom assailants. I had my own little pink-handled gun now, too, but randomly firing bullets at figments of my imagination might make my fellow campers a bit uneasy.

Stone would probably insist I catch my own supper in a rippling stream, too, and he should have learned from his first attempt to teach me to fish it was a recipe for disaster. He would spend his entire vacation untangling my fishing line and digging hooks out of somebody's flesh, most likely his own.

Stone and I own and operate a bed and breakfast lodging facility in Rockdale, Missouri, called the Alexandria Inn. Alexandria is my given name even though everyone calls me Lexie. We both lost our first spouses years ago, and met and fell in love back east when I was there investigating a murder case that involved the welfare of my only child, thirty-year-old Wendy.

Now we were celebrating our first anniversary and Stone felt we needed to get away for a couple weeks to rest and relax, and enjoy ourselves. Ever since he told me he was planning a secret vacation to celebrate the end of our newlywed status, I'd been hoping he had booked a western Caribbean cruise during which we could ingest entirely too many calories at a midnight chocolate bar, and stuff ourselves like throw pillows at the endless buffets. The onboard entertainment and nightly shows would, no doubt, be fascinating, and the ports of call would offer endless possibilities.

I could visualize myself snorkeling the second largest barrier reef in the world, in Belize, and riding a zip line through the forest in Roatan, Honduras. I hoped to swim with the dolphins in Cancun, as well. For some odd reason, being eaten alive by sharks or plummeting to earth from a high cable did not scare me as much as the thought of a boll weevil finding its way into my sleeping bag. A walking stick, no matter how harmless Stone assures me they are, can creep me out like nobody's business.

You see, I really do enjoy new adventures, but roughing it in a tent and having to squat behind bushes to relieve myself, were just not my cup of tea.

My idea of roughing it is when room service is late. I was preparing my rebuttal in my mind when Stone's next words made me stop in my tracks.

"Not tent-camping, honey. I've rented three class-C motorhomes, and reserved sites at an RV park in Cheyenne, Wyoming, during the largest outdoor rodeo in the world, called Cheyenne Frontier Days. I've even purchased tickets to several nightly concerts, including a couple of your favorite country music artists."

"Oh, well, that's different then. I can picture us driving down the interstate while fixing lunch at the same time," I said, my spirits lifted instantly.

"Yes, and these rigs have all the comforts of home, just in slightly smaller proportions in some cases. And not only that, I won't have to pull over at every single rest stop between here and Cheyenne, since you always have a cup of coffee in your hand. You can use the john in the RV at seventy miles an hour," he said.

"It's not just me who needs to visit the rest stops on a regular basis. You tend to need to stop frequently too," I said, a little insulted by Stone's comment.

"I can't help that I have an enlarged prostate, my dear. Besides, I was only teasing you. Getting out and walking around intermittently helps prevent blood clots from forming in our legs. We probably need to do that even when traveling in a motorhome. The exercise will be good for us, and adequate circulation becomes more of an issue at our ages."

"Isn't getting older a barrel of fun? I can remember the days when we never gave issues like those a second thought," I said. "Now, just forgetting where I laid my keys makes me panic, convinced that a rapid-onset case of Alzheimer's is kicking in. It does run in both our families, you know."

As Stone was responding, it suddenly occurred to me that I had lead us far away from the initial topic of conversation, and also that we must not be going on the trip alone. "Why did you rent three motorhomes, by the way?"

"I've talked Wendy and Andy, and Wyatt and Veronica, into joining us on our venture. I knew you'd be delighted to have them all along on the trip. They were sworn to secrecy, knowing I wanted to surprise you for our anniversary."

Wendy was living with Stone's nephew, Andy, who, like his Uncle Stone, had also relocated from South Carolina. I was certain it was only a matter of time before they tied the knot and began producing some grandchildren for me. So far, the closest they'd gotten to giving me grandkids to spoil, was adopting two baby alpacas, which they'd named after a '70s sitcom. I could just see us inviting Mork and Mindy to sit in on our next family portrait.

Wyatt was a dear friend of ours whom we'd met when a guest was murdered in our inn on its opening night. Detective Wyatt Johnston had served on the Rockport police force for sixteen years, and he dropped by nearly every morning to devour enough pastries to provide any normal person with his entire daily recommended caloric intake. His girlfriend, Veronica, was the only daughter of the murder victim from that inaugural evening at Alexandria Inn. She had moved back home to Rockdale from Salt Lake City after inheriting her father's historic Italianate mansion here. Like us, she had turned it into a bed and breakfast, which she called Little Italy Inn.

I thought highly of Veronica, but I wasn't totally convinced she'd be that delightful to travel with. All the lotions and potions she couldn't live without would more than fill the small bathroom in a motorhome, and probably the storage space under the bed, as well. High-maintenance was an understatement when it came to Wyatt's girlfriend. And the young lady couldn't ever manage to get anywhere on time, which drove me crazy at times. We couldn't join her and Wyatt on a run to Dairy Queen for ice cream cones without waiting an hour for her to get ready. How nice does one have to look to drive up to a window and have a chocolate sundae passed out to her by a sixteen-year-old, pimply-faced boy on summer vacation?

"How nice to have company on our trip," I told Stone. "Traveling with two younger couples will only enhance our vacation and keep us entertained and amused, I'm sure. Now that I know I won't have to share my bedding with a rattlesnake and my meals with a swarm of ants, I'm getting excited.. After all the murder cases I've unwittingly gotten myself involved in the last couple of years, I could use a vacation."

"Unwittingly?" Stone asked. "I'd describe it more as continuously throwing yourself in front of moving trains."

"Well, whatever," I replied. Then I quickly changed the subject back to our upcoming trip before Stone began reprimanding me for my habit of finding myself knee deep in doo-doo while investigating murder cases I had no business being involved with in the first place.

COZY CAMPING

**available in
print and ebook**

Jeanne Glidewell and her husband, Robert, live in Bonner Springs, Kansas. When not traveling or fishing in south Texas, Jeanne enjoys reading, writing, and wildlife photography. A member of Sisters-in-Crime, Jeanne is working on more Lexie Starr mysteries. You may contact her through her website, www.jeanneglidewell.com.

Jeanne is a pancreas and kidney transplant recipient and volunteers as a mentor for the Gift of Life program in Kansas City. The promotion of organ donation is an important endeavor of hers. Please be an organ donor, because you can't take your organs to heaven, and heaven knows we need them here.

9 781614 175186